THE TIME OF HIS CHOOSING

WITHIN AND WITHOUT TIME
BOOK FIVE

D. I. HENNESSEY

arkHarbor press
www.arkharbor.press

This is a work of fiction. Names, characters, businesses, places, events, and incidents are either the products of the author's imagination or used in a fictitious manner. Any resemblance to actual persons, living or dead, or actual events is purely coincidental.

THE TIME OF HIS CHOOSING © 2024, by D. I. Hennessey, (WITHIN & WITHOUT TIME - BOOK 5). You have been granted the nonexclusive, nontransferable right to access and read the text of this book. Unless otherwise stated, biblical quotations are based on the American Standard Version of the Bible, 1885 by the English Revision Companies. At least one Scripture reference is taken from THE MESSAGE. ©1993, 1994, 1995, 1996, 2000, 2001, 2002. Used by permission of Nav-Press Publishing Group.

ISBN 979-8-9859336-8-0 — (Paperback Edition)

ISBN 979-8-9859336-9-7 — (Hardcover Edition)

Version 0006252025

Dedicated to family

To the family that raised me.
To those who share the planet
and to those who now live in the stars.

May we always remember that,
while our days together are short,
our stories live forever.

CONTENTS

"May God give me a deep humility,
a well-guided zeal,
a burning love,
and a single eye,
and then let men or devils do their worst."

~ *George Whitefield, December 30, 1737*

KISSED BY HEAVEN

"He has chosen to anoint thee with a portion of faith seldom known to the earth." ~Ardent

Lobby doors blew open as paramedics and policemen burst into the emergency room, wheeling a stretcher. Juan was trying to speak... "BAIBI..," he gasped, "tell Baibina...."

"Don't try to speak," the EMT said, "save your strength."

"We found your address in your wallet, Reverend Rodriguez," one of the officers said, leaning over him, "a patrolman went to get your wife; she should be here soon."

The stretcher was pushed urgently through a set of double doors into a waiting trauma bay; Juan was lifted onto the bed, wincing in pain as they laid him down.

The scene was moving fast. The emergency room surgeon rapidly gave orders to a cast of attendants who continued to flow into the room. They quickly removed his blood-soaked clothes and prepped him for surgery, plugging him with intravenous lines and hooking him up to monitors; the room was a jumble of urgent voices, beeps, and buzzes. They covered his mouth with a mask connected to plastic tubes and turned up the oxygen flow. Sterile sheets quickly covered everything; they were preparing to operate.

The pace was frenetic. The monitors beeped erratically, reporting a mix of jumbled heartbeats and unnatural-seeming pauses. The doctor was barking instructions about mLs of this and milligrams of that. Juan grew calmer, the heaving of his chest slowing as he drifted into an anesthetized sleep.

As soon as the OR was ready, they rushed him into surgery.

A pile of reddened gauze was building higher in the attendants' stainless steel tray as they continued to fight the flow coming from Juan's chest. Two pint-sized bags of crimson fluid hung attached to his intravenous lines, traveling in an urgent torrent to his lifeless-looking arms. The reddened tubes stood out dramatically against the intense whiteness of the room.

Suddenly, the EKG monitor sounded a loud monotonic alarm, and his heartbeat flat-lined. The attendants scrambled frantically, pushing and prodding and injecting something. The doctor yelled, "CLEAR!" The room was suddenly filled with the warning signal from the Defibrillator. Juan's body jerked off the table and fell back again... the monitor continued its steady wailing. The attendants repeated chest compressions urgently as the AED (defibrillator) was recharged for a second attempt.

Another "CLEAR!" ...again, Juan was tossed violently... but still no response from his silent heart.

WHILE THE OR staff continued to work, they could not see the strange glow that began to appear on his arms and face. It grew brighter and brighter until the surface of his skin seemed to lose focus, like a TV image when the colors get out of sync. The brightness seemed to rise – emanating from him; it grew thicker and more distinct, taking on a recognizable form – his form. It rose quickly, floating into the air like a mist suddenly free of its confinement, except this mist did not dissipate. It rose in concise unison – a perfect likeness formed of transparent light.

The glowing likeness seemed to be sleeping as it floated higher, and then he slowly opened his eyes. He held an expression of utter wonder, not in the least burdened with confusion or fear but instead with an unmistakable sense of awe. He was intently gazing upward, beholding something immensely wonderful to him.

Suddenly, a thundering voice spoke to him. It boomed in the small room, causing Juan to turn and look toward the bright angelic messenger who stood near the door. The angel's countenance burned with compassion as he spoke. It was not out of sympathy for Juan's apparent death but rather because he was saddened by the news he had been sent to deliver to him.

"I am called Ardent. I have been sent to you, noble servant, with a difficult message. Thy heart cries earnestly for the reward that awaits above. Indeed, I can see that it aches most desperately for thy Master's meeting... still, ye have work yet to complete here below. There is much that ye still must do in the fields of His harvest."

Juan was drawn to the ground and appeared to stand, then bent and bowed low at the angel's feet.

"Nay! Arise thou heir of the Most High God! Bow not before a servant such as I, but stand and listen, for the word I have for thee is most urgent."

Juan didn't try to speak; he seemed awestruck by the imposing figure.

"Ye have done well, faithful one. The field of harvest in which ye have labored is hard indeed, but rest assured that our Master's word will not return unto Him void. Even now, the seed of thy message is gaining hold in the very enemies that have smitten thee.

"Ye have been faithful in small things; God will reward thee in large. Lo, He has chosen to anoint thee with a portion of faith seldom known to the earth. Ye shall be a powerful witness to this land in the closing days of your mortal time. Use thy gift well, for it is the final hope of countless souls. The hosts of darkness will fear and be powerless against thee, but be ever vigilant! Mindful be that no creature framed of the dust of this earth has yet resisted sin, save one. He faced the darkness alone to annihilate death, rendering all death's minions impotent.

"Yet ye know that mankind in their weakness, though thus freed, continue to wear sin's enslavement by flesh's unfettered will. Be strong, therefore! Watch carefully! For ye shall not taste death again before thy Lord's return!"

With that, the angel stretched forward his hand, with his palm facing upward and his index finger extended. On its tip, Juan could see a tiny seed that shined with glorious brightness as intensely as the sun. It gave such light to the room that it obscured everything else. The Heavenly Messenger touched the tiny fleck to Juan's forehead, where it quickly filled his entire being with its light. It came bursting from his fingertips in spectacular beams. He held his hands up, staring at them in amazement; his face filled with extraordinary peace and wonder.

Then, more suddenly than he had emerged – instantly – the room dimmed to its natural brightness as Juan returned to the motionless body behind him. His human form glowed momentarily with the outline of the glorious likeness that had the same instant stood before Ardent. Then, his body quickly changed from its cold white appearance to a warm, lifelike hue. He jolted as he gasped a massive gulp of air, and the monitors jumped back to life with the echo of his reinstated heartbeat.

The attendees, who had already begun recording his time and cause of death, turned in stunned disbelief at the miraculous recovery. A nurse raced to his side to feel the warmth of his newly ruddy skin and the pulse of his beating heart. The emergency room surgeon, who had already removed his gloves, quickly grabbed a new pair and returned to work on the untreated chest wound, muttering in disbelief as he discovered healed scar tissue on Juan's heart muscle. Nothing was left for him to do but close the surgical opening in his chest.

AN HOUR LATER, Baibina sat beside the bed in Juan's hospital room, anxiously praying. When he finally stirred, she took his hand and hugged it close, studying his face. A stream of grateful tears wet her cheeks as he smiled at her.

"I thought I lost you!" she cried through her tears.

"I'm fine," Juan assured her in a horse-sounding voice. He silently pondered his encounter with Ardent in the operating room but didn't share the incredible experience with her. Telling that story would require more strength than he could muster.

Baibina nodded at him thankfully and wiped her tears. "Rest," she encouraged him, "I'll be right here."

IT WAS after four in the morning when Juan awoke again. Baibina was asleep in the nearby recliner.

In the room's dim light, Juan was surprised to notice someone else standing near his bed. As his eyes focused, he could see that it was an old man. The man was dressed oddly, wearing a linen shirt with frills and a waistcoat that was short in the front and long in the back. His gray hair was probably shoulder length, tied behind his head. If Juan didn't know better, he would have described him as straight out of the eighteenth century. He couldn't make out the man's face.

"Hello, Juan," he heard the old man say in a friendly voice.

Caught off guard, Juan struggled to make sense of the strange man. "Wh-who are you?" he stammered.

"A friend," the old man answered. There was an air of nostalgia in the man's voice as if looking into Juan's face made him recall a lifetime of memories. Before Juan could question him further, the man motioned for him to keep silent.

"We don't have much time—listen carefully. By God's grace, I know what Ardent said to you in the operating room. Rest assured that Radison's heart is bending beneath God's call even as we speak. God has a great mission for the boy to do, and your mission is great as well.

"The days are now very short; the time of trouble is coming soon upon the whole world. I'm here to show you something that has been prepared beforehand for these closing days of mortal time. It is time for all of it to be revealed; this is the time of God's choosing."

ALL AT ONCE, Juan found himself standing with the stranger in a darkened space. The sudden change startled and confused him, making him gasp as he pressed a hand on his chest. There was no pain — no sign of the wound that nearly killed him.

His attention quickly turned to the place where they were standing. It seemed oddly familiar, giving him a strong sense that he had been there before. Light through an open hatchway above him revealed an old, tattered rug beneath his feet; the room's musty smell hinted of an old cellar. He finally recognized the place — the farm's old root cellar.

He watched the old man light a lantern and reach for one of the cellar wall's retaining bolts, removing it to reveal a slotted opening inside. Juan watched as the man used a strange-looking tool to open a hidden door in the stone wall and followed him as he was beckoned down the sloping passageway and along an underground stream of rushing water.

Juan got a better look at the old man's clothes as he followed him. He was wearing a knee-length coat underneath his waistcoat. He wore knee breeches on his legs, with stockings covering his shins and ankles. His shoes looked like they'd been made by hand, with buckles holding them closed.

They made their way to a second stairway cut into the cavern wall and climbed upward to a darkened doorway. When they entered it, the old man's lantern illuminated a bare room carved in the stone. He made his way to a large chest in the room's center and showed Juan how to open it using keys that the old man held in his hand.

Inside the trunk was a long metal box with a lid that opened lengthwise. The man opened it to reveal a pair of leather-bound journals, one appearing much older than the other.

As Juan tried to make sense of the sight, the man spoke to him again. His voice echoed in the cavernous room. "It's time now for these to be revealed— it's God's chosen time. Use these well; they will be a testimony to this generation in the final days of this age."

While Juan considered the weighty declaration, the old man lifted the metal tray holding the journals to show that the box underneath was nearly half full of neatly placed coin rolls.

"These will help you in the coming days. Use them for the work you're now called to do."

With that, he closed the metal box lid and resealed the huge chest. Juan followed the stranger with a continuing sense of wonder as they climbed the carved stone stairs for a long distance. The old man stopped a time or two to catch his breath, finally reaching another stone door.

They exited the tunnel and entered a large mausoleum. Juan recognized the place as he saw old Jim Van Clief's crypt and recalled the kind old man's burial there. Juan had performed the funeral himself.

Juan watched as the stranger revealed the location of another secret keyhole while the large door quietly slid closed. He finally led Juan up the mausoleum's marble steps and showed him a third large key, which he used to unlock the ornate iron gate.

The old cemetery felt cold in the deep night and seemed pitch dark beyond the light of the stranger's lantern.

Then, the old man looked again at Juan with a nostalgic expression and patted him on the shoulder. "Goodbye, old friend. I trust we'll meet again when the trumpet sounds," he said softly.

THE ODD OLD man had no sooner spoken these words than Juan found himself back in his hospital bed. He sat up and urgently looked around, searching the room, but there was no sign of his mysterious visitor.

He settled back onto his bed, his heart racing. He couldn't shake the feeling that there was something familiar about the old man. As strange as it seemed, Juan had a nagging feeling that he knew him.

⌘

2

THE DEEP END

"I tell you for certain that if you have faith in me, you will do the same things that I am doing. You will do even greater things..."
~ Jesus, John 14:12

As daylight lit Juan's hospital room the next morning, Baibina was surprised to wake and find him already out of bed. He was standing in front of the window, watching the sun rise above the horizon. His heart was full of swirling emotions that seemed to pour over him in a flood of immense peace and joy. Meanwhile, his mind was a jumble of amazing memories and puzzling questions.

Deep in thought, he didn't hear Baibina's question the first two times she asked it. It wasn't until she leaned against him and hugged his arm, repeating it again:

"What's going on? Why are you out of bed?"

He smiled as he looked at her, then turned to embrace her, giving her an eager kiss.

"I'm fine," he said, gently brushing her hair away from her face. "I'm ready to get out of here."

"Whoa…" she said in surprise. "I guess you're feeling better; that's a good sign."

"I mean it," Juan insisted. "I'm done here. There's something important that I have to do."

His wife looked at him, noticing the unassailable confidence in his eyes. She was used to Juan's fearless determination—she'd learned long ago that nothing could get in his way when he felt God calling him to a task. She'd seen him overcome impossible odds before, but the look in his eyes was different this time—they reflected a depth of faith and confidence she'd never seen before.

"B-but you're still recovering… you almost died…" she stammered in surprise.

He gently took her by the shoulders and looked at her closely. The flood of joy in his eyes seemed to wash against her soul as she studied his face.

"I saw Heaven," he shared in an enthralled whisper. Baibina shook her head slightly with a look of sudden wonder. Juan nodded to confirm what he'd just said. "I met an angel — he gave me a message. He said the days are short now — the Lord's coming is near!" Juan gripped her shoulders reassuringly as he smiled at her with a thrill in his eyes. "Baibi, I want you to help me. We have important work to do."

She nodded. "O-of course. Whatever God wants."

Juan swept her into his arms and held her tenderly. His joy was infectious! She laughed as a tear escaped her eye - a tear of sudden joy.

Juan's remarkable recovery confounded the doctors, but Juan didn't seem surprised by it in the least. Even the sutures in his chest had fallen out on their own — his wound was completely healed.

The city hospital where he'd been treated was massive, with nearly 3,000 beds. Per the usual protocol, Juan was wheeled in a wheelchair as they discharged him. Coming to a bank of elevators, he noticed a child being wheeled toward a set of doors to their right. The young girl's face was thin and frail looking, and her expression reflected the pain in her limbs, which were crippled and withered. Despite her lingering pain, she smiled at him as their eyes met.

"Where does that door lead?" Juan asked the hospital aide who had pushed him.

"That's the pediatric cancer ward — for kids with cancer. It's pretty sad," the Aide offered sympathetically.

Without a word, Juan jumped from his wheelchair and caught the closing door, following the child inside.

"Wait! You can't go…" the Aide called to him in surprise. He used his card key to reopen the door and chased him with Baibina following closely.

Juan was kneeling beside the child as they caught up with him. They saw Juan lay his hand on the young girl's head. The Aide stopped short when he saw the girl gasp in surprise and smile broadly. Juan stood and offered her his hand — the girl held it as she stood to her feet; her thin crippled legs had become strong and straight, and the gray pallor of her face quickly flushed with a healthy rose-colored hue. She laughed aloud and hugged Juan joyfully.

From just up the hall, there was a loud cry as the girl's parents gasped in surprise at the sight and came running — falling to their knees as they scooped the girl into their arms with sobs.

Juan immediately turned his attention to a group of children gathered in a nearby play area. No one moved to stop him; they all seemed frozen in awe as they watched Juan drop to one knee in the center of the room. A young boy came up to him, wearing leg braces and leaning heavily on a pair of crutches. The moment Juan touched the boy's head, his crutches dropped to the floor, and the boy stood straight. He turned and ran across the room to his mother, who had fallen to her knees, weeping loudly as she embraced the child.

Soon, the other children gathered around Juan, and he smiled and touched their heads and faces affectionately. Parents and hospital staff gasped in surprised shock to see each of these critically ill children suddenly running joyfully — completely well!

Before anyone could comprehend what was happening, Juan stood and closed his eyes, stretching his arms wide. Moments later, the sounds of children laughing and parents sobbing could be heard from rooms up and down the ward's corridors.

Baibina's cheeks were covered with tears as Juan walked to her and smiled. She fell into his arms in a joyful embrace, and the crowd who had gathered around broke into spontaneous applause.

JUAN TURNED to address the group standing around them.

"What has happened here today is a gift of God. This wasn't anything I've done — God alone deserves the glory for what you see here."

Feeling moved with tremendous inspiration, Juan began to share what was on his heart, delivering words of life to those gathered around him. Moved by his Spirit-filled words — and the miraculous evidence all around them, it wasn't long before many in the crowd were kneeling in heartfelt repentance as Juan led them to the Lord.

As JUAN and Baibina were leaving the hospital, it became clear that God's amazing mass healing had gone far beyond the pediatric ward. In every ward they passed, the hospital was abuzz with excited conversations about patients throughout the hospital who had experienced sudden miraculous healing.

Baibina kept looking at Juan in amazed wonder each time she heard of another miracle. Finally reaching the hospital's front door and stepping outside, Juan turned to her with a look of enthused joy in his eyes.

"This is what we've prayed for, for so long. God is moving the waters… we're in the deep end now, Baibi," he said as he flashed a huge smile.

STEPPING AWAY from the hospital's entrance, Juan walked toward a homeless woman seated on the ground nearby, wrapped in a blanket. He stopped and held out his hand, looking her in the eye. She reached upward curiously, and as soon as she grabbed his hand, a look of awestruck wonder filled her face. She immediately rose to her feet. Tears streamed down her cheeks as she looked down in amazement at her strong legs, which had been withered and crippled moments before. A fog appeared to lift from her eyes as her mind cleared for the first time in years. She seemed almost as surprised by her whereabouts as her healing. She kissed Juan's hand through her tears and hugged Baibina gratefully.

Juan quickly moved on, touching others as he went, leaving a trail of restored bodies and lives in his wake. By the time they'd walked several blocks, a crowd followed them — all formerly ill, addicted, or destitute. They were nearing the parking garage when Juan noticed the sign for the City Mission and walked inside; the crowd followed.

The crowd quickly filled the Mission's small waiting room. A familiar voice called out from the small office.

"Pastor Juan! What a surprise t' be seein' ya here. It's truly a blessed joy t' be seein' ya out o' th' hospital so quick like! What's all o'this? What's God doin' now?"

Juan smiled at Badrick, his old friend from Harbor City. "These people need shelter. I have a feeling some of them can help your team with the work here." Several in the group acknowledged Juan's suggestion, happily raising their hands to offer their services.

A few members of the Mission staff welcomed the group, inviting them into the dining room. Juan stayed behind with Badrick, calling him aside to speak quietly.

"Radison needs our help," Juan said, describing the events that led to his hospital stay.

"I figured it was Rad that had somethin' ta do wi' yer stabbin'. I can hardly believe y're walkin' about already!"

Juan pointed to Badrick's chest, acknowledging the scar he knew was there. Juan had been with him on the day God saved Badrick from a fatal gunshot. "You know how... better than anyone," he answered with a smile.

Badrick held both hands on top of his head, "Praise d' Lord! His miracles are never ceasin'!"

Juan gave a wide smile as he gratefully said amen. There was a lot more he could say about miracles, given the way his morning had gone. However, the urgency he felt inside was pulling him in another direction.

He turned to leave and looked again at Badrick. "God has a plan for Rad," he explained. He trusts you... he'll talk to you; keep an eye on him for me."

"Ya know I will. I'll be watchin' 'im like m' own kid brodder," Badrick quickly promised.

Juan patted him on the shoulder gratefully and hugged him.

———

IT WAS EARLY in the evening when Juan and Baibina finally made it back to Center Springs. Rather than making the expected turn toward their own home, Juan continued driving straight, turning onto Main Street.

"There's something I need to do — at the farm," he half-explained as he saw Baibina's confused look.

Juan hadn't shared anything with her about his mysterious late-night visitor. He was honestly still struggling to decide whether that experience was real or imagined. He had to be sure.

The farmhouse looked mostly dark as they pulled up the long gravel drive. Jimmy's pickup truck sat parked in its usual place near the house — beside Anna's small SUV. A few toys lay scattered beside a sandbox nearby. A fluttering of wings and cackles in the chicken coop signaled the hens' objection to their car's late-day arrival. Aside from that, the farmyard seemed eerily quiet, and so did the house. Juan checked his watch, confirming that it was just dinnertime.

They climbed the steps to the porch together, and Juan rang the bell. After waiting another minute, he rang again, this time ringing twice. After another silent minute, he opened the screen door to knock. When he did, the unlatched door opened as if inviting them inside.

Juan and Baibina looked at each other with worried expressions.

Carefully pushing the door further open, they surveyed the living room; it seemed neat and undisturbed. A single lamp was lit, and Jimmy's Bible was lying open on the coffee table. A stuffed animal was propped up on a small chair beside the Bible, along with a toddler's no-spill cup and some unfinished slices of cold toast, hinting that the family had been gathered around it not more than a day before.

Baibina squeezed Juan's arm nervously. Juan patted her hand reassuringly and motioned toward the kitchen.

"Jimmy...? Anna...?" he called out. "Is anyone home?"

Finding the switch for the kitchen light, Juan seemed stunned as the room brightened. He caught sight of what was sitting on the kitchen table: Jimmy's laptop and a large manila envelope. Beside those was an old wooden box. He cautiously lifted the lid and immediately recognized its unusual contents—they were the same strange-looking keys the mysterious visitor had shown him!

A letter was lying on top — it was addressed to Juan.

PJ,

I know this seems strange. Believe me; it's strange to us too.

Anna and I need to go away; God has made it clear that we're needed in the place we're going to. I can't explain where we're going or even how. But know that we're alive and well and in God's care.

On the table is an envelope with papers and a thumb drive. The drive contains a message we've recorded, explaining things the best we can. Please invite Mike and Lena, Pete and Angela, and the O'Malleys to watch it together. Uncle Ward can explain the papers; he helped prepare them for us. He recommended asking Sheriff Flanagan to officiate things. It'll be hard to explain what's happened to anyone else.

The envelope contains the deed to the farm and a signed letter transferring it to Pete and Angela. They've been a huge help to us on the farm and with running the food bank. A second letter appoints you in my place, along with Ward O'Malley, as trustees of the Legal Defense Fund.

I know you've been shown where to find a chest with other resources; those are also left to the church. We pray that they will be used to continue the work God is doing.

Thank you for everything. You've been a spiritual father to me and one of the strongest examples I've ever known of someone living a Christlike life. Working together in ministry for the past few years has been the most rewarding experience of my life. I will really miss you – Anna and I will both miss you and Baibina. We pray for God's richest blessings on you both.

In Christ's love,

Jimmy & Anna

P.S.

- Please give the enclosed letter to Lena and Mike
- You know what to do with the keys!

BAIBINA STOOD IN SHOCK, her hand over her mouth, as she listened to Juan read. She looked at him, confused. "What...? Where could they have gone? Why...?"

Juan hugged her and shook his head uncertainly. His thoughts were filled with the memory of Ardent's words: *'Ye shall be a powerful witness to this land in the closing days of your mortal time.'*

The closing days of time... those words reverberated in his mind.

Ardent's words were quickly followed by those of the mysterious visitor: *'Now is **the time of God's choosing** — it is time for these to be made known. They will be a testimony to this generation in the final days of this age.'*

JUAN LOOKED into Baibina's face. "I need you to trust me; there's something we need to do."

Baibina studied his eyes for a moment and nodded in agreement.

He grabbed the keys from the kitchen table and opened the pantry, pulling open the hatch to the root cellar. A flurry of memories rushed through his head as he started downward — from the days when Jimmy hid here from Athaliah and her powerful father, Bahal. It had been seven years since those incredible events shook the world.

Baibina had never seen the root cellar before now. "Where are you going? What is this?" she asked nervously.

"Don't be afraid," he encouraged. "It's just a cellar." He motioned for her to follow him, helping her down the old wooden ladder.

Juan switched on the lamp, recognizing the kerosene lantern sitting beside it on the room's old table; it was the same one that the old man used. He drew a wooden match from the nearby box of them, using it to light the lantern. Then he studied the wall, recalling where the old man had shown him, and located the fake bolt over the hidden keyhole. Feeling it lift free in his hand confirmed that the visitor's appearance was real. He inserted the large key and began to crank open the secret door.

"W-what's that? What's happening?" Baibina exclaimed in surprise as she saw the wall crack open.

"It's a door... don't worry," Juan assured her.

"Why is it hidden? Where does it go?"

Juan stood back and collected the key. "Why don't we find out?" he asked, sharing a nervous look. He offered her his hand; she nervously took hold as he held up the lantern, and they entered the passageway together.

If Juan's experience with the old man had been a vision, it was undoubtedly the most vivid he'd ever known. The passageway looked exactly as he'd seen it then — even the sound of the flowing water was familiar as it echoed off the cave walls. He vividly remembered the smell of the mysterious visitor's kerosene lantern and the curves in the underground path.

The second stairway appeared just where he remembered it, sending a renewed chill up his back as he peered upward into its darkened shaft.

Baibina cautiously followed him up the dark stairwell until they came to the underground room. She held the lantern as Juan retrieved Jimmy's strange keys and repeated the steps he'd seen the old man use to open the mysterious trunk. Once it was open, he found the journals exactly where he'd seen them before.

HE LIFTED the first journal in the lantern's light. Its leather cover was stiff with age, but he could make out the title on its opening page...

~

The Personal Journal of Amos Van Clief

JUAN RECOGNIZED the old diary from years earlier. He remembered Jimmy showing him its entries in the days when he hid from President Sheen. It was hard to believe it had already been seven years since those events.

~

After briefly thumbing through its pages, Juan laid that journal aside and lifted the second one. It seemed older than the first, with a stiff cover and pages that were yellowed and dark with age.

The cover had letters embossed on it, now faded and grey. They appeared to be a set of initials...

- JMM -

HE COULDN'T HELP NOTICING that the initials matched those on the outside of the trunk.

Oddly, this journal's earliest writing looked as if it was written with a modern ballpoint pen, yet the ink was badly faded, and the yellowed pages looked as if they were hundreds of years old.

⌘

3

GRADUATION

"Anna, hurry, we'll be late," Jimmy called from the front porch.

"We have plenty of time," Anna objected as she appeared in the doorway. Besides, how can they begin without their keynote speaker?" Her comment was a thinly veiled compliment; her tone revealed a little playful boasting about her young husband's having been given that honor.

"Yeah, well, they might regret their choice if I'm M.I.A. for the graduation ceremony," he answered nervously.

"Relax. You're going to be great. It's not every day that one of the graduates gets to give the keynote."

Jimmy jerked his head back slightly in a silent chuckle that dismissed her point. "All the honorary spots like Valedictorian and Salutatorian were filled; they had to get creative to make a spot for a third-string player."

MIKE AND LENA were waiting beside their car in the farm's wide driveway. They both clapped at the sight of Jimmy and Anna in their graduation gowns as they made their way down to join them. Anna's gown couldn't hide the fact that she was eight months pregnant with their first child. Lena kissed her daughter proudly as she helped her into the back seat.

"Thanks for driving, Uncle Mike," Jimmy said appreciatively as he approached the car.

Mike's marriage to Anna's mom technically made Mike his father-in-law, but that hadn't changed how Jimmy addressed him. Mike didn't mind; being a father-in-law and uncle to the same nephew was difficult enough to explain.

"How does it feel to be done with college?" Mike asked as he slapped Jimmy on the back.

"I'll let you know after the ceremony. They might change their minds about letting me graduate after they hear me," Jimmy joked.

"Ya got nothin' to worry about, kid. Schools in half the country would be happy t' have ya."

"Yeah... it's the other half I'm worried about," Jimmy quickly answered, brushing off the comment with a smile.

"How are things with the restaurant?" Jimmy asked as he settled into the back seat.

"Amazin'," Mike answered happily. "Lena's cookin' is a major hit."

Lena smiled as she shook her head to disagree with the last part of Mike's answer. "The Lord is blessing us; we're very grateful."

Jimmy nodded with a smile. "Sounds like it was a great idea buying that new location."

"Best thing we could'a done," Mike agreed.

THE UNIVERSITY WAS NEARLY an hour away; Jimmy and Anna had become accustomed to the trip, having commuted to campus for four years. Moving closer would have been convenient, but they had plenty of work to keep the farm going, and Anna didn't want to say goodbye to Elroy and Rosie — her pet goats.

The past four years had kept them incredibly busy. The events surrounding President Sheen and Athaliah had made Jimmy a well-recognized celebrity from the first day he arrived on campus. He remained uncomfortable with the notoriety, reluctant to accept any credit for those events.

They had only been at the seminary for a few weeks when revival broke out on campus. Naturally, Jimmy was right in the middle of it and soon emerged as the movement's most recognized face. Before the end of their freshman year, the revival had spread to campuses throughout the country. It was still burning four years later, leading to a thriving new nationwide campus ministry that was keeping them both busy. It was the success of that ministry that had prompted Jimmy's keynote invitation.

"I'M LOOKING FORWARD to seeing Mr. And Mrs. O," Jimmy offered quietly, looking at Anna. "We haven't seen them since our wedding. Can't believe it's been four years already."

"I know," Anna agreed. "Little Ryan is almost eight years old — he's gonna look so big."

"Speaking of looking big..." Jimmy said, affectionately placing his hand on her stomach. Mrs. O is going to freak when she sees you."

Anna placed her hand on Jimmy's and happily smiled in agreement.

"So, what are your plans now after graduation?" Mike asked over his shoulder.

"Are you asking me?" Anna joked. "You might not have noticed, but I'm planning to start a family."

Jimmy held his hand up to Anna's for a high-five before giving Mike a slightly more serious answer: "PJ and I are joining forces. We plan to combine the campus work and his work with the gangs. There are lots of kids from both groups who are anxious to help.

"And..." he added, looking over at Anna... "there's that starting-a-family thing too."

Just after Jimmy said this, a sudden feeling swept over him, and he paused thoughtfully. Anna noticed the sudden change in his expression.

"What is it?" She asked quietly.

Jimmy looked at her, seeming startled by her unexpected question. He took her hand reassuringly and silently shook his head, signaling she had nothing to worry about. She felt him squeeze her hand gently as he turned his gaze out the window, deep in thought.

Anna knew him too well to accept his assurance but kept quiet as she squeezed his hand. She'd seen that look on him before. It was a familiar feeling for Jimmy, but one he hadn't sensed in quite this way in a while. The unction awakening in his spirit nearly shouted its unspoken message... declaring to him that his *Traveling* days were not finished. Not by a long shot.

"OH MY GOSH... Ryan, look at you!" Anna exclaimed as they met the O'Malleys. Ryan looked embarrassed as he nodded hello and awkwardly accepted her hug.

"Ryan, my man!" Jimmy greeted in an exaggeratedly husky voice, offering the boy a fist bump. Ryan seemed much more comfortable with that greeting; he smiled broadly as he bumped his fist against Jimmy's, then hugged him around the waist.

Barbara O'Malley's eyes widened with her smile as she looked at Anna and wrapped her in her arms. "How far along are you now?"

"Thirty-two weeks and three days... but who's counting?" Anna joked.

"Yo, Ward... how ya doin'?" Mike greeted Mr. O. "How was th' flight?"

"It was smooth, thankfully. That's a welcome accomplishment these days." The men shook hands and slapped each other around the shoulders. Ward turned to Jimmy and did the same.

"Hi, Uncle Ward," Jimmy greeted, addressing him the way he had all his life. While not technically related, the O'Malleys had been like family longer than he could remember.

"Thanks for making the trip out here. It's really great seeing you guys."

Ward wrapped his arm around Jimmy's shoulders as they walked together. "We wouldn't have missed it for the world. Look at you... a seminary graduate."

"Well, almost. We'll see how that goes when this is over," Jimmy joked with genuine humility. "Anna is the genius in the family. Hope the baby takes after her."

"Says th' guy who's givin' today's keynote," Mike jabbed.

"That's right!" Ward agreed. "Congratulations. That doesn't happen every day."

"Well, thank the Lord for that; I wouldn't want to do this every day," Jimmy confessed nervously.

Ward hugged his shoulders supportively. "It'll be awesome. We're looking forward to it."

"Hey, you aren't plannin' t' declare another drought or nothin', are ya? Cause I might wanna stock up th' restaurant."

Jimmy shook his head with a smile. "I don't think there's any danger of Baal worship here today."

"Speaking of that, I watched your interview with Devlon Sheen on your blog. That was quite a coup," Ward noted admiringly.

"It was nice of him to do it," Jimmy admitted. "God has really done a work in his life. He's doing some amazing things with the prison ministry there."

"Speakin' o' th blog," Mike cut in, "is the keynote bein' broadcast today?"

Anna answered happily. "The college is letting us record it. It'll be posted later."

A FAMILIAR SHOUT interrupted their conversation. "Hey, guys - wait up!"

Pete and Angela ran to join them.

"Chrissy and Sean are covering the food pantry today," Pete explained. "We wouldn't have missed this for anything."

Jimmy stopped walking and looked at the faces of everyone around him. "It's like old-home week," he said happily. Thanks, everybody, for coming; it means a lot to us both." Anna smiled and nodded in agreement.

Just then, someone began calling all the graduates together for the ceremony. "I guess it's showtime," Jimmy said nervously."

"You'll do great! We'll be praying for you," Ward encouraged.

NEARLY TWO HOURS LATER, the graduates sat awaiting their diplomas as Jimmy's keynote drew to a close. His had only been a brief thirty-minute talk, but he followed a half dozen other speakers in the drawn-out ceremony.

Far from being bored, however, the audience listened in rapt attention as Jimmy's heartfelt address reverberated. He recounted stories of dramatic conversions and transformed lives through the college ministries, even pointing out a second-year seminary student in the audience who had been one of those converts to everyone's applause.

He grew quiet for a moment and then spoke earnestly into the microphone, addressing the graduates in particular.

"I SUPPOSE BY NOW, everyone has heard me say that the days are growing short. I feel that in my soul more strongly today than ever before. You are embarking from here on a mission that is the most important the world has ever known. It will not be an easy mission; it may require sacrifices — it may even be painful, but I can promise you it will be the most rewarding work you can imagine!

"Today, souls are hanging in the balance, waiting for you to come and offer them a saving rescue. You are the only thing standing between them and a lost and tragic eternity! You have the blessed mission of bringing to them the light of the good news of hope in Jesus Christ. You already know how glorious that work is — I've worked side-by-side with many of you as we've had the privilege of doing it together.

"I want to encourage all of you to remember the age in which you live. Remember the signs of the seasons that Jesus described... remember that you stand in the final days of time. No matter how hard it may be... no matter what tempts you to turn aside... no matter what catastrophe or calamity gets in your way — do the work! Be the messenger of light that God has made you! Remember the charge Jesus gave us: *Go into the highways and byways and compel them to come in!*

"In closing, I'll leave with you the words of C. H. Spurgeon, who said it better and more succinctly than I ever could....

"Do what the Lord bids you, where he bids you, as He bids you, as long as He bids you, and do it at once!"

⌘

4

SEASON'S CHANGE

"Learn a lesson from a fig tree. When its branches sprout and start putting out leaves, you know that summer is near." ~ Jesus, Matthew 24:32

TWO DAYS LATER...

R everend Wilkes was standing in the foyer of the new Living Springs Church building when Nyle entered.

"We'll be finished with the changes to the AV systems today," Nyle informed him. "The new cameras are totally automated. It'll take the LiveStream broadcasts to a whole new production level."

"I'm grateful for all your help, Nyle. Your work has greatly impacted our ability to bring the Gospel to so many." Rev. Wilkes paused and lowered his gaze, adding, "I must say, though, sometimes I miss the old tent meetings."

"I have to agree with you on that," Nyle conceded. "But God is still working here — the crowds are still coming, and this building is amazing!"

"Thank the Lord; you're right about that. None of this would have been possible without Jimmy's generous financial help, not to mention his gift of this land to build it on."

"It is cool having it here, right where the old tent was. I love how you built the auditorium with sides that open when the weather is nice, giving it that open-air feeling."

Rev. Wilkes admitted, "That was Anna's idea. She really loved the old tent meetings, too."

The thought brought visions of long lines of people lining up to enter the old tent and being miraculously healed. Nyle felt a familiar thrill as he recalled being one of those who were miraculously healed.

"Boy, those were some wild days, weren't they?" He said nostalgically. Do you think we'll ever see times like those again?"

Rev. Wilkes looked into the distance with an earnest gaze as he answered. "As a matter of fact, I do. I feel that extraordinary times may soon be upon us again. I feel it in my heart — the days until Christ's coming are growing short."

Washington, DC...
Later that afternoon

PRESIDENT JOSHUA GODARD was two years into his second term. He'd been elected to finish Devlon Sheen's term after the former President resigned and surrendered to authorities. In a reflection of the mood in the country at that time, President Godard was a strong advocate of religious freedom — he even invited Jimmy and Anna to the White House soon after his election.

In recent years, that mood had begun to change throughout the country. In the latest midterm Congressional elections, most of the candidates who ran on faith-based platforms were defeated. The President now found himself opposed even by members of his own party.

One of the most divisive issues he faced was growing pressure to adopt a new global cryptocurrency. Progressive members of Congress supported replacing the US dollar as a way to eliminate the national debt. They were also attracted to the new electronic currency's ability to track wealth and automatically collect taxes. The control it provided resonated like a holy grail for central planners.

As a man familiar with his Bible, President Godard could see that it was a clear move toward a centralized One-World Government like the one described in Revelation. In fact, it seemed that all of the efforts to expand government powers throughout the world were heading in the same direction.

"THE CURRENCY BILL is gaining support in Congress," Joshua worried, speaking to his Chief of Staff. "I can delay it with a veto, but it's only a matter of time."

"That's not the worst of our worries at the moment, I'm afraid," his Chief of Staff replied anxiously as he entered the President's office. The National Security Adviser followed him into the room and laid a folder marked Top Secret on the President's desk.

"Russia is moving ground forces into Syria in bigger numbers than we've ever seen. Our intelligence is reporting coordinated movements by Turkey, which is massing troops along their own southern border as well."

"Are they planning to fight each other?" Joshua asked in surprise.

"Not each other. The forces are all focused in the same direction. All indications point to a joint attack against..." he said, pointing to the map on the President's desk.

"...Israel," Joshua said as he understood. "How close are they to making a move?"

"We think it's mostly saber-rattling for now. A show of force. But it's adding heat to a pot that's already boiling."

Joshua silently prayed as he studied the map showing the Russian, Syrian, and Turkish positions. "What's your recommendation?"

"We want to move a carrier strike force into the area."

"Do it," The President agreed.

Geneva, Switzerland...

AT THAT MOMENT, the annual meeting of the International Monetary Fund was coming to order. Leaders of the world's most powerful economies had already been busy behind closed doors for days, and there was a strong air of anticipation that something significant was about to happen.

For months, news organizations had been reporting on the growing financial crisis that was sweeping the world. Rumors were becoming more persistent that the US Dollar was on the brink of collapse. US debt was quickly approaching the point where it would exceed any possibility of repayment. The country's tax revenues no longer covered even the interest obligations on the massive debt, making a default imminent. The US was officially bankrupt.

The Euro was not much better off. The spread of war and unrest had left several nations' economies in ruins. With those member states unable to repay their massive debts, the European countries that remained solvent labored under the burden of supporting their bankrupt neighbors.

Officials from China and Russia had been negotiating a secret proposal with the other leaders for months. Their own currencies appeared strong, although it was widely known that they had been artificially manipulated for years to appear more solvent. Nonetheless, their apparent economic strength bolstered their influence in the growing crisis. The price for their cooperation would be significant.

GRETA GRABALÓS, the IMF Managing Director, rose to the podium, flanked by leaders of the most prominent member countries. A hushed silence fell over the crowd as the clicking of camera shutters punctuated the moment.

"The annual meeting of the International Monetary Fund is now in session," she declared, striking her gavel on the large rostrum where she stood. She scanned the faces of the leaders beside her and those of the other member states seated below, acknowledging their acquiescent nods. They signaled that negotiations had been completed—the members were ready to vote in unison.

"As all of you know," Ms. Grabalós began... "the world is in the throes of a financial crisis. This crisis now threatens our very economic survival and the starvation of countless millions throughout the world's poorest nations.

"I am pleased to announce that this organization is ready to propose a far-reaching solution. One that will end the crisis once and for all and provide enormous benefits to mankind for ages to come."

THE MASSIVE SCREEN behind her was filled with an image depicting a new world digital currency.

"Today, we are happy to announce an international agreement to create the *EarthCoin*. A single world currency based on digital blockchain technology. This new global currency is 100% digital and will be managed by the World Bank. It will be issued with sufficient funds to cover all of the world's debt and wealth holdings, replacing all existing currencies. Citizens will be given ample time to convert their savings to *EarthCoins* at a predetermined exchange rate. At the same time, the nations' balance sheets will be reconciled to eliminate their debt burdens immediately.

"Before calling for a final vote on this proposal, the members will be given an opportunity to express any questions or concerns. Please welcome the brilliant mastermind behind the new *EarthCoin* and the monetary system that will support it, Maximiano Marata, who will explain more of the details."

A MAN WEARING oversized glasses and hair slightly askew entered the stage, stepping to the podium. He was young, appearing to be in his late twenties. He spoke in well-practiced English but with a thick Spanish accent. He began without introduction, diving immediately into the details of his presentation.

~

"Under the new digital currency, the movement of every digital coin will be tracked, showing a chain-of-custody record of each owner that holds it and providing a detailed ledger of all its transactions, investments, and purchases. Merchants worldwide will register with the World Bank to conduct commerce using a choice of simple mobile apps that will be provided. Onerous tasks, like the collection of taxes, will be handled automatically and reported back to the appropriate authorities in real-time.

"As I mentioned, the *EarthCoin* is based on a powerful blockchain algorithm. Every coin's movement will be infinitely traceable back to the moment of its creation, showing the unique identities of every business or individual who has possessed it, as well as the transaction details of those purchases. It is impossible to counterfeit and readily reveals any attempts to tamper with the transaction record. In this respect, it cannot be 'laundered,' to *coin* a phrase." He paused with an awkward smile at this attempt at humor. The audience remained silent and stone-faced. He cleared his throat nervously and pressed on.

"We are quite sure this unparalleled transparency will virtually ensure 'the end of stolen money.' Once all other currencies have been outlawed, that is."

Mr. Marata went on to explain how exchange rates would initially be calculated and the mechanisms for tracking commerce. It involved carefully negotiated exchange terms and a massive network of computer systems hosted at the World Bank, with backup systems distributed around the world. He didn't mention the fact that China and Russia had exacted especially favorable conversion rates for their own currencies as well as preeminent influence over the new monetary system.

Greta Grabalós returned to the podium after the presentation. The creation of the new currency was unanimously approved after just a single round of voting.

A DISTINGUISHED-LOOKING attendee smiled from the audience, nodding approvingly. He was obviously a wealthy and powerful man, surrounded by an entourage of bodyguards and clamoring staff. He looked to his right and then to his left, sharing looks of congratulation as he sat back with a subtle smile.

The distinguished dusting of gray in his hair had grown more pronounced, and a neatly trimmed gray beard now covered his face, but the man was not a stranger. He now went by a single name, *Bahal*.

FROM THE PODIUM, the World Bank's Managing Director nodded to him with a pleased expression as she hailed the day's achievement. Her words rang ominously through the vast auditorium.

"This is a great day!" She declared with evident pleasure. "We are witnessing the dawning of a new age for mankind!"

⌘

5

ENTWINED

"His story is to be entwined with thine own."

J immy stirred from sleep, surprised that morning had come so quickly, and immediately discovered that his surroundings had changed. He'd become accustomed to unexpected travels, which no longer surprised him, but he struggled to make sense of the scene this time.

HE FOUND himself on a mossy embankment beside a small stream. Judging from the warm sun and budding foliage around him, it was a pleasant sunny morning in springtime.

The sound of people talking caught his attention, and he climbed higher to look at a genuinely surprising sight. A small group of people were gathered nearby — an older couple with three young men; Jimmy soon understood them to be a family. Their father was a distinguished-looking man. They stood outside a rustic-looking log cabin in a clearing full of low-cut tree stumps, suggesting that it had been built with logs cut from the immediate vicinity.

The thing that truly surprised him was the way they were dressed. The men were wearing knee-length breeches with stockings and short waistcoats. Their father wore a linen shirt with frills and an odd sort of overcoat that was short in the front but extended down to his knees in the back. The men's shoes looked like they'd been made by hand, with buckles holding them closed. Jimmy couldn't see the woman's shoes beneath her long dress. Each of the men wore long hair that was tied behind their head, even the father's.

It was unmistakable to Jimmy as he gazed at them in awe — everything about the scene pointed to a time in the eighteenth century!

Two sons stood beside saddled horses; they appeared to be the older of the three brothers. Their mother hugged them and wiped a tear as she turned from one to the other. Their father embraced them both and spoke in a thick Scottish brogue as he addressed his sons.

"I'm proud o' ye William," he said to the younger of the two. "Ye'v done fine work with thy studies; a good man ye'v become by God's grace. Remember all ye'v learned here and ye'll be well equipped for thy calling."

"Thanks, t' thee, father," William said gratefully. He fought back a tightness in his throat that revealed the emotion in his words and then turned to his younger brother, "John... it will be thy turn soon to follow us. Keep fast to thy studies here." His younger brother nodded in a promise that he would.

"It was good to see thee, Gilbert," his father said to his oldest son with a hand on his shoulder. "Keep good charge of thy brother."

"I shall," Gilbert assured him as the young men mounted their horses.

"Are ye sure of the way?" their mother worried.

"Aye. It's a familiar journey," Gilbert reassured her. "It's hardly a day's ride... at this time in th' year, we should arrive before dusk."

With that, a shake of the reins and a gentle nudge with their heels set the horses walking. Their parents and brother watched them ride off, waving until they were no longer in sight. Their mother accepted her husband's embrace as she wiped the tears from her cheeks.

CHOZEQ'S familiar voice suddenly boomed close behind where Jimmy stood. "The lad's name is William Tennent," Chozeq explained. "Remember it. His story is to be entwined with thine own. His father's work here at this Log College has prepared many faithful men for God's work."

JIMMY WATCHED as the scene dissolved, placing him in a dimly lit room instead. The young William Tennent studied carefully at a small desk near the window.

His older brother Gilbert entered the room, looking at William with concern.

"Brother, I fear ye'll make thyself ill with thy exhaustive study," he said with notable concern. "By all counts, thy mastery of theology is unsurpassed. Why worry ye so over the Presbytery's examination?"

On closer inspection, Jimmy saw that William had grown thin and looked gaunt and pale. His hand was trembling slightly as he scanned the page with his fingers.

"Test me again in the Latin text," he requested, sounding distraught.

"Ye know quite enough of it, Will," his brother reassured him. "Few can wield it as well as thee."

William looked toward his older brother with a worried expression and suddenly grabbed his chest, appearing dizzy, then slumped over and began to fall from the chair. Gilbert caught him, calling for his wife to come and help.

They helped him to his bed, where he collapsed into unconsciousness.

"I'll go get the doctor," Gilbert said urgently. "Stay with him!"

"Of course," she quickly agreed, looking as worried as her husband.

It was night when Gilbert and the doctor arrived; although he had come at once, it had been a long distance. Jimmy was surprised that the doctor seemed so young, likely a recent graduate of medical school himself.

William was awake when they entered but seemed confused.

"He suffers from fever," the doctor quickly confirmed. "Has he had anything to drink?"

"He's refused it," Gilbert's wife answered, sounding worried and frustrated.

JIMMY WATCHED as the scene changed again, now several days later. William and Gilbert were talking. It seemed to be gibberish to Jimmy at first, but then he realized they were having a conversation in Latin. William was still in bed and looked weak; he held his head as he spoke as if he were nursing a bad headache.

All of a sudden, William passed out, falling as limp as if he'd dropped dead. He lay so lifeless that no pulse could be found. Gilbert frantically tried to revive him, but nothing he tried provided any response. By the evening, all hope was lost; it appeared that William wasn't breathing. After sitting vigil over his brother all night, Gilbert sadly began making funeral arrangements the following day.

They laid William's lifeless body on a board, as was typically done for a funeral wake, and soon, an invitation went out for anyone wishing to pay their last respects.

Late that evening, Jimmy stood alone, looking at William's cold frame. The eyes appeared sunken, the lips discolored, and the whole body cold and stiff. All chances of William's recovery seemed long gone.

TO JIMMY'S SUDDEN SURPRISE, the entire scene changed once again. He was enveloped in a loud and moving chorus of singing, surrounded by untold millions of worshiping souls gathered around a Heavenly throne. It was rapturous!

He was drawn into the amazing experience, losing all track of time as he joined in thundering praises. He eventually realized that Chozeq was standing in front of him with his hands on both of Jimmy's shoulders. Jimmy opened his eyes, looking up at his angelic warrior friend. Chozeq's face reflected all of the praises and rapturous joy that swelled in Jimmy's own heart.

At Chozeq's urging, Jimmy turned to see Ardent standing beside them, and, to his astonishment, William stood with him. It was evident that Ardent was attempting to get William's attention, but just as Jimmy had been, William was utterly engrossed in the enthralling worship. Jimmy could hear the message that Ardent was delivering to him…

"This is not thy time, ye must return…"

Jimmy looked to Chozeq, struggling to understand.

"William has not died," Chozeq explained. "There is still much for him to do in God's work. A very great move of God is coming in his time."

ALL AT ONCE, Jimmy was back in William's bedroom. He saw that the young doctor had returned and William had been moved back into his warm bed, but his body still appeared lifeless. The doctor was working urgently in his attempts to revive his friend. Gilbert entered the room, holding his head in dismay.

"I wish for my brother's recovery more than any, but this is madness! It has been nearly three days — look at him!" he protested. "I must insist that we go ahead with his funeral."

The people were again invited and assembled to attend the funeral. The doctor still objected, "Give just one hour!" he argued desperately. After an hour had passed, he begged for half an hour and finally for a quarter of an hour more. Gilbert was deeply grieved as he reluctantly conceded for a final time. He left the room to rejoin those already gathered for the funeral service.

"But they can't bury him!" Jimmy exclaimed in alarm, looking at the desperate scene.

The doctor noticed that William's tongue had swollen to the point where it threatened to crack. He was attempting to soften it by applying some emollient ointment with a feather when Gilbert came in. Mistaking what the doctor was doing for an attempt to feed him, he was horrified.

"It is shameful to be feeding a lifeless corpse!" he exclaimed, demanding that the funeral should begin immediately.

Jimmy looked at Chozeq imploringly... "He's not dead — They can't!" he urged.

At this critical moment, William opened his eyes and gave a dreadful groan, then sank again into apparent death. Gilbert gasped with alarm as he saw this, his eyes wide with astonishment. This put an end to all thoughts of burying him, and all Gilbert's efforts quickly turned to helping the doctor revive his brother. In about an hour, William's eyes opened again with another heavy groan, and again, all signs of life vanished. A full hour later, he seemed to revive with more power and regained consciousness to the great joy of the family and friends gathered around. Some stood astounded, who had been ridiculing the idea of restoring a dead body to life.

JIMMY SAT up straight as he awoke again in his bed, nearly breathless. The scene shocked him, not because he thought it unbelievable, but because he could never have guessed that such a miracle had happened at such a time—just before the American Revolution. Everything about it implied the beginning of a great move of God... a mighty revival.

Chozeq's words resounded in his mind as he tried to make sense of them... *'His story is to be entwined with thine own.'*

He wondered how the life of someone who lived so long ago could have any bearing on his own. Furthermore, Chozeq's clear message was not that William Tennent would merely pass down a legacy that would influence Jimmy's life but rather that the timelines for their lives would be *entwined*. That was far different; it suggested that Jimmy's life would somehow influence William's as well.

The puzzle kept Jimmy up for most of the night as he struggled with its meaning.

⌘

6

SLEEPLESS

*"**This hope** will not disappoint us, because God's love has been poured out in our hearts through the Holy Spirit who was given to us." ~ Romans 5:5*

SIX WEEKS AFTER GRADUATION....

The baby's crying shattered the room's temporary calm, waking Jimmy from a light sleep. Beams of early morning sunlight peaked around the edges of the bedroom's window shade as he rose. Anna was unmoved, still sleeping soundly — the victim of pure exhaustion. She'd been up half the night.

Jimmy lifted their infant son from his cradle and jostled him gently, inserting a pacifier to quiet the hungry child.

"Good morning, VJ," he whispered, using his son's initials, which were short for Vincent James. They'd named him after the two men Jimmy loved most: his father and old Jim Van Clief.

He kissed the tiny boy's head and smiled as little fingers wrapped tightly around his pinky. Then, nestling the two-week-old baby against his shoulder, he patted the child's back as he paced the floor, soon distracted by his thoughts.

Ever since their graduation, he hadn't been able to shake the feeling that something was coming; a new change was on the horizon. The news from Geneva had added to his sense of foreboding. The new global currency was one more puzzle piece falling into place. Nearly every other part of the world order described in Bible prophecy was either already apparent or poised to fall into place.

Unrest among nations was getting worse; anger and lawlessness were on the rise once again. The brief sunshine of revival that swept the country after Athaliah's defeat had dimmed. Jimmy knew that the tide of opinion could turn against believers at any time—he'd seen it firsthand. Liberty, especially religious liberty, was increasingly fragile.

If it weren't for his travels to future events, he'd be expecting Christ's return at any second, but he knew other developments were yet to come. That thought reminded him of the first time he met Chozeq when he first traveled—that night still seemed as vivid to him as ever, even seven years later. In his mind's eye, he could practically see the hideous devils that filled the skies that night — it was the same night he saw PJ being stabbed by Rad.

That memory brought a flood of others — of PJ's near-death experience on that night and the words that Ardent would speak to him in the emergency room. Jimmy's mind jumped from those memories, recalling Chase's prison execution and Rad's eventual conversion. None of those events had happened yet.

Rad's conversion drew Jimmy's thoughts to another memory... his future meeting with Rad, PJ, and Badrick at Pastor Jerome's Calvary Hill Church in Brooklyn. That experience was still jarring in its implications. For one thing, Jimmy had been surprisingly visible when he met them, even though he'd traveled through time. It wasn't the first time he'd been visible when traveling — there were those other times at the New Year's services and the Glass Cathedral — but those travels weren't through time. Its implications have haunted his thoughts for five years.

During that same meeting, he and Radison were transported

together to another future time, which was even more surprising. It remained as clear to Jimmy as if it had just happened. The sights and sounds of the old European city where they'd found themselves... the mixed smells of food wafting from small cafés... and Bahal's cigar. The memory of Bahal's face suddenly seized him, sending a chill up Jimmy's back. He didn't need to hear another supernatural voice to know that the time was coming soon when Bahal would be revealed for who he was — the little horn that speaks great words... the coming Beast.

"OH... HEY..." he heard Anna say in a sleepy voice as she stirred. "How long has he been up?"

"Not long. Just a few minutes," Jimmy assured her.

She came alongside and offered her husband a kiss as she accepted their baby from his arms. She settled into the nearby rocking chair while Jimmy grabbed some work clothes.

"I should go see how Pete's doing with the chores."

PETE WAS PLACING two filled milk cans in the barn's walk-in refrigerator as Jimmy caught up with him.

"Thanks for your help here this morning. It's been great having you here a couple of days a week."

"No sweat," Pete assured him with a smile. "Many hands make the work light... or whatever that saying is."

"Well, it's nice of you to do it. I know it's tough to get up so early."

"I kinda like it," Pete dismissed, "Especially when the weather is nice like this." He looked at the clear sky, "Looks like it'll be a beautiful day."

Jimmy grabbed a gallon of milk from the barn's walk-in. It was Pete who had the epiphany that he didn't always need to carry one of those huge milk cans into the house. "What a brilliant idea," Jimmy joked in a humble admission of how dumb he'd been for not thinking of that sooner.

As they walked together into the yard, Pete could see that Jimmy was distracted. "I've seen that look before," he noted. What's up?"

Jimmy seemed surprised by the comment. He looked at his friend with a subtle shake of his head. "Nothin... everything's fine. The baby was up a lot last night."

Pete nodded his silent reply; they stood quietly for a moment. "Did you see the news last night about that new International Peace Force the UN is creating? If you ask me, it looks more like an army; they're merging NATO into it."

Jimmy looked at him with a nod, acknowledging he'd seen the news, then he turned and looked distractedly toward the new church building in the north field — on the old tent grounds. "It's happening fast now," Jimmy said as he took in the sight of the gleaming new auditorium. He thought to himself about the feeling he'd been having, silently repeating the words that kept going through his mind: *The days are growing short.'*

Jimmy's recent thoughts about Rad came to mind again. He glanced at Pete, "Have you heard from Radison lately?"

"Radison?" Pete repeated, seeming surprised by the question. "No, I can't remember when I last heard from him. He stopped answering my messages when he quit school and moved out of his last foster place. What makes ya ask?"

"Not sure," Jimmy admitted. "I was just thinking about him this morning. I think God still has a plan for him — know what I mean?"

Pete rubbed a hand across the top of his head as he sighed. "That's a tall order... it'll *take* an act of God to get through to *him*, that's for sure." After thinking briefly, he added, "Maybe his dad knows where he is; they were starting to keep in touch."

"That's a good idea," Jimmy agreed. "I'll ask PJ when he gets here. I know he's still visiting the prison every week; he can ask Chase for us."

.   .   .

WHILE THEY WERE STILL TALKING, the sound of a car on the farm's gravel drive drew their attention. They turned to see PJ park it and climb out.

"You're up early," Jimmy said, checking his watch. Just as he said that, Baibina climbed from the passenger seat.

"Baibi couldn't wait to see the baby," Juan smiled.

With remarkable timing, Anna emerged just then onto the front porch, holding little VJ.

Baibi ran to her with a broad smile and was soon cradling the infant lovingly in her arms. The women wandered back inside the house, chattering happily.

PJ slapped Jimmy on the back and shook Pete's hand as the ladies disappeared inside. "What were those serious looks I saw as I drove up?"

"Nothing really," Jimmy dismissed. "We were just talking about Radison; I wondered how he was doing. Has Chase heard from him at all?"

PJ grew serious as he considered the question. "No, as a matter of fact, Chase is pretty worried about him. We pray about it every time I'm there."

"Think he's still in Brooklyn?" Pete asked.

PJ was about to answer uncertainly, but Jimmy cut him off; "Yeah, he's definitely still in the city, near the waterfront." Pete and PJ looked at him curiously, surprised that he seemed so sure of his answer. They had a strong suspicion of how he knew it.

"What have you seen?" PJ asked quietly.

Jimmy gave his friends a concerned glance and then looked down distractedly. "Just that things are starting again — things are in motion. It won't be long... the days are getting short now."

PJ grew serious as well. "I sense it, too. The past few years have been incredible... we've seen an amazing move of God. I've lost track of how many workers have been commissioned through the City Missions — they've gone out all over the world. But things are different lately; the fire is cooling. Persecution is getting worse, too."

"Yeah, looks like the country's turnin' cold again," Pete weighed in.

"If things keep goin' the way they are, it won't be long till we're back to how it was under President Sheen."

"Maybe worse," Jimmy added ominously.

LATER THAT EVENING....

JIMMY SAT ALONE at the old desk in the guest bedroom. This had been *his* room when old Mr. Van Clief — Uncle Jim — was alive. The setting brought back a flood of memories from those days. Jim remembered the nights he spent here reading from Amos' journal and the days he spent writing in his own.

Maybe it was Pete's mention of President Sheen that triggered those thoughts. For such dramatic events, he admitted that he thought surprisingly little about them. He'd spent the past five years trying to get out of the shadow of those events, not to mention being busy with finishing college and growing the campus ministry. Jimmy thought about the amazing night when Sheen gave his heart to Christ. The transformation in his life had been undeniable. The two of them remained in touch, though their calls had become rare. The prison where Sheen was held was too far away to visit very often.

Jimmy thought again about the way Amos' journal had chronicled all those events, recording even small details. Amos' own words about those days still rang in his mind... *'You're livin' in the true end of days, son.'*

It was odd that Amos' journal ended with the conclusion of those events — he wrote nothing about events after Athaliah's defeat. Amos' visits had stopped after that. It was one of the great puzzles of Jim's life; if those times marked the last days, why hadn't the Lord come back yet?

Jimmy rested his chin in his hand as he leaned forward and silently breathed a prayer.

~

. . .

"HELLO, SON..." The sound of Amos' voice startled him. Jimmy turned quickly to see his old friend standing with his thumbs in his pockets. He was an older man but not the oldest that Jimmy had seen him. The oldest was on the night before Amos died, on November 26th, 1919. Judging from his apparent age this time, Jimmy guessed he was a few years younger than that. He reminded Jim of old Mr. Van Clief, Amos' grandson.

"A-Amos! It's been a while... five years..." Jimmy said in surprise.

"Has it now..." Amos answered, seeming as surprised as Jimmy by the fact. He paused for a moment as he glanced around him, seeing that the room's bed had been removed and replaced with a pull-out couch. Jimmy noticed his glance and explained...

"I don't sleep here anymore; Anna and I are in the main bedroom. We have a son; he's there in the next room."

Amos nodded with an approving smile. "I must say I'm not surprised. Seems congratulations are in order."

"Thanks."

"Well, if it's been five years, I suppose the days are gettin' pretty dark by now. I confess I haven't been shown much of these times — not since those events with Athaliah and the drought's ending."

"Things have been mostly calm, actually. The revival that started back then spread everywhere — it changed the world!" Jimmy paused, considering the burden weighing on his heart lately... "At least until recently."

Amos took a seat, leaning forward attentively with his elbows on his knees. His attention coaxed Jimmy to continue.

"Honestly, I've been feeling something lately... like God wants me to do something. It feels like it's time to do something new."

Amos seemed to be contemplating something, deciding whether to share it. "To be perfectly honest, my travels to these times haven't completely ended; there have been a few more that I was told not to write down in my journal. I can't help feelin' like my visit here today is for the purpose of sharin' what I've seen."

It was Jimmy's turn to lean forward, elbows on his knees as he listened carefully.

"It's to do with Bahal, mostly," Amos shared. He'll be fixin' to pick up where he left off. He's pullin' the strings behind the scenes, even here in America, where he's still got powerful allies."

"I saw him too," Jimmy revealed. "He's the Beast, isn't he."

Amos nodded, "If he's not, then he's awfully close to the man who is. He'll be the one who's behind establishin' a single world currency and gettin' the governments to come together."

"That's happened; the move to a world currency has started already," Jimmy explained. "They just announced it last month. Bahal is behind that?"

"Yup. He's got his hands in the whole thing, pullin' it all together like a puppeteer. The currency comes first, and then the single-world government will follow. He'll sell it as a way of stopping the nations from war by joinin' 'em all under one alliance. If the change in currency has started, the rest'll be happenin' soon after."

Jimmy considered what he was hearing; it was no surprise that Bahal was involved in the IMF's plans. Yet the prompting in his spirit at the moment was for something different. Something else comes first.

"Is that all you've seen?" he asked Amos tentatively.

Amos studied Jimmy's eyes for a moment, avoiding a direct answer. "You've become quite an accomplished traveler yourself, even doin' some things I haven't, like travelin' backward in time to see me. God has a purpose in that — the gifts He gives are always for a purpose. You'll have to trust Him to show you what the purpose is."

⌘

7

ETERNAL CHAINS

"Whatever you bind on earth shall be bound in heaven."
~ Jesus, Matthew 18:18

A FEW DAYS LATER....

"That's the last load for today," Angela said as she waved goodbye to the final delivery driver.

Pete dropped a huge bag of feed grain from his shoulder and wiped his hands. "I hope you're bein' careful," he said, placing his hand on his wife's belly protectively. "I don't want ya workin' too hard."

She dismissed his concern with a kiss. "Look who's talking... just because you're strong enough to move a whole silo of grain by your-self doesn't mean you should."

Pete shrugged. "God's been blessing this place. The silos are full, an' we're still bringin' in more." He nodded at the neatly stacked pile of filled bags on the pallet in front of him. "We get ten times as much sellin' it direct to the wholesalers once it's bagged."

As they were talking, Anna joined them. She beamed a smile at Angela as she admired the growing evidence of her friend's expected baby. "We appreciate you guys so much! We could never run this place without you."

"We love it," Pete assured her. "Besides, where else could a guy like me earn this much?"

"Worth each penny... both of them," Anna joked. It honestly wasn't much of an exaggeration.

"Seriously though," she placed her hand on Angela's shoulder in a friendly gesture, "we're going to need others to help soon — you can't keep working like this for much longer."

With a smile, Angela accepted Ana's admonition, looking down at herself gratefully.

"That's what I'm sayin'," Pete chimed in. He hugged his wife's shoulders supportively. "Speakin' o' help... I need Jimmy's help with the milking machine — it's makin' a funny noise. Do you know when he'll be back?"

"He's at the Mission in Harbor City with PJ today. They could be back any time now or late tonight. You never know with those two." Anna didn't smile as she answered; there was a detectable hint of worry in her eyes.

It was Angela's turn to place a consoling hand on her friend's shoulder. "They'll be fine. They've been through times a lot worse than this. God has His hand on them — if that's true of anyone, it's true of those two."

Anna nodded gratefully. She couldn't argue the point. Still, the sense of danger she felt wouldn't go away. She looked at her friends seriously...

"I'd like to pray for them... can we?"

Pete and Angela immediately agreed, joining hands together as they began to seek the Lord.

HARBOR CITY...

PJ AND JIMMY climbed the stoop to the old brownstone's front door and rang the bell. Lorena, the young woman who lived there, had been part of the City Mission team since its beginning. Her voice had immediately raised PJ's concern when she'd called them earlier that morning. She was asking for prayer — her ex-boyfriend, the father of her child, was on his way over to see her. PJ knew Lorena was right to be worried.

Raul had been the leader of one of the city's rival gangs; he'd been in prison for seven years — since before God's move swept through the city's gangs at the start of the City Mission. Lorena was now a very different person than she had been then. She was clean from drugs and was now a respected member of the community, active in her son's school, and a vital member of the Mission team.

She had just opened the door to greet PJ and Jimmy when Raul's voice startled her. He was standing in the street, along with a dozen of his former *associates*. The former gang members looked at PJ with detectable fear in their eyes. They remembered all too well the day they saw him stop a shower of hot lead and knock hundreds of gang members to the ground with just the sound of his voice. All of them had been among the group who fled in panic that day.

Raul hadn't seen any of that. In fact, the reason for the demise of the city's gangs was a mystery to him. He only saw it as an opportunity to step into the void and return things to the way they were... with himself at the head of it all.

One of the guys leaned close to speak into Raul's ear, pointing at PJ. Raul's eyes narrowed as he looked at him.

"I hear you're the dude that split my bloods — broke up my posse. I'm here ta bring it back again." He looked at his group and shook his head. "What're you Rudeboys afraid o'? This guy ain't nothin'."

He turned toward PJ again. "What're ya doin' with my woman? She don't need you no more, Raul is back in town.

"Hey Lorena, get y'self out here - you're with me now. I got some catching up t'do baby..." he looked to his friends with a sly smirk... "ya know what I'm sayin'?

"An' bring me my kid; I wanna show 'im the ropes... teach 'im the family business."

PJ spoke quietly to Lorena, "Get inside and lock the door. Stay upstairs with Pablo. If things get crazy out here, call 911 right away."

Lorena didn't argue. She vividly remembered what happened that day on the street six years ago and clearly recalled Jimmy's encounter with Athalia on national TV. If anyone could handle Raul, it would be these two!

Jimmy didn't take his eyes off Raul and his men. He could see that the unsavory team of gang members was not alone — a small host of sinister creatures was also gathered around them. Jimmy noticed others also hovering near the street corner and beside an alleyway. The creatures glared at Jimmy and PJ with looks of seething hatred but also nodded deferentially to Raul as if he were their leader. Jimmy quickly detected why — seeing Raul's eyes flash red as they blinked, with the snake-like eyes of a demon master.

"These guys aren't alone," Jimmy whispered.

"How many?" PJ quietly asked, immediately understanding Jimmy's message.

"A few dozen, plus more across the street and over by the alley. By the way, Raul is possessed."

"That figures," PJ said with a slight grimace. "What about on our side?"

Jimmy looked right and left, pressing his fist to his chest in a familiar salute to his angelic friends. "Do you remember that angelic army that appeared at the tent grounds? The one that filled the skies?"

"How could I forget?"

"They're all here," Jimmy said with a smile.

"Right," PJ said, suddenly feeling much more confident. "So, who's doing this, you or me?"

Raul interrupted their private conversation by shouting at them, "What're you two jabbin' about? I'd wipe those dirt-eatin' grins off yer faces if I was you."

He flipped open his switchblade, signaling the others to do the same. "Boys, get ready t' serve up these losers. We're takin' our city back."

Jimmy closed his eyes as he silently sought the Lord, then opened them with a piercing look that bore into Raul. His shout practically thundered, echoing loudly from the nearby buildings.

"VILE BEAST — TELL US YOUR NAME!"

THE DEMON that possessed Raul cried out immediately in an inhuman, snarling growl.

"ODIUM..."

...the creature shrieked loudly.

JIMMY STEPPED FORWARD, challenging the beast.

"IN THE NAME of Jesus Christ and the power of His might, you're commanded to come out of this man... come out in Jesus' name!"

ODIUM EMERGED, visible and in full view of the surrounding gang members, revealing his blood-red form. He rose on leathery bat wings and bared his massive talons, shrieking like a prehistoric monster.

The already jittery gang members immediately turned tail and fled in terror at the sight, abandoning Raul as they escaped in every direction like roaches fleeing daylight.

The hoard of demonic imps that surrounded Odium did not flee. In fact, to Jimmy's surprise, they all suddenly materialized and rushed together toward Jimmy and PJ with their vicious claws extended.

Angel warriors immediately met the demons' attack, materializing visibly to meet their enemies. More demon forces soon joined the battle, which converged on the surreal scene from all directions like a swarm of angry wasps that filled the air and covered the open streets. It was some kind of hellish ambush!

Ardent and Chozeq appeared at once, shielding PJ and Jimmy from the vicious attack and driving the creatures back with bright flashes from their huge swords.

Lorena watched wide-eyed from her apartment window above, able to see the battling demons and bright angels as they clashed in their titanic struggle. She fell to her knees in desperate prayer. When PJ had talked about things getting crazy, she was pretty sure that this was not what he had in mind! Calling 911 didn't seem like much of an option under these circumstances.

In all the chaos, Raul stood unmoved, unafraid of the fiends swirling around him. In fact, he seemed to be directing them! Jimmy suddenly realized that the demon hoards had not been deferring to Odium after all. It was Raul who commanded them!

The fearless gang leader glared hatefully at Jimmy, then pointed toward the upstairs windows and shouted to his demonic minions, "Bring me the boy! Kill the woman if you have to!"

A massive swarm of sinister creatures flew toward the upstairs windows but were swiftly blocked by a battalion of angelic protectors. The angel warriors took up positions, standing guard over Lorena's apartment. Jimmy looked up at the attacking swarm, infused with righteous fury. He cried out with a shout that echoed like thunder:

STOP!

To Raul's astonishment, the entire hoard of fierce hellish beasts was instantly frozen, appearing paralyzed as they began falling to the ground. Odium resisted the longest, charging at Jimmy in bloodthirsty rage.

. . .

"In the name of Jesus Christ — BE STILL!" Jimmy shouted at him.

The force of his command struck the demon like a cannon blast, throwing him backward and sending him skidding across the ground, finally landing at Raul's feet. Jimmy raised his arms as he yelled the Spirit's judgment over the entire demonic throng:

"By Heaven's decree, your time here has ended—today, you are banished to eternal chains!"

The ground began to open around them, swallowing the beasts as they shrieked in a terrified panic. Odium began to sink and looked up at Raul, watching the way Raul dismissed him with an arrogant sneer. Suddenly, Odium burned with hatred for this man who had led him and his demon brothers to this terrible demise. His talons grabbed hold of Raul's ankles, shocking the gang leader, who seemed to believe he was impervious to harm. As Odium was pulled into the earth, Raul felt himself being dragged down with him. He screamed a terrified howl and clawed at the ground in desperation, shouting obscenities and cursing God along with the evil beast who was betraying him.

The screeching of howling beasts, mixed with Raul's curses and terrified cries, lasted for over a minute until the ground finished swallowing the sentenced creatures. Raul disappeared, screaming, as he was sucked beneath the earth. The fissures closed as quickly as they'd opened, leaving no trace of the astonishing event.

The angel armies were soon gone as well. Ardent nodded to PJ, acknowledging the astonished Pastor's thanks. Chozeq placed his hand on Jimmy's shoulder supportively, and then they both spread their enormous wings and disappeared in flashes that streaked into the sky.

PJ looked at Jimmy in stunned silence over the unbelievable events they'd just witnessed. "Wow..." he finally said. "I definitely didn't see that coming."

⌘

8

WITH OR AGAINST

"They won't be able to claim ignorance; people will have to either be with Him or against Him."

On their way home, PJ and Jimmy discussed what they would tell their wives about the day's events to avoid scaring them. They finally decided to keep it vague, leaving out the terrifying details.

When they finally arrived, Anna was rocking on the porch with the baby. Jimmy climbed the stairs to meet her, with PJ following close behind. Anna looked at her husband seriously, studying his face. He detected that she'd been crying recently.

"What's wrong?" he asked with concern.

"I've been praying for you all afternoon," she confided. "You were fighting demons again, weren't you?"

Jimmy was stunned by her comment. He looked over at PJ, who was clearly as shocked as he was. As he scrambled for a reply, it quickly became apparent that none of the plans he and PJ discussed on their way home made sense any longer. He had a disarmed expression as he humbly answered. "Um... well... yes, actually."

Anna rose suddenly from her seat and hugged Jimmy close, leaning against his shoulder as she nestled their infant son between them. She sniffled emotionally as she spoke. "I'm so glad you're alright. I was so scared!"

"I'm fine... Jimmy assured her tenderly. "We're on the winning side, remember?"

"I know..." she admitted. "It just looked so scary; they showed it on the news."

Jimmy and PJ looked at each other in surprise. "Th-the news?" he asked.

"Well, they only had video from a few blocks away — it was from someone's phone who recorded it. It looked like there were so many of them... we could hear all their screeching... it was terrible!"

Jimmy coaxed Anna to sit down, then carefully took a seat beside her. PJ leaned against the railing close by, providing moral support. "We were visiting one of the women from the Mission... Lorena. She's a single mom. Her ex-boyfriend just got out of prison, so we went to make sure she was alright."

Jimmy went on to describe the whole chain of events as they'd played out.

After he finally finished, Anna sat quietly for a moment, then spoke in a voice straining with emotion.

"It's a good thing you were there.... That poor woman and her son... imagine if you hadn't been there!"

Jimmy smiled at the purity of his wife's heart and gently took hold of her hand. "Thanks for praying for us."

She just nodded and raised her eyebrows playfully. "I almost activated the Blaze global prayer chain," she admitted, only partly kidding.

Jimmy looked at PJ and then back at her. "You know what? That would have been just fine. Feel free to do that anytime you want."

"Amen!" PJ agreed with a laugh.

Jimmy kissed little VJ and then tenderly kissed his wife.

"I'd better get going," PJ said, suddenly feeling like a third wheel. He waved goodnight, already thinking about the conversation with Baibina that awaited him.

THE NEXT MORNING...

HARBOR CITY WASN'T the only place seeing a sudden rise in crime and unrest. It was a growing international problem. Cities everywhere were seeing mass shootings, rioting, rampant drug deaths, and gang violence. Much of Africa and the Middle East were overrun by war as factions battled endlessly, catching millions of innocent civilians in the crossfire. Even Europe was embroiled in escalating tensions. The unprecedented interruption of food production caused by these conflicts was quickly leading to widespread famine across the globe.

Jimmy and Anna sat watching the morning news together as one report after another described troubling world events.

"Crime and gun violence continue to rise despite ongoing initiatives by the United Nations," the news report explained. "It has been a year since the United States joined European nations in banning private gun ownership, yet gun crime in all of those countries has proliferated since then.

The UN Security Commissioner announced new steps today to combat the problem, including increasing the size of the new UN Peace Force. Member nations will now be required to commit one-tenth of their active military personnel to the new force, which is being deployed to assist local authorities throughout the world.

"In economic news, the rollout of the new EarthCoin currency is expanding as planned. The transition of the US national debt to the new currency is being hotly debated in Congress. Proposals are gaining support to replace US dollars with EarthCoin for government salaries, Social Security pensions, T-Bill interest payments, and all government expenditures.

"Here to debate the transition's merits are the United Nations' Lucius Sonos and the House Ways and Means Chairman, Barbara Shekel.

"Mr. Secretary, some critics of the transition to a World Bank currency have warned that it will weaken the US. How do you respond?"

"Eliminating one hundred trillion dollars of national debt would surely be a historic accomplishment. The country will be in a much stronger position as a result—not only because of this debt forgiveness but also because of the enforceable constraints on US spending going forward. Politicians will no longer be able to spend and borrow indiscriminately."

"Congresswoman Shekel, it seems like something can be said for the secretary's points. What would be the downside of the country's debt elimination, not to mention the other benefits of the new cryptocurrency?"

"Well, for one thing, the national debt would be transferred, not eliminated. All existing T-bills and securities will still owe interest, except now those payments would be in a foreign currency—the EarthCoin. The World Bank would enforce the budgetary constraints the Secretary spoke of. In exchange for this assumption of the US debt, the UN will dictate how much the US can spend on our national programs and military defense. Meanwhile, Russia and China have been able to ramp up their military budgets dramatically.

"Wow," Anna said as they watched the report together, "it just keeps getting worse and worse."

A reply quickly ran through Jimmy's mind: *'We haven't seen anything yet... it's going to get a lot worse.'* He kept the thought to himself...

"The world needs Jesus," he answered instead.

Anna nodded and took his hand in hers. "It seems like He could come back any second... how long do you think it will be?" she asked quietly.

A flurry of scenes of future events rushed through Jimmy's mind as he considered his answer. "That's in God's hands. For now, we have to keep working — save as many as we can."

"Speaking of work... I need to catch Pete before PJ gets here."

Anna squeezed Jimmy's hand, "Remember, call me if anything crazy happens today, and I'll launch the prayer chain."

Jimmy considered her request as an image ran through his mind of him asking a hoard of angry demons to wait while he called his wife... he just smiled and assured her, "Don't worry, God has got this. We should be home in time for dinner."

Pete was emerging from the dairy barn when Jimmy met him. He took one of the huge milk cans from Pete's hands. "I oiled the pumps and adjusted the pressure; how did it seem this morning?"

"Awesome... like new," Pete answered. "Thanks for checkin' it out; I know you've been busy at the Mission."

After the milk cans were deposited in the walk-in, Pete stood beside the door, removing his gloves. "I saw the news last night about that crazy demon thing in Harbor City. You wouldn't happen to have been involved in that, would ya?"

"Yeah, actually. It was pretty nuts," Jimmy answered humbly.

Pete straightened and took a deep breath. "I thought those things...

demons and angels... were supposed t' be invisible. Why are they showin' up so much nowadays?"

"I'm not sure, to be honest. It just seems like God is making it harder for people to deny that these things exist — it's like He's making sure nobody has an excuse. They won't be able to claim ignorance; people will have to either be with Him or against Him."

AS THEY TALKED, the sound of a car in the driveway announced PJ's arrival.

"Hey Jimmy..." PJ suddenly called out from his open car window. "Chief Fernandez just called — there's been a bombing. We have to go!"

Jimmy could tell from Anna's look that she was worried. "I'll call with info as soon as I have it!" he promised her, jumping into the car with PJ as he sped off.

AN HOUR LATER — HARBOR CITY...

THE BOMBING WAS at the historic downtown church that had become the Mission's headquarters. It looked like a crude pipe bomb had been thrown into the sanctuary through the front door.

Investigators were snapping pictures of the occult symbol that had been spray-painted on the door.

PJ and Jimmy met Homer Martin, one of the city's pastors, as they approached the scene. He greeted them each with a handshake and evident sadness over the damage to the historic church. He managed a friendly smile as he greeted Jimmy. "It looks like your victory yesterday ruffled a few feathers."

"God's victory," Jimmy said humbly. He looked at the door, trying to make sense of the painted symbol. "Do you recognize that?"

"The pentagram?" Pastor Martin answered. "It's not unique to any particular group... it could have been anyone."

"Looks like intimidation," the detective said as he walked up to join them. "Thankfully, no one was inside at the time; the damage was extensive."

"I agree; it could've been much worse," Pastor Martin offered, "— something like this during a service could've killed a lot of people."

"You're right about that," the detective agreed. "If it was a fire-bomb, you probably would've lost the whole building."

"Thank the Lord for His protection," PJ said sincerely. "These are just material things. All of this can be replaced."

"Amen, " the others readily agreed.

JIMMY SURVEYED THE SCENE INSIDE. A large hole had been torn in the floor of the main sanctuary, leaving shattered beams and splintered wood piled in the fellowship hall below. Several rows of pews had been destroyed, and debris was everywhere.

"How is the building's insurance?" Jimmy asked, looking at the extensive damage. "I think the Defense Fund should be able to help if you need it."

PJ placed a hand on Jimmy's back appreciatively. "It's insured; thanks for the offer."

JIMMY AND PJ shared a glance that conveyed what they both were thinking. Neither one of them could avoid being reminded of events seven years earlier when Jimmy himself had been targeted. Back then, Bahal was behind the attacks. The unspoken sense they both felt was another confirmation that times were changing once again. The peaceful hiatus they'd experienced for the past several years was ending. It seemed certain the world had now resumed racing toward its final appointment with *the Day of the Lord.*

MEANWHILE — BROWNSVILLE, BROOKLYN...

BADRICK WALKED PURPOSEFULLY DOWN Union Street. His keen eyes noticed every alleyway nook and shadow he passed. It was second nature to him, one of the survival skills he'd mastered as a kid growing up on the streets.

That skill, and a handful of others, had once ensured his rise to power as one of Harbor City's most feared gang heads. That life was now a dimming memory, he acknowledged gratefully. Nonetheless, a few of the skills it taught him proved valuable in his new life as an urban missionary.

That's not what he called himself, of course. People had a hard time accepting that America needed *missionaries* despite the godless evidence all around them. He went by the official title 'Outreach Coordinator' — or just 'Preacher' as the local street kids called him. He'd found pretty good success since arriving in Brooklyn to open the new City Mission. More than a hundred 'kids' had been rescued from these streets in the five years he'd been here. All of them were former gang members.

They were the blessed few. Unfortunately, most of the kids Badrick met on the streets were not quick to give up gang life; there were hundreds — if not thousands of holdouts.

Many of the old tenement buildings he passed were just burned-out shells — a legacy of the bitter riots and unrest that swept the country half a decade earlier. The crumbling structures hadn't been demolished yet, let alone rebuilt. Some that still had enough of a roof to provide shelter from the rain were occupied by squatters. The rat-infested buildings had no plumbing or electricity, but at least it was better than sleeping on the sidewalk.

This section of Brownsville was the worst area in Brooklyn. Local businesses had either fled, been burned down, or been robbed into oblivion long ago. Badrick wasn't here to shop. He had a destination in his sights — at the far end of the road. The building he approached was old but still served as an actual apartment building, meaning it still had power and running water. That was not to say it was the lap of luxury — its cracked or boarded windows and filthy hallways made it barely distinguishable from the abandoned structures behind him.

The instructions he'd been given said to look for the second steel door on street level — the one to the left of the building's front stoop. The cheap camera mounted on the door jam was a pretty good clue that it was the door to a Bando or Trap House — a base where drugs are sold.

BADRICK SAID a prayer for protection and prepared to press the buzzer.

⌘

9

PRODIGAL

"Our Lord has heard your prayer" ~ *Chozeq.*

J ust as Badrick was about to press the call button, the door
swung open to the sound of loud shouting and cursing.
Badrick jumped aside defensively as a pair of scruffy-looking
guys were shoved through the open doorway and tumbled
onto the sidewalk.

"Keep yer sorry selves away from here if ya know what's good for
ya!" He heard Rad shout through a cursing rant as he waved a gun at
them threateningly.

The pair scrambled to their feet and took off, fearing for their
lives.

As they disappeared up the block, Rad noticed Badrick beside the
door and waved his gun toward him....

"Yo... Donde? *(Where are you from?)* he demanded.

"Badrick!...! de name's Badrick." He responded, raising his hands
in surrender. "I be lookin' fer Rad. Got a message to 'im from his
dad."

"My dad's El Condado (*in the county jail*). You Farmero? (*a member of a prison gang.*)"

"No, no, mon. PJ sent me," Badrick answered quickly, trying to explain.

Rad studied Badrick's face intently for a moment and then tucked his gun into his belt and pulled a cigarette from the pack in his shirt pocket. He placed the cigarette between his pursed lips and struck a match, then blew the smoke into Badrick's face.

Several others stood behind Rad in the doorway. Badrick guessed they couldn't be more than seventeen years old, probably younger; the street had a way of aging kids like these.

There was a ruthless — half-crazed look in Rad's eyes.

"You seen my dad?" he asked with a sneer.

Badrick quickly clarified, "No, I ain't seen 'im me-self. It's PJ who sends yer dad's message to ya." All four boys stood staring coldly, waiting for him to continue.

"PJ is sendin' his regards too. He's been wantin' t' come an' see y' his self; that's a fact."

Rad shrugged dismissively. "Ain't seen *that* dude in years. Figures it'd involve the old man — only time he comes 'round is when he's tryin' t' get me t' visit the guy. I practically forgot 'bout him, to be honest." Rad looked around at his friends as he shrugged his shoulders self-consciously, doing his best to look unfazed. The truth was, he thought about his dad almost every night.

"How'd ya know where t' find me?"

"It took us some searchin' an' prayin', that's for sure," Badrick admitted. "We been askin' around. "Word on th' street said this was where you'd be."

"Word on the street, eh?" Rad looked at his friends, seeming pleased... "Guess we're famous!" His smile quickly changed to a threatening scowl — "You ain't a Narc,[1] are ya?"

"Me? No way, mon... I'm jus, a mission worker with th' City Missions. I'm real glad we found ya — PJ an' your dad, they been worried about ya."

Rad dismissed the comment. "It ain't like they been lookin' out for me or nothin'. They ain't real family. This right here... this is my family."

"Yo, right, that's th' truth," Nacio, Scamp and Jay-Jay all agreed, bumping their fists together with Rad's.

JUST THEN, they heard the screeching tires of a speeding car racing toward them. Badrick recognized the car's occupants as the scruffy pair who'd just been thrown out, and his eyes were immediately drawn to the gun being aimed out its window. His instincts kicked in — he dove against Rad, pushing him through the open doorway and onto the floor, knocking the others down in the process. They had no sooner hit the floor than the doorway was filled with a barrage of bullets.

It ended as quickly as it began, as the racing car sped off down the block. Badrick checked to be sure the coast was clear before getting up, still shielding Rad with his own body.

Rad was quiet as he sat up, looking up the block for the car. Badrick climbed to his feet and then offered a hand to help Rad up.

"Thanks, man," Rad said self-consciously, realizing that Badrick had just saved his life. After an awkward silence, Rad turned to his friends and let loose a stream of expletives that ended with a vow to get even with the pair who'd just fired on them. He eventually cooled enough to turn back toward Badrick, acknowledging him with a nod. "I owe ya one," he said, dusting himself off.

He stood in the doorway and lit another cigarette to replace the one he'd lost.

"What kinda message did my dad want ya t' give me?"

Badrick stood beside him on the door stoop and joined him in watching the street as he answered. "He wants ya t' know he loves ya an' is prayin' for ya."

Rad bobbed his head back as if he couldn't believe what he was hearing. "You came all the way out here to say that?"

"He also wants t' know how yer doin' an' where y'be livin' deez days," Badrick added.

Rad turned and waved toward a mattress on the floor in one corner. "That's my pad over there. At least it ain't in a prison cell."

Badrick recognized the flash of pain in the boy's eyes as he answered and could tell that his tough-as-nails attitude was an act. He scanned the small basement space; it had no kitchen. The boys looked like they hadn't had a decent meal in a while.

"I'm from City Mission in Bed-Stuy. You guys 're welcome dere— the beds 're clean, and the meals ain't bad.'"

"You a preacher?" Rad questioned in surprise. "We're jus' fine right here where we're at — ain't that right guys?" His friends nodded at him assuringly.

"Jus' th' same, the food ain't bad if yer ever needin' a free meal." Badrick drew a few printed cards from his shirt pocket and gave one to each of the boys. "Here's de' address. Ya can call me on dat number anytime."

The boys all glanced at the cards and stared at Badrick, unsure what to make of him. With his long dreadlocks and street clothes, they'd never met a preacher anything like him before. The impression he made was bolstered by the fact that he'd clearly just saved their lives.

"Well... I guess I better be gettin' back now. It was good t'be meetin' ya Rad. I'll be hopin' t' see ya at de Mission one o' deez days."

MID-JULY — CENTER SPRINGS...
20 Months ago

"You have taught children and infants to tell of your strength, silencing your enemies and all who oppose you..." ~ Psalm 8:2

———

SUNDAY MORNINGS at the new Living Springs Church building brought a thrill to Jimmy's heart. The building's location and layout reminded him of the old tent meetings, stirring a blizzard of familiar memories of those miraculous events. The mid-summer morning was clear and calm, with a gentle, refreshing breeze that blew through the open-sided auditorium.

Jimmy sat on the outside aisle nearest the open field at the end of the first row. Anna was beside him, holding little VJ against her shoulder — drawing endearing looks and smiles from people seated behind her.

As much as he enjoyed their surroundings, Jimmy couldn't help feeling nostalgic about the 'old' days. It had been only six years since Athaliah's defeat, yet the spiritual temperature in the country had already cooled. Even here in Center Springs, things weren't the same as they'd been then.

The change happened so gradually that he'd hardly noticed it. At first, the occurrence of miraculous healing slowed, and then the services that were happening nightly were reduced to a few services weekly. The worship, which was still vibrant, had begun to seem more scripted, beginning and ending in planned time slots. Services seldom extended past their designated ending times, let alone going all night as they had in those early days.

People still loved the Lord; there was no question about that. The church was still packed. It just seemed like things had become... 'normal.'

Jimmy, on the other hand, was beginning to feel restless. The week's events in Harbor City had reawakened his spirit. Being ambushed by an army of hideous demons had a way of doing that, he reasoned to himself soberly. He breathed a prayer for God to rekindle the move of the Spirit they'd known before.

With Angela at the piano, the music team was leading the congregation in worship. People were engaged in worshiping, many with their eyes closed and hands raised. Yet Jimmy's heart ached for more of the deeper move they'd once known — when the stirring of the Spirit had regularly knocked people off their feet or drawn them to their knees. It brought healing and life to desperate souls!

"Lord, move in us again..." Jimmy prayed under his breath.

While he was still breathing these words, a strong breeze blew across the field outside, blowing papers and the pages of hymnals as it swept through the open auditorium. Jimmy couldn't help being reminded of the breeze he and PJ felt on that first summer afternoon — the day they consecrated this very ground to God's work.

It started with the youngest children...

In the middle of the song she was playing, Angela suddenly stopped and sat with her eyes closed, then placed her hands on the baby in her womb as a tear ran from the corner of her eye. Within moments, the rest of the music team had also stopped playing; a silence fell across the congregation.

In the silence, they could hear a commotion coming from the Children's classrooms — it sounded like it started with the youngest classes and then quickly spread to older kids. Soon, the Junior High and High School kids were heard even louder than the others. Everyone in the congregation turned to look, immediately recognizing the sound!

Through the large glass panels that separated the classrooms from the sanctuary, they could see the children — from the youngest to the oldest — all standing with hands raised and tears streaking their young faces. They were crying out loudly... in worship!

The Spirit's move quickly spread through the parents, who watched their children. Tears flooded their own eyes. Soon, many were moved with a deep awareness of the Spirit's loving touch as it swept across the auditorium. Jimmy watched in awe as people bowed under the immense sense of the presence of God that quickly filled the place, causing some to fall to their knees as others cried out with hands raised or held onto loved ones in urgent prayer.

Jimmy looked down at little VJ in Anna's arms, seeing the infant laugh as the baby's eyes lit with joy. He followed his son's gaze — recognizing from the child's reaction that he could see the huge angel standing beside them.

"OUR LORD HAS HEARD YOUR PRAYER," Chozeq said in his booming angelic voice.

The sound of his words brought tears of joy to Jimmy's eyes while little VJ laughed aloud!

⌘

MIRACULOUS MEETING

'God is getting ready to do something....'

**NORTHAMPTON, MASSACHUSETTS —
DECEMBER 1734...**

J onathan Edwards trembled with fear. The visions in his head
shocked and terrified him.

He saw the faces of people in his congregation — one after
another, and to his horror, they were dropping unprotected
into a thundering pit of horrendous flames. The accusing looks on
their faces haunted him as they fell to their eternal doom. What had
he done to warn them of their terrible destiny? As their minister, he
was responsible for warning them of the eternal terror that awaited
them — he was their watchman!

Turning from the sickening sight of their condemned souls in
eternal torment, he saw an enormous angel standing beside him. The
angel's flaming sword pointed to the tragic sight as he charged
Edwards....

"Behold the end of these to whom thou wast sent! Was it not thy duty to warn them?"

The accused minister shook violently as he fell to his knees in wrenching remorse. He knew he was guilty — he was without excuse. As he knelt weeping, the powerful angel dropped to one knee and placed his huge hand on Edwards' shoulder. The tone of his thundering voice was consoling as he spoke again.

"Remember this that thou hast seen; it is a shadow of things to come. There is yet time to alter the destiny ye witness here."

The trembling Edwards looked up hopefully as he comprehended the angel's words. "A shadow...?"

"Aye, faithful one," the angel confirmed reassuringly. "To thee has been shown what must soon come to pass. Take heed and be diligent in the task thy Lord has entrusted to thee. Many souls hang upon the work that ye must do; more than these — more than thou canst know."

Edwards looked at the powerful emissary with a pleading look. "I- I'm only a man... how can I turn the hearts of so many?"

"Simply speak the words thy Lord gives thee. Leave unto Him the inward working in hardened hearts."

THE NEXT MOMENT, Edwards awoke lying on the cold ground where he'd knelt to pray, a clearing in the Northampton woods. The sun shone brightly in a clear sky, and the air was oddly still on this late November day. Fresh snow covered the ground, revealing the trail of his footprints leading to where he knelt. From the corner of his eye, he was startled to see other fresh footprints as well — following them quickly to the sight of a young stranger seated on a nearby log. The young man was dressed oddly and sat rubbing his crossed arms, appearing unaccustomed to the cold.

"Hello, Reverend Edwards," the stranger said in a friendly voice.

Edwards nodded back uncertainly.

The young man looked around at the pristine clearing, taking a deep breath of the fresh, clean air. "It's a beautiful day. I see why you like to come here; it's a perfect place to seek the Lord."

Edwards' caution softened; he nodded again in agreement as he climbed to his feet and looked at the young man carefully. "I perceive ye are not a citizen of this place. Whither art thou?"

"Far away," the stranger answered. "I've come to offer my help. I think you've sensed that God is getting ready to do something here — something extraordinary."

Edwards fought a sudden chill up his back; he knew it was not from the cool weather. He didn't have to ask the young man how he'd come to find him in the deep woods — a task that would take the skill of an experienced tracker. Nor did he wonder greatly how the stranger knew his name. Even the fact that the young man had no horse did not surprise him. Instead, it was the stranger's words that reverberated in Edwards' soul… 'God is getting ready to do something….'

"Art thou a Heavenly messenger? Hast thou been sent by Divine hand?

"Sent, yes. I suppose I'm a messenger, but not in the way you may be thinking. I'm not an angel if that's what you're wondering."

Edwards studied his face as though he was trying to solve a puzzle. He glanced around at the ground, noticing that the stranger's footprints ended at the edge of the clearing as though he'd been dropped there from the sky. The baffled Edwards was momentarily speechless as he looked back at the young man again.

"How I arrived is unimportant," the stranger responded, reading Edwards' unspoken words. "The work you've been given is urgent— that's what we need to focus on. Souls need saving — you've been shown the faces of some whose souls are dangerously lost; there are thousands more like them."

Edwards wiped a sudden tear from his cheek with the back of his hand. The memory of his recent vision of hell's fire was still vivid. He studied the young stranger with a pleading look. "What can a man such as I do to turn these from their course? Can the mere words of a preacher change such as these?"

"You're right; *mere* words cannot, but *anointed* words certainly can. Under God's anointing, words can change far more than that."

"I perceive ye speak the truth. Yet what may a man do to compel God to move in such a way?"

"He needs no compelling; He desires to do it. The work that's needed is in our own hearts, first of all… you have made a good start of it," the young man said, nodding toward the place where Edwards had knelt. "Prayer is the thing that moves His hand."

Edwards cautiously walked closer and sat on the log beside him. He was more convinced than ever that the unassuming messenger was from the Lord.

"The work that is about to happen here is from the Lord," the stranger continued, answering Edwards' unspoken thoughts once again. "Some things are likely to seem strange to you if you've never seen them. When the Holy Spirit begins to move upon people's hearts, it can make them do unusual things. Don't be surprised if some of them cry out or shout. Tears and deep remorse can be expected. If things get stirred up, you could see some of them drop to the ground as if they've fainted; don't worry about that. It's how some people react when they suddenly encounter God's power in their life." He nodded toward the place Edwards had been lying moments before… "you've experienced something like that yourself."

Edwards looked overwhelmed by the young man's words and struggled to make sense of what he heard. He rubbed his hands together as he stared at the ground. "I'll admit they don't teach such things in seminaries. The things ye describe sound like emotional outbursts; are they to be condoned in times of solemn worship?"

"That's the best time for them," his new acquaintance encouraged. "There's not an instance in scripture when a person has encountered God and not been moved by it emotionally. God's essence — His deepest character— is love. That can't be experienced in a human heart without emotion. It's the most fundamental part of our nature; it's how we're created to experience Him."

He looked into the afternoon sky, judging that the day grew late. "You'd better be starting back; you have a long ride."

"Shall I see thee again?"

"That's in God's hands, but I suspect that you may, Lord willing," the stranger answered with a humble smile.

With that, he turned and walked a few yards to the edge of the clearing, waving over his shoulder as he continued. Edwards watched in awestruck disbelief as the man faded from sight!

NORTHAMPTON — SEVERAL DAYS LATER...

ARDENT STOOD on a ridge of the steeple at the old Northampton church, gazing out over the village below. Chozeq's sudden appearance beside him did not surprise him; he seemed expected.

"It is a great task that our Lord has given the man," Ardent shared. He looked down at the small parsonage below, where a lamp had just been lit in the early morning darkness.

"Great indeed," Chozeq agreed. "Yet he will not be alone in his task. Nor will the Lord's strength be withheld from him."

Ardent gave a single nod in trusting confirmation. His eyes fixed on the horizon as the first light of a new day began to dawn in the distance. "Our enemies here are gathering; this work shall not be unopposed," he predicted.

"Aye. The battle will soon be joined," Chozeq agreed. The two angelic sentries searched the skies vigilantly, each with a hand on the hilt of their gleaming swords.

THE CHRISTMAS SEASON was the busiest of the year for Reverend Edwards and helpers at the prestigious church. Before Edwards, it had been his grandfather's church for decades — the Reverend Solomon Stoddard. He had been widely known throughout New England as a respected and influential theologian; following in Stoddard's footsteps was a great honor for the 31-year-old Edwards.

However, despite the church's long history — or perhaps because of it — Edwards had to admit that many of its congregants did not take their spiritual condition seriously. There was a great apathy toward the true things of God. There was far more enthusiasm for rituals and traditions and upholding the church's 'good name.'

This was seldom more pronounced than during the Christmas season. With the Fall harvests complete and several inches of early snow already blanketing the frozen ground, people were anxious to turn their attention to feasts and festivities. The church choir had already been practicing its Christmas program for weeks.

EDWARDS MADE his way from the parsonage to the church's rear door and kicked the snow off his shoes before stepping inside. The building's elderly caretaker, old Tom Witherbee, had started the stove's fire, but it was still barely felt in the auditorium's cold dampness.

"A good morning t' ye, Tom," he said as he warmed his hands beside it.

"Mornin' Reverend," Tom replied. "A cold mornin' it is, most surely."

Edwards shook a chill from his shoulders. The weather may have been partly to blame, but the real reason for his shudder was the constant memory of his unexplainable encounter in the woods, along with the memory of Hell's thundering roar that still haunted his thoughts. He contemplated his prepared sermon for the morning service, so engrossed that he missed the question Tom was asking, causing the old man to repeat it for a third time.

"Will ye be needin' anything else, Reverend? I need to attend to the front steps...."

"No... Thank ye, Tom." The second part of the older man's remarks finally registered. "Permit me to help with the steps; it's surely a younger man's work."

Tom waved dismissively, "Think me not that aged. Surely, I'm still able to wield a shovel."

"Doubtless!" Edwards conceded. "Nevertheless, it would favor me to be so engaged... for a chance to warm myself ."

He finally convinced the old man, who agreed to confine his effort to pushing snow off the upper stoop while Edwards cleared the steps. The two of them made fairly short work of the job. The physical activity did Edwards some good, taking his mind off the troubling thoughts in his head.

"Ye've been caring for this church a good many years," Edwards admired as they worked.

"Greater than fifty, I would suppose," Tom admitted. "Leastwise, it was nearly as long as Reverend Stoddard served. A good man he was, that I'll say truly."

Edwards agreed, of course. He admired his grandfather without question. Still, it had been Stoddard, more than any other, who convinced the greater part of churches in New England to discount the need for true conversion, opening the sacraments to many whom Edwards perceived to be clearly unconverted. Participation in the church had become a civic duty rather than a firm belief. That was undoubtedly the cause of so much apathy among the church's congregants, many of whom, Edwards was convinced, had never aspired to true faith.

The thought again brought many of their faces to mind — lit with the horror of eternal flames. As the familiar flurry of images rushed past his eyes again, he realized that old Tom's face was not among them. It didn't surprise him that Tom was not among them. The kindly old man had a spirit about him that reflected a genuine walk with Christ.

. . .

THE TWO MEN hung their shovels on pegs in the church foyer and made their way back to the coal-burning stove to warm their hands. Edwards cleared his throat to interrupt another momentary silence. "In your years here... do y' recollect many sermons on the doctrine of Hell?"

"Hell!?" Tom repeated, sounding as if the very sound of the word was the most shocking part of the question. He thought for a moment... "Not that I can honestly recall," he finally admitted. "I suppose that's been thought a difficult topic among polite society."

"Why should it be difficult?" Edwards challenged. "Jesus himself often spoke of it. In very fact, He spoke more of it than He did of Heaven."

Tom nodded as he conceded the point. "I'll admit, likely, there are many today who have never considered it very seriously."

"Why not? Do they not believe in Hell?"

"I would suppose they believe their church attendance and taking of the sacraments will be enough to keep them from it."

"Do you believe that?" Edwards questioned directly.

"I'm too sure of the guilt in my own heart to be foolish enough to believe I can save myself by my own works," Tom quickly explained. "It's faith in Christ alone that saves a man. I am a sure witness to that."

Edwards smiled as he placed a hand on Tom's shoulder... "Amen, my friend." Returning his hands to the stove's warmth, his face again grew serious. "I covet thy prayers for this morning's sermon. We shall see how well polite society suffers a difficult topic."

⌘

THE TIME OF HIS CHOOSING

*"...it shall be for a revelation to this final age of man at the appointed time –
in the time of His choosing."* ~ Chozeq

CENTER SPRINGS, LATE AUGUST...
19 months ago

Anna switched off the living room TV, silencing endless images of war-torn devastation from every continent. It seemed like the whole world was at war. Whole swaths of the planet had already been reduced to famine-stricken wastelands. While the nations in Europe wrestled over scarce energy resources, the Middle East was boiling once again with violent unrest — most of which was directed toward Israel.

The Americas were not exempt; violent gangs and powerful drug cartels controlled most of Central and South America and indiscriminately carried out their attacks inside the US as well.

. . .

"IT'S HARD TO WATCH," Anna complained sadly. "What kind of world will VJ have to grow up in?" She nestled their two-month-old son against her shoulder protectively.

Jimmy pondered what he knew about coming events and thought about the words Amos had once shared: *'You're living in the true end of days, son.'* Jimmy tenderly placed his hand on their baby's head and silently prayed for his family's protection.

"We're in God's hands — there's no safer place than that," he softly reassured her.

He stepped to the front door, peering through it at the gleaming church building in the old north field. An urgency burned in his spirit — he knew God was getting ready to use him for something new. Whatever the new calling was, it seemed imminent.

"God's not done... there's more that He wants us to do," he shared.

Anna came alongside and leaned against him. "The Services over this summer have been incredible," she agreed. "We haven't seen God move like this in a couple of years."

"There's more coming; I feel it," Jimmy said with conviction. "The darker the night becomes, the brighter His light will shine."

THAT AFTERNOON...

PETE PULLED the farm's new combine into the barnyard, filled to the brim with freshly harvested corn.

"This new combine did the job in a fraction of the time," he noted with a smile as he jumped down from the driver's seat.

Jimmy agreed with a nod as he surveyed the shiny new machine. "It's a beauty. But I still like Old Bessy," he said nostalgically, referring to old Jim Van Clief's beloved tractor. It had been retired to a parking spot inside the barn but still ran like a charm. "At least we got a good deal on this new one," Jimmy added.

Pete agreed. "Yeah, they're really pushin' the new electric ones now — who knows how long we'll be able to keep using diesel units like this one. It's kinda crazy; food prices are already nuts, and they keep addin' mandates for stuff like electric vehicles that raise 'em even higher."

"It's lipstick on a pig," Jimmy said, shaking his head. "The world is careening toward Armageddon, and the policymakers are worried about whether the planet might be one or two degrees warmer in a hundred years."

Pete agreed with a shake of his head. "A hundred years...," he repeated dismissively. "The world 'll be lucky to see another ten if ya ask me."

Jimmy didn't answer but nodded that he thought his friend was right. *"We have to work while it's day... the night's coming,"* he said, half under his breath. He caught himself and looked over at Pete. "That's why this food mission is so important. The work you're doing here won't go unrewarded," he encouraged him. "This mission is still being used to change lives. I have a feeling it's gonna be more important than ever soon."

Pete agreed. "The demand has been growing in the cities especially. The city missions that PJ has been planting are takin' care of more and more families."

The sound of a truck on the gravel drive drew their attention. The first of the day's delivery vans arrived to be loaded.

"I'll give you a hand," Jimmy offered, smacking Pete on the shoulder.

BEDFORD-STUYVESANT, BROOKLYN...

RAD and his three closest friends walked along Fulton Street, carefully eying the burned-out shells of buildings as they passed. This area of Bed-Stuy was no better than their own neighborhood in Brownsville. It looked like one of the war zones on TV. In fact, the wars that raged around the world hadn't left behind any devastation worse than this.

The remains of cars and vans lay abandoned in overgrown parking lots, many burned or overturned. A few of the old relics that still had windows and doors were being used as makeshift shelters.

The boys came to a garbage-strewn park, and Rad pulled out the tattered business card that Badrick left him, rereading the address. "We should turn here on Lewis Ave," he said, waving at the next inter-section. "We take that up t' Halsey Street."

Rad's friend Nacio pulled open the neck of his teeshirt to cool off and squinted ahead. His friends all called him Juice — the kid was like a live wire. "I remember when there was buses runin' here... could use one now."

"Yeah, you ain't kiddin'," Scamp agreed. Scamp's mom had named him Sabas, but he could barely remember when anyone called him that.

"There used t' be people livin' here in real buildings and open stores an' stuff, too," Jay-Jay pointed out.

Rad shrugged. "There used t' be a lotta things... come on an' keep goin'." His intense focus showed that he was on the lookout for any sign of those thugs that shot up their doorstep. He didn't like being vulnerable, out in the open like this.

The Mission was easy to spot. It filled the ground floor of a small apartment building that also served as housing for the Mission's resi-dents. The building stood out for its clean appearance among the rundown properties surrounding it.

Rad and his friends approached the door but didn't enter, stopping to peer through the front windows to see who else was there. Badrick noticed them and quickly stepped outside.

"Greetins bredren, Wat a gwaan? (*What's going on?*) he said as he welcomed them with a handshake. It's good t' be seein' y' here. You've picked a good day fer comin'... it's Beef Stroganoff day — there be plenty for ya!"

Rad licked his lips revealingly; he couldn't remember the last time they'd had a real meal. Jay-Jay, Juice, and Scamp stood waiting for Rad to respond before acknowledging Badrick's invitation; they didn't dare cross him despite the growling in their empty stomachs.

"What's it cost?" Rad asked suspiciously.

"Be no cost," Badrick assured him. "It's a free meal t' any who're needin' it."

Rad stared in through the window at those inside who were happily eating; it looked pretty good. "Well, I guess since we're in the neighborhood...," he conceded.

Badrick smiled in welcome and led them to a table inside. "Help yerselfs," he offered with a wave toward the buffet table.

The three boys loaded their plates and returned to their seats, digging into them like they hadn't eaten in days. Badrick arrived with a pitcher of iced tea and filled their glasses. Setting the pitcher down, he slid into a seat beside them.

"Ya ever seen more o' dose hoodlums wat shot at ya?" he asked them curiously.

Rad and the others just shook their heads, still busy eating. They ate as if they were afraid someone might take their plates away at any second. Badrick smiled with an understanding nod.

"De food's always free here at de Mission. You brodders are always welcome. While yer here dough, it's fair for ya t' listen to de word we're sharin'."

Rad gave him a cold stare and continued eating, not saying a word.

"PJ told me about yer grandma. He said she was a Christian lady. She took ya t' church an whatnot. He said yer dad talked to ya about God too."

Rad didn't respond, pretending to ignore Badrick's words.

"Well, ya know den dat Jesus has His hand out to ya. Trust me sayin dat dere ain't nothin He can't forgive. I'm livin proof o' dat."

Rad stared into his plate as he continued to eat. He knew he had plenty that needed forgiving, but remorse was something he didn't let himself feel. He was doing what he had to to survive, he argued to himself.

Badrick seemed to understand the boy's thoughts. He nodded quietly and breathed a silent prayer for God's Spirit to intervene. He decided to change the subject.

"Ya know, yer dad wants t' see ya. PJ says it's been a while since ya went t' see 'im."

Rad shrugged. "I hardly know the dude... seriously."

"He's still yer dad. Trust me sayin' dar will be a day when ya regret not seein' 'im."

Rad glanced at Badrick, reading a hint of regret in the preacher's eyes.

"I ain't got a car," he answered defensively.

"Jus' say de word — I'll pick ya up meself," Badrick promised without hesitation. He could see that Rad was still resisting. "Life it be short my friend," he counseled. "An' de way things is goin' in de world, this all could be over pretty soon anyways. It's truly de End Times... hear what I be sayin'?"

As HE SPOKE, someone yelled from across the room: "Hey, can you turn up the TV?"

One of the Mission staff lifted the remote to raise the volume....

───────────────────────────────

The scene showed columns of tanks and armored vehicles on the move as a reporter described developments.

"The historic agreement between Russia and Turkey has surprised Western leaders with its depth of military cooperation and what the two nations have called their mutual interests. The focus of these interests appears to be the Middle East — particularly Israel.

"Now, just hours after the agreement's signing, it is evident that the two nations have begun jointly amassing their armies along Israel's Syrian border."

Badrick turned back to the boys and spoke soberly... "De times maybe even shorter, den we think."

SEVERAL DAYS LATER — CENTER SPRINGS...

JIMMY SAT ALONE in the farmhouse's old root cellar, reading his journal. He had just finished recording the events of the demon attack in Harbor City and flipped through the rest of the journal's empty pages — more than half of them remained blank.

Memories of Athaliah's defeat and the end of the country's terrible drought flooded his mind as he scanned the written accounts. They seemed even more incredible now that some years had passed; it almost seemed like a different lifetime. A stirring in his spirit told him that the past few years had only been a pause in God's relentless timeline for the world. Amos' words had begun to echo loudly in his mind... *'You're living in the true End of Days, son.'*

The pages fell open to one of the journal's first entries; he remembered it well. The events it described were experienced on a busy rainy night while working at his Uncle Mike's Sub Shop. It was the night he first met Anna.

Memories of the scene replayed clearly in his mind as he read it....

A loud noise behind me drew my attention. As I turned, the room suddenly changed around me. I was surrounded by a flurry of activity, with people running everywhere. I recognized that some were wearing what looked like medical garb. The room had completely changed - I was standing in an emergency room!

He read through the Journal's account of PJ's near-death experience and meeting with Ardent—events that still hadn't happened. The memories it spawned for Jimmy were just as remarkable as the events themselves. He knew now that he'd *traveled* to those future events, recalling how confusing it had all seemed at the time.

He soon came to the account of his encounter with Chozeq amid swirling time — *'Without Time'* as Chozeq called it. It sent a chill through him as he read it....

Instantly, a hand was in mine. My eyes followed the strong arm upward to Chozeq's steadfast face... Somehow, I knew we were standing amid swirling time.

All of the emotion and thrill of those moments washed over him once again as he read the account. Chozeq's familiar charge pulled at his heart once more:

"But heed this carefully! Ye must tell no one of this that thou hast seen nor yet shalt see! Only write what thou seest and most cautiously guard it; for it shall be for a revelation to this final age of man at the appointed time - in the time of His choosing."

As Jimmy read these words, something suddenly jolted him. It was like the Spirit was taking hold of the words and lifting them off the page. They reverberated in his mind like an earthquake gaining strength: "a revelation to this final age of man at the appointed time—*in the time of His choosing.*"

AN UNSPOKEN VOICE seemed to add... *that time is coming soon.*

At the same time that he sensed these words, something else came over him. The words carried another unspoken message — reminding him that the journal's accounts of future events were not his to share. Like Amos, his charge was to write them for the future. They were recorded for others — *after he was gone.*

The thought was sobering. He tried to shake it off, wondering if it was just an enemy assault meant to make him afraid. But he wasn't scared. The implied message didn't inspire fear at all. In fact, there was a growing confidence within him that only grew stronger the more he considered it.

Closing the journal, he dropped from the chair onto his knees on the cellar's old, worn carpet and began to pray. The more he prayed, the more he felt peace and a deeper confirmation of the same unspoken message...

...he'd be leaving soon.

⌘

1 2

A NEW CALLING

"Thy labors are greatly cherished noble one; to thy Lord thou art well-beloved."
~ Ardent

HAMPSHIRE, ENGLAND — 1734...

George Whitefield had just finished a strenuous day. His itinerant preaching continued to draw huge crowds, today's perhaps the largest so far. Unfortunately, his unorthodox methods of outreach had drawn more than crowds—they had also drawn the disapproval and ire of the official clergy.

Because of his troubles with the clergy in London, he'd been residing for the past two months in Dummer, a little rural parish in Hampshire near Basingstoke. He found himself among poor, illiterate people there, but he was soon reconciled with it and spent his days conversing with the poorest residents, finding them eager for the simple gospel message.

Because the Church of England refused to permit him at their pulpits, he'd resorted to open-air preaching. It turned out that the open air was an even better venue than the churches for his unique brand of preaching. He was reaching out to common men and women — the factory workers, coal shovelers, chimney sweeps, housemaids, livery drivers, and garbage collectors. And they were turning out in droves; thousands at a time filled the squares where he preached from makeshift pulpits. Their heartfelt cries for mercy and shouts of praise echoed throughout the city.

Whitefield knew it wouldn't be long before his enemies in the clergy shut down his outdoor meetings as well. There was already talk of having him arrested. He prayed about this as he knelt in his small boarding room, seeking God's help.

The thunderous voice of a stranger interrupted the silence, startling him.

"Thy labors are greatly cherished noble one; thou art well-beloved by thy Lord."

The kneeling preacher's heart leaped at the sight of the heavenly envoy. The huge angel's countenance glowed in the room's darkness— especially his enormous, radiant wings. Whitefield bowed his head low in awestruck reverence.

"Rise, dear one. I am a servant just as thou. Thy faithful work here has been of great worth; indeed, its fruit will resound in eternity with the praises of redeemed souls. Yet there is something more that thy Lord calls thee to — an even greater work than this.
"A message is making its way to thee even now... it is a call from the American colonies. Fear not to accept the call; The Lord's Spirit goes before thee, and He has prepared thy way. Ye are called to a great harvest of souls, which shall resound for many generations!"

The angel's words rushed against Whitefield like a flood of waters, taking his breath away. He struggled to find his voice as he carefully asked him....

"Surely it is a call I earnestly welcome; I desire nothing else! Yet I have no means to pay the price of such a journey, and surely no church here would be wont to lend me support for such a mission."

"Thy passage has already been secured; ye need only follow thy Lord's leading. Others are also called to join with thee there; thou wilt know them soon."

Whitefield nodded gratefully, accepting the angel's answer without the slightest doubt. The news of it made him smile joyfully.

"What is thy name?" he carefully asked the kindly envoy.

"I am called Ardent."

CENTER SPRINGS, MID-SEPTEMBER...
18 months ago

JIMMY AND ANNA sat outside with Pete and Angela beside a fire. It was a rare night of relaxing together at the end of a busy summer.

Angela held little VJ affectionately, anxious for the birth of her own child, which was due within weeks. Anna glanced at Jimmy and held his hand, obviously feeling sentimental about how Angela and Pete doted over their baby.

Jimmy smiled back and leaned closer as Anna rested her head on his shoulder. He looked around at the old farm with its farmhouse and barns, enjoying a comfortable breeze rustling through the surrounding fields of corn. He couldn't help but feel blessed with it all, especially as he glanced again at their young son, surrounded by so much caring attention.

Yet something was troubling him. Deep in his spirit, he felt that all of this was temporary. He was being called to do something; he didn't know yet what it was.

Pete dropped another log into the fire, sending a cloud of sparks into the air. Jimmy watched the crackling fire with its yellow flames and bright red embers, feeling its comfortable warmth as the stars brightened in the darkening sky.

All at once, the scene dramatically changed....

JIMMY FOUND himself standing beside a man he guessed to be in his early thirties. The man was dressed in a manner that no longer surprised him, wearing a linen shirt with frills and a long waistcoat that was short in the front and long in the back. Jimmy recognized the man's dress from his visions of the Tennents—it was the way men dressed in the 1700s, around the time of the American Revolution. Chozeq's presence couldn't be missed, standing beside the man.

But most striking of all was the place where they stood. Jimmy recognized it immediately—engulfed in the deafening sound of its terrifying cries and the strong stench of burning sulfur. He turned to look at the dreaded scene, which brought a flood of vivid memories— he'd seen it before; the memory brought tears to his eyes.

This time, instead of peering across a vast chasm, he looked directly into the flaming pit. He saw the faces of people—one after another—as they were dropping helplessly into a thundering pit of horrendous flames. The man standing beside Jimmy appeared to recognize the people's faces. Their accusing looks haunted the man as they fell to their eternal judgment as if it had been his job to warn them of their terrible fate.

Jimmy watched as the shaking man turned from the sickening sight of these condemned souls and saw Chozeq standing beside him. Chozeq's flaming sword pointed to the tragic sight as he thundered....

"Behold the end of these to whom thou wast sent! Was it not thy duty to warn them?"

Jimmy saw the accused minister shake violently as he fell to his knees in wrenching remorse. Chozeq dropped to one knee and placed his huge hand on the man's shoulder. The tone of his thundering voice was consoling as he spoke again.

"Remember this that thou hast seen; it is a shadow of things to come. There is yet time to alter the destiny ye witness here."

IN THE NEXT MOMENT, Jimmy realized he was standing in a secluded clearing in deep woods. The ground was covered with freshly fallen snow. Lying there on the cold ground, deep in prayer, was the same man he'd seen with Chozeq. The air was oddly still, making the sun feel warm against his skin despite the snow-covered ground.

Jimmy made his way to a fallen tree and sat against it, waiting to discover the purpose of his traveling here. The fresh snow revealed the trail of his own footprints, prompting him to realize that this was more than a typical travel — he was surprisingly visible here, the way he'd been on a few rare occasions in the past.

Chozeq's voice drew his attention, and Jimmy turned to see his angelic warrior friend standing beside him. Chozeq's steps left no prints in the snow — angels' steps never did.

"His name is Jonathan Edwards," Chozeq explained, looking toward the man in the clearing. "He is a servant of uncommon acclaim among the annals of God's people."

THE NAME WAS familiar to Jimmy. "You mean *the* Jonathan Edwards? He preached in the 1700s… is that where we are?"

Chozeq nodded. "It is a rare calling God has for thee, a mission rarely given." He briefly looked again at Edwards, drawing Jimmy's attention to him. "This man's work will begin a great awakening here, but he will need much help in such a work. In his day, such a move of God has not been seen before. It will be strange to him and, for the most part, troubling.

"Ye have seen God's move and know the workings of the Spirit in a time of great revival. Ye are sent to give guidance to this man of God."

"Me? How can I guide *him*? Shouldn't *you* guide him like you've guided Amos and me?"

"It is God who plans the work of His servants. His ways are unerring and need not be questioned," Chozeq gently reminded.

Jimmy silently struggled to take in what Chozeq was saying to him. He looked again toward Edwards, "What sort of guidance does he need? I'm willing... you know I am — I guess I wouldn't be here if that weren't true. But I have no idea how to give him advice. Besides, why should he listen to *me*?"

Chozeq placed his hand on Jimmy's shoulder, and suddenly, a flurry of scenes rushed through his mind, showing encounters with Edwards among worshiping crowds. People were falling on the ground or crying loudly in repentance. He was shown a sweeping revival as whole communities and cities sought the Lord in massive crowds throughout the American colonies. The scenes seemed familiar to Jimmy; he'd seen such things before. In fact, he'd lived through far more dramatic events than these. He looked back to Chozeq with a comprehending gaze.

"I think I understand," he accepted, then looked again toward Edwards lying nearby.

JIMMY BARELY NOTICED that Chozeq had gone. He watched as Edwards stirred and slowly rose to his knees in the snow. He saw him catch sight of Jimmy's footprints from the corner of his eye — following them quickly to the nearby log where Jimmy sat.

Jimmy rubbed his crossed arms, unaccustomed to the cold, which was becoming more difficult to ignore. "Hello, Reverend Edwards," he said in a friendly voice.

Edwards nodded back uncertainly.

Jimmy looked around at the pristine clearing, taking a deep breath of the fresh, clean air. "It's a beautiful day. I see why you like to come here; it's a perfect place to seek the Lord."

Edwards' caution softened; he nodded again in agreement as he climbed to his feet and looked at the young man carefully. "I perceive ye are not a citizen of this place. Whither art thou?"

"Far away," Jimmy answered. "I've come to offer my help. I think you've sensed that God is getting ready to do something here — something extraordinary."

Jimmy spoke with the famous preacher for several minutes, doing his best to explain that he wasn't an angel but had been sent to offer his help.

"The work you've been given is urgent," Jimmy emphasized. "You've been shown the faces of some whose souls are dangerously lost; there are thousands more like them."

Edwards wiped a sudden tear from his cheek with the back of his hand. The memory of his recent vision of hell's fire was still vivid. He studied the young stranger with a pleading look. "What can a man such as I do to turn these from their course? Can the mere words of a preacher change such as these?"

Jimmy felt awkward giving advice to this giant of the faith, but his answers seemed to come easily.

Edwards cautiously walked closer and sat on the log beside him.

"The work that is about to happen here is from the Lord," Jimmy continued. Some things may seem strange to you. When the Holy Spirit begins to move upon people's hearts, it can make them do unusual things." Jimmy described some ways he'd seen people act under the moving of the Spirit. "It's just how some people react when they suddenly encounter God's power in their life." Jimmy nodded toward the place where Edwards had been lying moments before... "you've experienced something like that yourself."

Edwards looked overwhelmed by Jimmy's words and struggled to make sense of what he heard. "The things ye describe suggest emotional outbursts; is that really to be condoned in times of solemn worship?"

"That's the best time for them," Jimmy argued with a smile. "There's not an instance in scripture when a person has encountered God and not been moved by it emotionally. God's essence — His deepest character— is love. That can't be experienced in a human heart without emotion. It's the way we're created to experience Him."

Jimmy looked at the afternoon sky, judging that the day had grown late. "You'd better be starting back; you have a long ride."

With that, Jimmy walked a few yards to the edge of the clearing, waving over his shoulder as he continued. Edwards watched in awestruck disbelief as each step made his strange visitor less visible until he'd faded from sight.

JIMMY WAS SUDDENLY LOOKING AGAIN into the warm fire, recognizing the reassuring sounds of the fire's crackle and summer crickets in the fields with the feeling of Anna's head against his shoulder.

Anna raised her head and looked at him suspiciously, sensing that something had changed. Jimmy gave her a reassuring smile and placed his hand on hers, coaxing her to rest her head again. Things would be all right... everything was going to be all right.

⌘

13

AWAKENING

"There is a way that appears to be right, but in the end, it leads to death!"
~ Proverbs 16:25

NORTHAMPTON, MASSACHUSETTS
December, 1734

The Northampton church slowly filled for the morning service as the town's prominent members arrived. The usual combination of polite greetings and self-righteous whispers could be heard as they filed into the pews dressed in their holiday finery. The choir took their places in the choir stalls, smiling proudly in anticipation of their well-practiced holiday selection.

All was proceeding in the service as expected thirty minutes later. Announcements of the season's events were made, prayers had been prayed, hymns sung, and offerings collected. The choir had just finished their seasonal medley and taken their seats.

The congregation was silent as Reverend Edwards climbed to the dais. Some smiled sentimentally, expecting a traditional message to usher in the Christmas season. Some of the town's more prominent citizens appeared bored, with one or two glancing at their pocket watches impatiently.

Edwards thought again of the stranger's words: *'Under God's anointing, words can change far more than that.'*

The sermon that burned in his heart seemed to have been inspired — *indeed, breathed* — by the very Spirit of God. Looking down from the pulpit, he saw the faces of men and women he'd so recently seen illuminated by the flames of Hell. It tore his heart, causing him to bow his head in a silent plea for God's help.

His message this morning was not about Hellfire, however. It was, in fact, about Heaven — or more accurately, about Heaven unattained — about missing it. It seemed to him that to warn souls away from Hell, he had better first give them a view of the alternative. He drew a breath and began....

~

"On a recent ride in the woods, I alighted from my horse in a retired place, as my manner commonly has been, to walk for divine contemplation and prayer. It was there that I had a view with the eye of the spirit that for me was extraordinary, beginning at first with the glory of the Son of God, as the mediator between God and man, and his wonderful, great, full, pure, and sweet grace and love, and meek and gentle condescension.

"As I first knelt there alone, this grace that appeared so calm and sweet appeared also great above the heavens. The person of Christ appeared ineffably excellent, with an excellency great enough to swallow up all thought and conception – which continued, as near as I can judge, about an hour. I must confess that it kept me in a flood of tears most of that time, weeping aloud. I felt an ardency of my soul to be, what I know not how otherwise to express, emptied and annihilated; to lie in the dust, and to be full of Christ alone; to love him with a holy and pure love; to trust in him; to live upon him; to serve and follow him; and to be perfectly sanctified and made pure, with a divine and heavenly purity."

"I have had views of the same nature several other times, and they have had the same effects.[1] Indeed, never have I experienced more rapturous joys than at those times when I have wept at the foot of the cross."

HE BRIEFLY THOUGHT of his vision of Hell and his meeting with the remarkable stranger that followed the events he'd just described. He quickly determined that sharing those encounters would be more than anyone could be expected to believe. He decided to keep his comments focused on his times of prayer.

The congregation stared at him, startled by the imagery and humility in his words. This did not appear to be a traditional Christmas message at all.

"IT IS this Christ that I will speak of to you this morning. He is a Christ most glorious, enthroned in the Heavens. The God-Man, who has purchased our redemption with His own blood. He is our great High Priest who is very-greatly touched by the feeling of our infirmities and now makes intercession for us.

"He Himself was the sacrifice that has taken away the sins of the whole world. He is the ark of safety into which sinners may run to find shelter from God's great and just wrath. He is a shelter most glorious, in whose presence is fullness of joy and pleasures forevermore."

EDWARDS STOPPED and looked over the congregation with eyes that seemed to pierce their souls. Tears began to well as he urgently continued.

. . .

"YET, I fear that many here today have not yet entered that ark. Ye stand afar off, looking upon the ark's great safety and assuming that because you have looked upon it, you will be secure. Yet know this day that you shall **not** be!

"Indeed, if ye have not entered into that covenant which was sealed in Christ's blood, then ye still have no part in His salvation. Though ye have walked with Christians, ye are not a Christian. Though ye have been seated with worshipers, ye have not worshiped. Though ye have even partaken of the sacraments, ye have not partaken of the true blood of Christ.

"I say to thee this morning that ye are **not** secure! If ye were called from this life into eternity this very day, ye would **not** find shelter from God's just wrath. The glories of Heaven would **not** be thine!

"Scripture is right in its profound declaration — 'There is a way that seemeth right unto a man, but the end thereof is death!'"

EDWARDS' message continued for nearly an hour. As he pleaded God's case, a deep and profound supernatural anointing filled his words, making them like arrows that pierced hearts throughout the dumbfounded assembly. Before he had finished his message, several in the audience had begun to openly weep in remorse, and many were being deeply and eternally affected.

AN EXTRAORDINARY BATTLE raged while Edwards preached. It swirled around the men and women in the old church, filling the air inside and the skies above the church. It was an immense clash as vicious dark enemies tried to snuff out the kindling spark of revival that was beginning to glow. The hideous demonic forces sensed that this fire was especially dangerous — it was the defining fire of a *new work of God*.

Heaven's bright defenders were not absent. They drove the ugly demon hoards back in waves. Only to have the ugly creatures clamor back again in their desperate efforts. The demons whispered with silken tongues to people in the crowd who had been sitting in the same pews all their lives, telling them they were surely secure. The preacher surely could not be talking about *them!*

Seeds of bitterness were blown onto others — like angry, poisonous weeds that stung their souls. How dare the young minister speak accusingly of *them*, the beasts suggested. After all, they were respected church members with wealth and great social standing!

Still, others were afflicted with numbing tiredness that sought to shroud their minds with distracting or menacing dreams.

However, these attacks were swiftly and repeatedly obliterated under the tremendous unction of Edward's Spirit-filled preaching. They were washed away in the flood of Heavenly anointing that now filled the old church from its lowest floorboards to the tip of its steeple. This flood was like fuel poured upon the kindling sparks ignited in people's souls. The fire quickly grew into a roaring blaze, causing more and more of those in attendance to weep and cry out in genuine repentance with great distress.

Edwards remembered the stranger's words about people's emotional reactions, recognizing that they were indeed encountering God's presence. He'd never seen anything like it before but rested in the assurance that their outbursts were Heavenly-inspired.

BY THE TIME EDWARDS' message was finished that morning, a profound change had been worked in the Northampton church. It marked a turning point in the town that would soon spread throughout Massachusetts. Edwards would not be alone in leading this God-breathed move — God was in the process of raising up others throughout the Colonies to join the work. For now, though, this newly ignited flame was a singular wonder.

The supernatural enemies who fought so hard to stop it knew what it truly was—the birth of a generation-defining movement. On this extraordinary night in 1734, God established a beachhead for revival in the American colonies. It was the start of a great awakening.

In fact, the awakening it spawned would soon be felt beyond the American colonies, impacting even the British throne.

⌘

14

A MISSION RARELY GIVEN

"It is a rare calling that God has for thee..."
~ Chozeq

CENTER SPRINGS, LATE-SEPTEMBER...
18 months ago

A week had passed for Jimmy since his meeting with Jonathan Edwards. He mulled over the scenes that Chozeq had shown him— they were sights of vast crowds and packed churches. It occurred to him that it wasn't just Edwards he'd seen preaching in many of those scenes; there were others, especially in the preaching to open-air crowds.

Jimmy began to research historical accounts of Edwards' life and the Great Awakening and soon realized that there were several great preachers who made an impact during that time. The one who especially intrigued him was George Whitefield.

He read how Whitefield worked his way through Oxford as a servitor since his family lacked the money to pay his tuition. He was ordained at a young age in the Church of England. From what Jimmy could tell, Whitefield had great talent as an orator and loved the theater. Ironically, those talents set him at odds with Church clergy, but they also opened doors for his ministry that rocked the world.

Jimmy sat in a rocker on the farmhouse porch, pondering his meeting with Edwards. What could Chozeq have meant when he spoke of Jimmy's new mission? The angel's words echoed in his mind: *"It is a rare calling that God has for thee, a mission rarely given."*

It seemed odd to Jimmy that God would use someone from a future time to help with events in the past. As he thought about it, though, he realized it wasn't much different from someone in the past traveling to the future or, in Chozeq's case, from outside of time altogether. Some of the Bible's prophets had been shown events in the past just as much as the future — Moses wrote Genesis, after all.

Jimmy realized that whether someone in Edwards' time traveled to the future or Jimmy traveled to the past, the purpose was the same— to help the ones being guided. So, what exactly did they need help with?

WHILE JIMMY CONSIDERED THAT QUESTION, a sea of unfamiliar sounds suddenly filled his ears. He opened his eyes with a start, realizing he was now sitting on a bench beside a set of docks. It was a vibrant seaport.

Several ships were unloading passengers and cargo, and the docks were bustling with activity. Jimmy was not surprised to see that the boats were sailing ships—three-masted vessels like those he'd seen in pictures from the 1700s.

"Excuse me, lad. Is anyone seated here beside ye?"

Jimmy was not expecting to be visible; he looked up in surprise at the man who had asked the question. "N-no," he stammered, caught off-guard.

"I dare say ye dress a bit strangely here in the Colonies," the man noted with a detectable Scottish brogue as he took a seat.

Jimmy looked at his clothes—he was wearing sneakers and running shorts with a teeshirt that said 'New Dad' on the front—a gift from Anna. He didn't respond to the man's comment, quickly deciding it could lead to a complicated explanation.

"Have you just arrived?" Jimmy asked him instead.

"Aye, by God's grace," the man replied, extending his hand to shake. "I'll be forgettin' my manners... I've just arrived from London. Whitefield's the name... George Whitefield."

Jimmy reached for his hand in absent-minded shock, barely believing what he'd just heard. Gathering his thoughts the best he could, he introduced himself. "Jimmy... Jim Moretti," he said as they shook.

"Strange names here as well," Whitefield cracked with a hint of wit. "Hello, Jimmy-Jim Moretti. Nice t'be makin' yer acquaintance. A peddler of trinkets are ye?"

"Trinkets?" Jimmy asked, confused by the question.

"Thy attire bears the moniker *New Dad*... I suspect a play with the term Doodad. It is a clever turn of the phrase, I might add."

Jimmy's face reddened as he realized the Scotsman's mistake. "No, Dad is a word for Father. I'm a new father; our son is three months old."

"Ah, my apologies. I see I have a fair bit to learn about the culture here. Hearty congratulations t' ye, nonetheless."

"Thanks. Is this your first trip to America?"

"It is. I'm here in response to an invitation to speak... I am a preacher of sorts."

"I know," Jimmy confessed, "...I mean, I know who you are."

"Well, now, there's another surprise," Whitefield said. He stopped and looked at Jimmy closely. "I perceive ye are of a different sort. A follower of ecclesiastical affairs, are ye?"

"You could say that, yeah."

Jimmy paused, considering what to share with his new acquaintance. Their meeting was far too great a coincidence not to be divinely ordained, so he decided to share what he knew.

"I know you've come in answer to an invitation from your friends,

John and Charles Wesley," he revealed. "God plans to use you here in a tremendous revival - not just here in Georgia but all throughout the colonies."

"Are ye a friend of the Wesley's?" Whitefield asked hopefully.

"No, I've never met them," Jimmy confessed. "Not that I wouldn't welcome the chance."

Whitefield lifted his head, taken aback by Jimmy's words. "How is it then that ye know such things?"

"I've been sent to help you, as well as Reverend Edwards in Massachusetts and others. Like I said, God is planning something incredible - a great awakening."

"Are ye a friend of Reverend Edwards then?" Whitefield asked, still trying to make sense of Jimmy's words.

"Well, we've met once; it was a meeting similar to this. God has already begun the work there in Massachusetts; it will be fertile ground when you get there."

"Well, if Reverend Edwards is inclined to have me, I'd surely be wont to accept his invitation. I'm encouraged by thy faith in me, nonetheless."

WHILE HE WAS STILL SPEAKING, a man cried out from several yards away: "Whitefield! George! It's good to see you, my friend!"

Whitefield stood with a smile to greet the Wesley brothers, old friends since their college days at Oxford. He turned back to introduce Jimmy but found the bench empty. Scanning around the docks, there was no sign of him anywhere.

THE FLASH that returned Jimmy to his place on the farmhouse porch did not shock him. He'd become accustomed to his travels by now. But the meeting with Whitefield *had* been a surprise. Jimmy wondered what God had wanted him to say to the famous preacher. It didn't seem to him like he had anything to share that was of any significance. He thought of the men who called to Whitefield just as Jimmy was taken from the scene. He was sure they were the Wesley brothers. He would have loved to meet them — it seemed that such a meeting was not in God's plans.

"Hey, Jimmy! Can ya lend me a hand over here?" Pete's voice interrupted his thoughts. "I've been trying to fix this grain bag loader; it looks like something's jammed."

Jimmy followed him into the barn and examined the temperamental machine. "I see what's wrong," he said, turning toward the workbench for a few tools. They worked together for the rest of the afternoon, finally clearing the jam.

LATER THAT NIGHT, Jimmy sat alone again on the front porch. He'd finished cleaning up from dinner and showered to remove the grime from his repair work. Anna had gotten the baby to sleep and gone on to bed.

His thoughts returned to his meeting with Whitefield. Aside from introducing himself, he repeated the conclusion that he hadn't offered anything helpful to the famous preacher as far as he could recall. There must have been some reason for their meeting - it didn't seem likely that God would send him more than 200 years through time for just a handshake.

His thoughts turned again to Chozeq's message about his coming mission—"a mission rarely given," he heard the words repeat in his mind. The urgency in his spirit was growing; he was becoming increasingly restless to get started with his new calling—whatever it was. Jimmy's eyes closed in prayer as he sought the Lord for help with the odd puzzle.

ONCE AGAIN, the sound of bustling crowds stirred him to open his eyes. He was sitting on a stoop beside a busy city street. The street's pavement was cobblestone. The sidewalks teemed with people while horses and carriages rode past in a bustling flow. Everyone seemed to be dressed formally in waistcoats, jackets, and hats; the women wore long, frilly dresses that covered their shoes. It was obviously some time in the 1700s.

A look down the long boulevard drew his eyes to a familiar building still under construction. Jimmy recognized it as the Pennsylvania State House from its distinctive copula and bell tower — it would one day be called Independence Hall. He was in Philadelphia.

Lying on the step beside him, he noticed a discarded newspaper—it was not much more than a—pamphlet with the name *Pennsylvania Gazette* emblazoned across the front page. Curious, he lifted it, surprised to read the headline in large type:

WHITEFIELD DRAWS THOUSANDS.

Its date made clear what year it was — 1739.

Jimmy guessed that the paper was at least a day old. He read the article with interest; it described one of the open-air rallies being held in the city, recounting Whitefield's preaching to large crowds who seemed greatly moved by his messages. It said the rallies were continuing all week.

Jimmy stood excitedly and stopped a man walking past....

"Excuse me. Can you tell me how to get to this square? The one where Whitefield is speaking?"

The man looked at Jimmy strangely, eying his clothes... Jimmy was wearing an old T-shirt, sweatpants, and slippers—he'd been dressed for bed. (Jimmy noted that it'd be a good idea to pay better attention to what he wore when he prayed these days.)

The man seemed indignant as he answered, "How is it ye know not the way from here to the square? Ye'll find it right there, just beyond the new State House." The man shook his head in apparent disgust as he continued on his way.

Jimmy smiled as he thanked him and tucked the paper under his arm, setting off toward the place. Groups were already gathered, and more were arriving from all directions. Jimmy made his way through the growing crowd toward the square's main platform, finally arriving near where he expected Whitefield to stand.

The makeshift platform was large and partly filled with an orchestra of musicians. He noted flutes, clarinets, trumpets, drums, several violinists, and even a harpsichord. A man rose to the podium and announced a familiar hymn; the orchestra erupted in song as the crowds joined in the singing with impressive gusto.

The hymn was followed by a soloist who held the crowd's rapt attention with her beautiful performance. From the time the music had first started, the crowd quickly doubled in size.

When she finished singing, Whitefield rose to lead the next hymn, and then he enthusiastically led another. The crowd was deeply stirred as he eventually introduced his message and began to preach.

⌘

15

UNLIKELY FRIENDS

"Ye are called to a great harvest of souls... which shall resound for many generations!"
~ Ardent

PHILADELPHIA, NOVEMBER 1739...

"It is again a great honor to preach the Gospel of Christ in this fine city," Whitefield bellowed loudly.

A scattering of clapping and cheers rose from among the crowd. Whitefield turned, thanked the orchestra seated behind him, and stood quietly gathering his thoughts. Jimmy got the sense he was seeking God for His leading. There was a palpable feeling of God's presence over the place, and the crowds grew silent in anticipation.

"Some may ask the question, why... why bother with this preaching of the gospel? Why roam from city to city and traverse the ocean to do it? Why travel the highways and byways of strange lands for it?"

He paused as a sly smile grew... "I mean no offense in calling these lands strange... only that they are strange to me!" A wave of laughter rolled through the crowd.

He grew serious again... "What is the purpose of such preaching? Such endless preparation and ceaseless roaming?" He raised his voice and shouted: "What is God's intention in it?"

He paused again - silence subdued the enthralled crowd.

"I will tell ye what it is! It is to speak the words of the almighty God to lost and helpless sinners!" Whitefield's voice boomed with words that echoed from his surroundings. "It is to reach lost men and women who have never ventured inside a church or understood the purpose of it. Men and women who do not know that their souls are destined for a tragic eternity of burning Hell!"

AN OVERWHELMING SENSE of God's presence had descended on the spellbound gathering. Jimmy could see faces staring in rapt attention as their eyes clouded with sudden tears.

Whitefield raised his voice even louder. "Christ's ministers must do the work of fishermen! They must not wait for souls to come to them but must go after souls and 'compel them to come in.' Christ did not sit tamely by his fireside, like a cat on a rainy day, mourning over the wickedness of the land. He went forth to beard the devil in his high places. He attacked sin and wickedness face to face and gave them no peace.

"In the same way He did, we must dive into holes and corners after sinners. We must hunt out ignorance and vice wherever they can be found so that we may save those poor souls who are imprisoned by them[1].

"You are a sinner as ye stand here today!

"I do not say that *some* of you are sinners—all of you are, as am I! Everyone in this great throng deserves a destiny of burning Hell, separated from God's great holiness. But there is good news, friends— Christ came to save sinners, of whom I am chief!

"Christ seeks sinners! He came to seek and to save those who are lost. He pursues them across years of time and seasons of life. And when He finds them, He wraps them in gleaming robes of righteousness, cleanses them of every sin, and makes them sit in Heavenly places!

"Some who hear my voice at this hour know that it is thy destiny to meet Him soon — perhaps even today. It may be that some here will not see a tomorrow in which to meet Him; none of us know the length of our lives. Today, if ye hear His voice, harden not thy heart!"

Whitefield lowered the Bible he'd been waving in his hand and placed it gently on the podium, opening it.

"I feel that God is leading us to look into the great Fall of man, in Genesis chapter three, and the promise of redemption that He decreed even then to provide for the fallen creation.

"In His judgment upon the serpent we read in Genesis 3:15…

> "And I will put enmity between thee and the woman, and
> between thy seed and her seed, it shall bruise thy head, and
> thou shalt bruise his heel."

"On reading these words, I could address you in the language of the holy angels to the shepherds, who were watching their flocks by night: 'Behold, I bring you glad tidings of great joy!' For this is the first promise that was made of a Savior to the apostate race of Adam. We generally look for Christ only in the New Testament, but Christianity, in one sense, is very near as old as creation.

"It began with the promise in the text, which the elect lived upon until Abraham's time. Afterward, at sundry times and in diverse manners, God spoke to the fathers through the prophets until, at length, the Lord Jesus himself was manifested in the flesh and came and tabernacled amongst us.

"The promise appeared dark to our first parents, yet, dark as it was, they built upon it their hopes of everlasting salvation.

"How they came to need this promise, and what is the extent and meaning of it, I intend, God willing, to make the subject of your present meditation.

"The Fall of Man is written in characters too legible not to be understood: Those that deny it, by their denying, prove it. The very heathens confessed and bewailed it: They could see the streams of corruption running through the whole race of mankind but could not trace them to the fountainhead. Before God revealed his Son, man was a riddle to himself. And Moses unfolds more in this one chapter than all mankind could have been capable of finding out of themselves, though they had studied to all eternity.[2]"

JIMMY HAD FORGOTTEN THE CROWDS. He stood, enthralled, as Whitefield opened the scriptures with vivid imagery. He preached for over an hour with no notes that Jimmy could detect. When he finished, the wave of weeping people who pressed forward left no doubt of its effect.

———

IT WAS NEARLY sundown when Whitefield finished praying with the last of those who'd come forward. The music had ended, and the crowds had thinned. Jimmy made his way over to him, feeling nervous that Whitefield might not remember their last meeting. As he approached, however, the tired preacher called to him in greeting.

"I had hoped to see thee again, my friend. Earnestly have I prayed for it." He reached out a hand to shake, "It's Jimmy-Jim, is it not?"

Jimmy couldn't help laughing. "It's just Jim... or Jimmy... whichever."

Whitefield's head bobbed back as he realized his error. He smiled humbly and nodded, indicating that he understood. "We last met in Georgia, as I recall. What brings thee to Pennsylvania?"

"Well, you do, I suppose," Jimmy answered honestly. Whitefield's bewildered look made him feel like he needed to explain. "That is, I go where God sends me... he sent me here."

"I perceive thou art an odd fellow... by that, I mean a man of uncommon calling," Whitefield quickly clarified.

"Uncommon," Jimmy repeated, "Yeah, you have no idea."

Whitefield lowered his eyebrows as if studying a puzzle.

"I'm not sure I can explain it," Jimmy hurried to add. "I doubt you'd believe me if I told you... I wouldn't blame you if you didn't."

"Perhaps ye can answer me this," Whitefield said, stroking his chin contemplatively. "Art thou acquainted with the messenger who is called Ardent?"

Jimmy's eyebrows raised, hinting at his surprise at the mention of Ardent's name.

"It looks like you've met him," Jimmy observed without answering the question.

"Aye, and so have ye, I perceive."

A VOICE CALLED out just then, interrupting their exchange... "Reverend Whitefield!"

Whitefield acknowledged the man who called and leaned closer to Jimmy. "We must finish this a bit later. I wish to speak more of it," he said in a hushed voice.

At that moment, the calling man reached them, and Jimmy stared at him; the accomplished-looking man in his early thirties looked vaguely familiar.

"Jim, this is Mister Franklin. I am here in Pennsylvania at his invitation."

Jimmy couldn't help being awestruck as he shook the man's hand.

"Benjamin Franklin, at your service, sir," the man said with a smile as they shook hands.

"Jimmy Moretti, sir."

"Moretti," Franklin repeated. "An Italian name, if I'm not mistaken. An uncommon origin here in the Americas... although, I suppose there was Columbus...." His voice trailed off as if lost in thought for a moment. "In any case, it is a pleasure to meet any friend of Reverend Whitefield's," he concluded with a slight bow of his head.

"You'll have to forgive Mr. Frankin's obsession with names," Whitefield cut in. "He's just been appointed postmaster of this fine city."

Franklin grunted with a smile and nodded with a self-deprecating gesture. His voice was excited as he turned to Whitefield and lifted a journal notebook. "Your vocal projection is quite extraordinary. I took specific measures... you could be clearly heard from a mile away! I'm going to write about it in my Almanak."

Whitefield tilted his head: "Was it only the *volume* of my message that registered to you?" he asked with a sly smile.

"Of course not," Franklin quickly accepted, "It was a fine exposition — very moving indeed. It is wonderful to see the change soon made by your preaching in the manners of the inhabitants of Philadelphia. From being thoughtless or indifferent about religion, it seems lately as if all the world is growing religious.[3]

"On the other hand, I must say that your singing voice, while equally boisterous, does leave something to be desired."

Whitefield burst out with a loud guffaw as he gave Franklin a friendly slap on the shoulder. "That, sir, is why God has appointed better-equipped soloists to His work."

"Indeed," Franklin agreed with a smile. By the way, I've had a man write notes of your message today. With your permission, I'd like to publish a pamphlet of it."

"Notes, you say. I'd much appreciate an opportunity to review them before printing. I've had the unfortunate experience of seeing several of my sermons taken down in shorthand by reporters and published without correction. Those men appeared to have done their work very indifferently and were evidently ignorant alike of stopping and paragraphing, of grammar and of gospel. In the way that they wrote it, sense and connection were destroyed by injudicious, disjointed paragraphs, turning it into nonsense. The resulting works they attributed to me turned out to be a "mingle-mangle" and a complete mess."

Franklin smiled and humbly assured him, "I completely understand. I assure thee that nothing will be printed unless ye have agreed." He lifted the watch from his vest pocket and glanced at it in the lamplight. "Speaking of complete messes, I'd better be off before the evening post is delayed."

With that, he hurried off across the open square, which was now mostly empty.

"WELL THEN," Whitefield said, turning back to Jimmy. "I should very much like to continue our earlier conversation. Whither art thou boarding for thy stay here?"

"Boarding? Well... nowhere... that is, I'm not staying here." Jimmy studied Whitefield's puzzled look for a moment. It reminded him of how Jonathan Edwards looked in an earlier conversation. He grew serious as he continued.

"It's been made clear to me that God wants me to help with something He's doing here in the colonies. It's a great awakening... a great revival. Its outcome will change the course of history — not just here in America, but everywhere."

A chill ran through Whitefield as he remembered Ardent's words: *'Ye are called to a great harvest of souls — one which shall resound for many generations!'*

He looked at Jimmy intently, realizing that this young friend had also received the same charge, perhaps from Ardent as well.

"Are ye a Minister then? What work is He calling thee to do?"

"No, I'm not a minister... not really. Not in the way you'd expect. Honestly, I'm not completely sure what he wants me to do. I've learned that the important thing is to follow... and say yes."

"Hmmph," Whitefield intoned with an accepting nod. "I see in thee a maturity in the things of God. It takes great faith to step into thin air, as it were."

Jimmy accepted the comment with a humble nod. His new friend had no idea how accurate his words about stepping into thin air were. Glancing around, he saw that the square around them had emptied, and the nearby streets were quiet.

"...Anyway," Jimmy interrupted the brief silence, "I have a feeling we'll be seeing each other again."

He held out his hand to shake... "It was good to see you."

Whitefield grasped his hand with a firm handshake and agreed.

THEN JIMMY TURNED TO LEAVE — walking three or four yards before Whitefield watched open-mouthed as Jimmy faded from sight.

⌘

16

MATTHEW TWENTY-FOUR

"...and then shall the end come."
~ Matthew 24:14

CENTER SPRINGS, EARLY OCTOBER...
17 months ago

Lena flinched in her sleep. The dream that ran through her head made her heart beat wildly; her hands were clasped into tight fists as her eyes darted rapidly beneath her closed eyelids. The visions in her dream were not unfamiliar; she'd seen them before.

SHE DREAMED of a vast field of golden grain; it stretched as far as she could see in all directions. It was endless. The sky was crystal clear and vivid blue... so blue that it was awe-inspiring... and the air was perfectly still and calm. As she watched, a commotion appeared in the center of the field — it was small at first, like a gentle rustling, then it grew into a swirling breeze that was barely strong enough to move the grain tops, tracing a circular pattern across the surface. The wind soon grew stronger until it created what looked like a whirlpool in the center of the field, making the grain stalks bend low as the wind touched them. The wind didn't beat down the stalks... it was more like they were bowing as it touched them.

The swirling wind kept expanding larger and larger, filling more and more of the field, and the wind swirled faster and faster. It began pulling the grain off the stalks and sending it flying into the air, forming a colossal funnel cloud... like a tornado. It stayed in one place, just growing larger and larger... swallowing more and more of the field. As it grew, it came closer and closer to where she stood. Then, when it was nearly upon her, she could see that the wheat grains had become sparks flying upward... it was beautiful. She could see them gathering into a giant pillar — like a pillar of fire. It was loud... like a tornado, but with the sound of a raging inferno... its power was frightening and awesome. Still, it was so incredibly beautiful.

Suddenly, she was standing outside the church at Maria's memorial service. The rumbling sound of the huge fiery pillar drew her attention upward, and she watched the amazing sight with renewed awe.

That's when it exploded outward, instantly flooding the air all around as far as she could see. It was so amazing! It filled everything with swirling light and warmth. It made her tremble and gasp ...its beauty thrilled her soul with overwhelming joy -- it was astonishing!

It burned like that for a while, but not very long. Soon, the surrounding sky turned cold and dark, and an icy, freezing rain began to fall. At first, the fire drove the rain back, but a cold mist crept over the ground, slowly killing the stalks of wheat and causing the fire to shrink smaller and smaller. Finally, she could see the last sparks flying away upward — disappearing through the shrinking blue opening in the darkened sky. As the fire retreated, the rain and ice beat the field harder, crushing what was left of the wheat until the entire field was frozen and lifeless. As she watched it, she was struck by a deep feeling of despair. Seeing everything frozen and dead made her feel sick and heartbroken, and the cold made her shiver terribly.

LENA AWOKE WITH A LOUD GASP, sitting bolt upright and breathing frantically as she wiped a sudden stream of tears from her cheeks.

"What's wrong!" Mike asked in alarm, waking with a start. He sat up beside her, studying the tears and deep concern on her face in the early morning light.

"It was a dream," she explained without looking at him. Her thoughts were racing. "A dream I've seen before...," her words trailed off as she spoke. The feeling that it stirred in her was ominous.

"It was about the firestorm... you know, the one at Maria's memorial. I'd seen it before then... before it happened. It was in a vision... on the first night of the tent meetings. Maria saw it too...."

Lena paused silently as she considered the poignancy of the fact that it was Maria who saw the vision — a vision that was fulfilled at Maria's own memorial service.

LENA FINALLY LOOKED AT MIKE, collecting her thoughts. "There was more. The fire died out; then everything got so cold." Her eyes narrowed as she remembered something else... "Matthew twenty-four!"

Lena reached for her Bible on the nightstand and opened it as she explained....

"In her vision, Maria saw a message... a scroll. It had verses from Matthew twenty-four on it. Here..." she said as she found the place and began to read.

And Jesus answered and said to them, Take heed that no man deceive you. For many shall come in my name, saying, I am

Christ, and shall deceive many. And ye shall hear of wars and rumors of wars: see that ye be not troubled: for all these things must come to pass, but the end is not yet.

For nation shall rise against nation, and kingdom against kingdom: and there shall be famines, and pestilences, and earthquakes, in divers places. All these are the beginning of sorrows.

Then shall they deliver you up to be afflicted, and shall kill you: and ye shall be hated of all nations for my name's sake. And then shall many be offended, and shall betray one another, and shall hate one another.

And many false prophets shall rise and shall deceive many. And because iniquity shall abound, the love of many shall wax cold.

But he that shall endure unto the end, the same shall be saved.

And this gospel of the kingdom shall be preached in all the world for a witness unto all nations; and then shall the end come.[1]

"Do you think you dreamed it for a reason?" Mike asked quietly.

"I don't know... it seemed so real." She stared into space, deep in thought. "Do you ever wonder about all the things that happened five years ago — all those incredible things with Jimmy? With the drought and seeing all those angels and demons... back then, it seemed like the Lord would return any minute. The past five years have been so... normal."

"Normal ain't a bad thing," Mike noted with a hint of a smile.

She leaned against him, and he put his arm around her shoulders. "I know...," she agreed, "but it seems like we're in a waiting period — like God is just waiting for something. I can't help feeling like it's just a matter of time before everything gets crazy again."

The words from Matthew twenty-four replayed in both their minds as they pondered her point; neither spoke. Mike supportively squeezed her closer. She sat distracted by her thoughts as she laid her head against him.

SUNDAY MORNING...

SERVICES at the Living Springs Church had been incredible throughout the summer. God's move there still resembled that of five years ago. The fires of revival had become even brighter over the recent summer weeks.

The church in Center Springs was not alone. Churches all over were experiencing the same rekindling lately. It was especially evident among the kids, from college-aged to the youngest.

Though not technically on staff, Jimmy was a regular speaker at the Living Springs Church. His national notoriety from the events of five years earlier had not dimmed either.

That notoriety meant that the world's eyes remained on him. His reputation as 'the prophet who stopped the rain and called down lightning' followed him everywhere. It was especially hard for him during his college years; fitting in hadn't been easy, at least not at first.

More than anywhere else, he could be himself here in Center Springs. To most people here, he was still the kid they knew growing up.

He preferred it that way. He was still the same person, despite saluting angels and starring-down demons — not to mention his trips through time. For him, the past few years had been busy with studies and helping out with the Mission in Harbor City. Still, even he recognized that his work had been quieter the past few years. He knew in his heart that things would not remain quiet.

His recent meetings with Edwards and Whitefield had driven home that point. The puzzle of his involvement with them now occupied him constantly. Why was he needed at that time in history? What could he possibly offer to those giants of the faith?

Chozeq had said it was because of his experience with revival. It was hard for him to grasp just how unusual a spiritual revival was in the 1700s. Even Whitefield and Edwards had never seen anything like it.

Jimmy had to admit that there was at least one advantage to being in the 1700s—it was easier for him to blend in, his clothes notwithstanding.

These thoughts were rambling through his head as he took the platform. Looking out over the packed church, he refocused on his message.

"Some may ask the question, why... why bother with this preaching of the gospel? Why should missionaries roam from city to city and traverse the ocean to do it? Why travel the highways and byways of strange lands for it?" ...he began.

The inspiration for his message still burned in his memory — he'd borrowed much of it from Whitefield's stirring sermon in Philadelphia.

EARLY NOVEMBER...
16 months ago

HARVEST TIME WAS the busiest season on the farm. Jimmy was grateful to have Pete's help, along with a few others who usually worked at the food pantry. Angela had taken Anna's advice and confined herself to light work. Her baby was nearly due.

The new combine tractor made the job easier. Pete was smiling broadly as he climbed off. "Man, this thing makes the work a breeze!"

"I'll say," Jimmy agreed. "Looks like it practically drives itself."

"They have some that do that...," Pete reminded him. "That Autonomous AI[2] stuff worries me, though; it's gettin' *too* smart."

"Yeah, I gotta agree with you," Jimmy said. "Especially with what the military is doing with it. Did you see those unmanned fighter jets and tanks? They're even talking about giving it control of the nuclear launch codes."

"It scares the heck outta me," Pete agreed. "Don't those people ever go to the movies? There have been, like, a hundred of 'em about evil robots takin' over the world."

"The problem is that all the world's major powers are using it. Everyone's afraid of being left behind." Jimmy paused, thinking about his own words... "They should be worried about a different kind of being *left behind*."

Pete grew serious. "Do you think it'll happen soon... the Lord's coming?"

"I pray that it does..." Jimmy answered sincerely. Inside, he was considering some of the future events he'd seen in his travels. He knew that things were going to get pretty rough.

THEY WERE INTERRUPTED SUDDENLY by Anna's excited voice as she burst onto the front porch, letting the screen door slam loudly behind her....

"ANGELA IS IN LABOR! You need to leave for the hospital **right now!**"

⌘

17

NIGHTFALL

'The surrounding priestesses fell to their faces before her...'

BROWNSVILLE, BROOKLYN -- LATE-NOVEMBER...
16 months ago

B adrick pulled up to the one-room basement hangout that Rad called home and blew his car's horn. Rad appeared on the doorstep with his arms crossed, looking like he hadn't yet made up his mind whether to get in.

"Yer dad's expectin' us at two o'clock. He's anxious t' see ya, mon."

Rad was still uncommitted as he stepped nearer, debating whether to go through with it. Badrick read the boy's uncertainty and knew just the way to coax him.

"I get that you're fearin' it... It takes a brave man t' go dar to de prison. If yer too afraid, we can cancel."

Rad looked back at his friends standing around him and straightened tall.

"I ain't afraid. I ain't afraid o' nothin'." With that, he pulled the door open and got in.

———

THE CAR RADIO was tuned to a news report that vividly depicted the world's growing crises. Suspicion between nations was at an all-time high, which had already spurred a new arms race in developing autonomous weapons and artificial intelligence. Tenuous alliances were being tested between suspicious allies. At the same time, surprising new alliances were being formed between former rivals — leaving the US increasingly isolated.

Meanwhile, tensions in the Middle East were still the most significant headline. The radio report described the latest developments:

———

The Russian-led Northern Alliance continues to amass battle groups along Israel's border. Its ships have begun a blockade of Israeli ports in the Mediterranean, disrupting its shipments of natural gas to Europe. Israeli protests to the United Nations have gone unheeded.

In other news, the World Bank's new EarthCoin currency has now been accepted by 190 nations, including the Vatican's Holy See. Israel remains the most prominent hold-out against the single-world currency.

———

BADRICK WHISTLED THROUGH HIS TEETH. "Mon, I'm tellin' ya, it be like hearin' the Bible's pages on de radio. Trust me mon, Jesus is comin' back real soon!"

Rad shrugged off his words. "People been sayin' that my whole life. I'll believe it when I see it."

"When you're seein' it, it'll be too late, mon. Some rough times'll be comin' den; de worst the world has ever known."

"Ya don't have t' tell me about rough times. In case ya ain't noticed, some of us ain't got it so great already. I got nothin' t' lose."

"In dose times, you'd be wishing' fer today's troubles. Believe it — this ain't nothin.'"

———

THEY WERE STILL DEBATING the point when Badrick finally pulled into the prison parking lot. It had been over two years since Rad had last visited his father, and the guards' scrutiny of him was decidedly greater this time. PJ had prearranged for them to meet Chase in the prison chapel. It so happened that they'd arrived during one of Chase's prayer group meetings. The chapel was filled with inmates who'd come to Christ through PJ's prison ministry — most of them through the efforts of Chase himself.

Rad sat in the back, staring uncomfortably at the floor. Chase had seen him come in and couldn't wait to wrap up the meeting. Rad watched as Chase sent the men off, embracing some of them as they parted, and then he made his way to the back while the chapel slowly cleared.

"HELLO, SON. IT'S GREAT T' see ya again." Rad had grown since the last time he'd seen him; he was more man than boy now. Chase wanted nothing more than to wrap his arms around his son in welcome but could see in the boy's eyes that he wanted no part of it.

Rad avoided eye contact, still questioning his decision to come.

Badrick broke the awkward silence, saying hello to Chase with an embrace. "That was an awesome meetin' mon. Dose men, dey love de Lord, it's bein' clear seen."

"Thanks for bringing him, man; it's good to see you again," Chase said sincerely to Badrick.

Badrick smiled with a nod. "I'll be 'round when you're done," he said as he patted Chase's shoulder and left them alone.

Chase offered Rad a chair and sat beside him.

"How've you been doin'?"

"I'm gettin' by. Almost got killed a few times... I guess you probably know what that's like." Rad's sarcasm was sharp and obviously intended for injury. Chase studied his son's eyes, ignoring the comment's intent as he recognized the pain it conveyed.

"I do, actually," Chase admitted. "That's not something I'm proud of. I'm sorry to hear it."

Rad shrugged.

Chase leaned forward with elbows on his knees. "I hear you left your foster place. Where are you stayin'?"

"I got a pad. Me an' some bros got it together. It's got a camera in the door an' everything," Rad bragged. He left out the fact it was one room in a basement with a small filthy bathroom and no kitchen.

"That's good, that's good," Chase repeated, trying to be encouraging. Parenting was a skill he'd never had a chance to learn; he was admittedly at a loss as a father. He breathed a silent prayer for help.

"How's school going? I guess it's summer break. You're gonna be startin' your second year o' high school, right?"

"I quit that last year. School ain't for me. I ain't got time for that s***. I got my troop... my bloods — we're fierce; nobody crosses us, man."

"You mean a gang?" Chase asked in alarm. "Radison, trust me, that ain't the way t' go. Killin' an' drugs — that'll only land ya in a place like this!"

"My name's Rad," he answered coldly. "I'm just followin' in my old man's footsteps... Ain't that what a kid's supposed t' do? That's all y' ever gave me, man... that's yer legacy."

Chase looked crestfallen. The truth in his son's words cut deep.

"Look, son, I know it's been hard on ya... all this. I'm sorry, I really am. You deserved better."

RAD SLAPPED his knees and stood to his feet in a sudden fit of anger.

"Stop... just stop it! Stop actin' like ya know me. Like, ya got any idea what kinda life I had. Ya wanna know what my life is like? My life has been hell — a livin' hell!" He clenched his fists in seething anger, using all his willpower to keep from punching the nearest wall. The now familiar rage inside him was quickly rising to a boiling point. "I don't know why I even came here. S***, I can't even do this... I'm getting outta here."

Chase stood and took hold of Rad's shoulders. "Wait, son! I'm sorry..." His words were cut off as Rad's rage exploded.

"Don't touch me! Get yer hands off me! To hell with you!" Rad shoved Chase away and swung at him with an angry fist. The punch caught Chase hard in the face, knocking him backward. "I don't wanna see ya no more. I NEVER WANNA SEE YOU AGAIN!" Those words echoed in the empty chapel as Rad stormed off, slamming the chapel doors.

CHASE CLIMBED off the floor where he'd been knocked down, now alone in the empty chapel. He wiped a stray tear from his cheek — it was from his son's words, not his angry strike. He sat on a chapel bench and bowed his head sorrowfully, then turned and slid to his knees; he would spend the rest of the hour urgently lifting Radison in prayer.

BEIRUT, LEBANON — EARLY DECEMBER
15 months ago

AN ENTOURAGE of two dozen young women gathered in ceremonial robes around an ancient statue. They were priestesses of the goddess Anath, sister of the ancient Phoenician god Ba'al.

The ancient sect had scattered following the death of Athaliah, their former High Priestess, but was now beginning to resurface. Four had been singled out; all four had served with Athaliah and knew the ancient rites well.

"Tonight, Anath will choose from among you the one to become her new High Priestess," an older woman declared. She held a sacred dagger and stared at the four with a fierce, piercing gaze.

A young goat sat tethered at the older woman's feet. It brayed softly and shivered in the cold night, unaccustomed to being separated from its mother. Ancient-looking silver chalices filled with milk from the kid goat's mother were presented to each of the four candidates. They held their cups in offering toward Anath's statue as the older woman plunged her dagger into the young kid. Then, she raised the knife over the women's cups, dripping the young goat's blood into them, mixing with the milk.

"Oh, great goddess of Love and War. We offer to you these symbols of life and death. Make known the one you will choose among those who stand before you. The one to be your high priestess — the mouthpiece of the great Anath, goddess of our people!"

The older woman bowed low before Anath's statue and then stood tall with her arms raised high....

"DRINK! DRINK ALL OF IT!" She commanded loudly.

The four women drew the cups to their lips and eagerly swallowed, draining them completely. Immediately, the four fell heavily to their knees, their eyes tightly closed. One of them began to convulse violently and was thrown backward to the ground, her mouth frothing as her eyes turned entirely black. Within moments, a second had fallen in the same way, and then a third followed. The stricken women snarled and growled unnaturally as their eyes rolled back, finally falling silent, barely breathing.

The young woman who remained rose suddenly to her feet, and her eyes snapped open — fierce looking and yellow, like the eyes of a large predatory cat. In a trance-like state, she let her robe drop to the ground and took a cup from the older woman's hand, filled to the brim with a blood offering drained from the young goat. Placing it to her lips, she tasted it, letting it overflow down her chin to run down the front of her. Then she poured it out into the statue's cupped hands, allowing the blood to run down its white marble arms.

She turned, blood-covered, to accept a new robe and headdress — the garments of the high priestess. Her yellow cat-like eyes radiated with an eerie glow as a look of sadistic cunning filled her blood-stained face.

The surrounding priestesses fell to their faces before her, praising Anath and fearfully chanting their loyalty to the new high priestess.

⌘

18

SIGNS

"...many false prophets will arise and will deceive many."
~ Jesus, Matthew 24:11

SAN FRANCISCO, CALIFORNIA — CHRISTMAS EVE
14 months ago

Mark Ostenhizer's video posts on social media were drawing attention. Calling himself *Aurora, the Mouthpiece of God*, he was widely known as the 'Prophet of Mission Bay,' named after the San Francisco neighborhood where he lived. He'd recently gained national notoriety for helping police solve a high-profile murder, claiming to have seen visions of the crime.

A large crowd gathered to hear him give a well-publicized Christmas Eve announcement. As usual, he was dressed in a flowing robe and sandals, bearded with hair that ran down his back. He walked onto a wide platform as the sound of the Beatles' song, 'All You Need is Love,' played in the background. As the music ended, he stepped to a lone microphone, and his voice cut the waiting silence.

. . .

"IN RECENT YEARS, our country has been plagued with many crimes of selfishness and greed," he began. "We have been divided by bigotry and hatred, enduring all kinds of evil and pain caused by people who say they're trying to help us.

"Some have told us that these ills were our own fault and that it was God who was judging us for sins. We remember the boy prophet — the one I call the Fire Prophet, who used his power to hurt rather than heal the country.

"We saw the Fire Prophet call down lightning on people, including the president's wife and cabinet. He hurt our planet with his disastrous drought, leaving behind the terrible destruction that we still see today. That is not the kind of love that God requires of us.

"I have come to show a better way. We must abandon all selfish ambitions to find self-actualization. Those who follow me are learning that love brings peace."

HIS PIERCING EYES widened in excitement as he lifted his arms dramatically and raised his voice....

"Today, I bring good news, which shall be for all people. I have seen a vision of a coming leader — a great one who will bring peace to this troubled world. The time will not be long. Lift your heads, all people! The great time of peace for all the world is near!"

KOLKATA, INDIA — DECEMBER 25TH

"Many shall come in my name, saying I am Christ..."

KALA MEHMOOD KAUSALYA stood in front of the Mother House Of The Missionaries Of Charity with his arms outstretched. His appearance was striking: He stood more than six and a half feet tall, with long, wavy hair and a large, full beard. His robes reached the ground, hanging like curtains from his outstretched arms.

The place where he stood — on Bose Road in the heart of Kolkata, the city once called Calcutta — was teaming with the city's populace along with pilgrims drawn there to the site of Mother Teresa's tomb. Kala's voice boomed with an unnatural volume.

"My beloved people of Kolkata! In this place rests the one you called Mother Teresa. I bring you greetings from Agnes Gonxha Bojaxhiu — the one you once knew as Saint Teresa."

A flurry of gasps ran through the crowd as people checked with each other to see if they'd heard correctly. Some who heard him waved and muttered derogatorily, dismissing him as a lunatic.

"There are skeptics among you, I understand. Yet know that this dear one has found rest with me these many years since she departed from you. Today is a great day, a day that Teresa longed to see herself. A day that is glorious for the whole world. I come to bring peace to the earth. Today, I reveal myself for who I truly am — the returned Messiah! The incarnate son of God!"

AS THE PEOPLE WATCHED, Kala waved toward a random passing truck carrying bottles of water, causing it to stop. Walking up to it, he placed his hand on one of the water jugs....

"Behold... come and taste!"

The truck's driver looked at his load in astonishment. All of the giant water jugs had turned the color of red wine. He poured a small taste from one of them, and his eyes grew large. "It is wine!" he shouted.

People rushed to taste the converted waters, then turned to Kala and fell to their knees in an expanding wave of stunned worshipers.

NEWS COVERAGE of Kala's appearance filled the airwaves. Jimmy only had to glance at the TV to see the powerful influence behind it. The dark spiritual overlord controlling Kala was a deceiving spirit like none he'd seen before.

Anna sensed it, too; although she couldn't see the demon lord the way Jimmy could, the sense of its presence was plain to her spirit.

"Those poor people," she said sadly.

"You're right," Jimmy agreed. "The thief comes to steal, kill, and destroy," he added, quoting Jesus' words.

Anna looked at him forlorn. "Everyone's repeating what that Aurora guy said about you. They're saying you're the evil one."

Jimmy could see the distress on Anna's face. Taking her by the hand, he muted the TV and leaned closer. "It's nothing I haven't been called before, remember?" he reminded her. He squeezed her hand gently, "It's been clear for a while that the times are getting darker. The Lord's coming is close; I can feel it."

Anna felt a shiver as something inside her echoed a confirmation of his words.

CENTER SPRINGS — JANUARY
13 months ago

JIMMY SAT ALONE in the old root cellar. It had been two weeks since Kala made his dramatic appearance on Christmas Day. Jimmy's thoughts were consumed with something else, however: his encounters with Edwards and Whitefield. He still struggled to understand what kind of help he could possibly give to either of them; the two men were already giants of the faith.

He thought about his growing sense that time was drawing short and couldn't help wondering about God's choice of mission assignments. God could choose from any number of more qualified people throughout history to help Edwards and Whitefield — why choose *him* now when the Lord's return could honestly come at any moment? Jimmy knew from his travels, of course, that the shortness of time was not a problem for God; He wasn't constrained by time — He could squeeze a lifetime of traveling into an eye blink. He would surely provide all the time needed, one way or another.

WHILE JIMMY WAS CONTEMPLATING THIS, his surroundings changed once again. He found himself at a construction site and understood immediately that more than his location had changed; the weather was warm — it was summer.

The structure was framed with large timbers in an old style, in which the building's heavy frame was built first before any inner floors or walls were added. He remembered his dad calling it balloon framing. From that detail and others, it was clear to Jimmy that he was back in the 1700s. The building seemed large for a house, given the likely time in which it was being built. The place where it stood was picturesque — atop a small hill surrounded by white oak trees. As he studied it further, he noticed that a set of vertical beams rose above the half-framed roof line — a steeple, he quickly guessed. Carefully moving nearer, he located a new cornerstone with a recently carved date: '1731.'

"Canst thou lend me a hand?" Jimmy heard a man call from nearby. Turning, he recognized the man who had called to him; he was roughly Jimmy's own age, dressed in long trousers and a plain white shirt with the sleeves rolled up. The man's hair was tied behind his head. From the look of him, he'd been hard at work most of the day.

Although he was older than the last time he'd seen him and in much better physical shape this time, Jimmy knew who he was.

"Sure," Jimmy agreed, no longer surprised that he could be seen. He grabbed one end of a thick beam and helped the man carry it to where it was needed.

"I'm William; I see thou art newly arrived here," the man said in welcome, extending his hand to shake.

"Yes, you could say that," Jimmy agreed. "I'm Jim Moretti."

"Greatly pleased to meet thee, Jim; thy help is surely welcome in this work." He introduced Jimmy to the other workers, who welcomed him warmly. "This is our Pastor... my brother, John," he said as the younger man firmly shook Jimmy's hand.

"John Tennent," his brother greeted with a smile. "What brings thee to Freehold?"

Jimmy acknowledged John, remembering the youngest brother he'd seen at their father's log college. He hadn't realized that John would be ordained before his older brother but assumed it was due to William's illness and prolonged recovery.

Jimmy repeated their names silently as pieces of the puzzle came together — *John* and *William Tennent*, the church they were building, would be a central fixture of the coming Awakening. From his reading, he knew that both Edwards and Whitefield would preach here. William himself would become a central figure in American independence.

"I've been sent here," Jimmy answered carefully. As he spoke, he rolled up his sleeves and mopped a bead of sweat from his forehead. He wore a white sweatshirt with a pair of white carpenter's pants and white sneakers; he'd been dressed for a snowy day in January, after all.

"Who has done us such a favor as to send thee?" the Reverend asked.

"Just the Lord's leading; no one else. He wants your work here to succeed; there's a great awakening coming."

The brothers looked at one another seriously. John examined Jimmy's face and the clothes he was wearing; his white pants and sweatshirt nearly glowed in the bright sunlight. "Where is it ye hail from?" he asked, sounding as if he almost feared the answer.

"Not far from here, actually," Jimmy admitted. That much was true; Center Springs wasn't far from there, at least geographically— give or take two or three centuries.

John and William looked at one another again; William raised his eyebrows.

"Wouldst thou walk with us?" John invited, nodding toward the wooded path.

As soon as they were out of the other men's hearing range, John sat on a nearby rock, inviting Jimmy to follow suit. The three sat facing one another in a small gap in the woods.

"Ye used the phrase 'Great Awakening,'" John began, leaning forward as he spoke. "What is it ye meant by it?"

Jimmy sensed that the expression resonated with the two of them. His meeting with them was obviously no coincidence. He looked at both of them curiously. "It sounds like you've heard it before."

William looked to his brother, exchanging a resigned glance, then explained. "Tis true. We've heard it in our dreams — both of us. It's been a mystery to us, honestly.

"A great revival is coming," Jimmy explained. It will stir people's hearts toward salvation—thousands will be saved throughout the Colonies. God plans to use both of you as leaders in this movement of His Spirit, and the church you're building will be used as well. Jonathan Edwards and George Whitefield will preach here, along with others."

"Edwards and Whitefield?" John exclaimed with surprise. "Here?"

William leaned forward with his hands on his knees. "How is it ye know such things?"

"I'm afraid you'll have to trust me on that," Jimmy answered. He looked at William, remembering the scene of Heaven's glory that they shared during William's brush with death. It was evident that William had no memory of Jimmy's presence in those events. "You've seen the glory of Heaven — remember how beautiful the worship is there?

God wants to bring some of that here. He's planning a revival of hearts like that — a move of His Spirit here on earth."

William looked as if a chill ran through him as the thrill of those memories washed over him. His words came breathlessly as he studied Jimmy's eyes in surprise. "How...?"

"That's not important," Jimmy assured him. "The work God is doing is what's important. There are thousands of souls at stake. I'll help you all I can — in whatever way the Lord leads. For now, the best thing we can do is pray about it; prayer is the most important thing we can do to bring it about. We need everyone in your church to pray for God to awaken souls to the reality of their need for Him."

IN STUNNED AGREEMENT, the men dropped together to their knees, following Jimmy's lead, and bowed their heads to seek the Lord. They each prayed aloud, with Jimmy praying first. John Tennent was the last to pray; when he finished, and the brothers opened their eyes, Jimmy was gone.

⌘

19

GROWING DARKNESS

*They embraced the 'new enlightenment' as their eyes became shrouded in a
deep spiritual darkness.*

NOGALES, MEXICO -- FEBRUARY...
Twelve months ago

L eyla Athaliah Majedah emerged from her private jet, joining
the small entourage of young women who waited on the
tarmac. The girls bowed their heads as she joined them,
raising their pressed hands to their foreheads in a praying gesture.
Since Leyla's ascension to high priestess, the other priestesses of
Anath were careful to give her the honor that her position demanded.
It was far more than a formality—none would dare offend the unnatural power that now possessed her.

Leyla had chosen to honor the former high priestess, Athaliah, by
taking the name as part of her own. A name was not all that she and
Athaliah shared; Leyla had welcomed the dark power that had occu-

pied her predecessor. With eyes that briefly flashed yellow and cat-like, she basked in the girls' reverent praises with a sinister smile.

"Have preparations been completed?" Leyla asked, speaking quietly as she turned to her head of security.

"All is ready," he answered, extending his hand in invitation toward a waiting group of large SUVs.

Leyla followed him to the first vehicle while the others loaded into the vehicles behind it, each accompanied by heavily armed body-guards. The cover of darkness shrouded their desert surroundings as the convoy made its way onto the road.

"How far to the border?" she asked, peering into the darkness ahead.

"Our route will be through the mountains—about an hour's drive," he explained. From there, we should reach the US compound by morning. The others will be waiting for us there."

IT HAD BEEN NEARLY an hour to the minute when their dust-covered vehicles pulled up to a worn-looking gate in an old section of border wall. The unpaved road they drove on was little more than a dirt trail, missing from maps and nearly invisible on satellite images. Their convoy was alone in this deserted expanse of desert, the only vehicles for miles. As arranged, the gate was unlocked and ajar; border agents were conveniently occupied elsewhere.

Two men from their security detail scouted the terrain and then pushed open the wall's tall gate, waiting for the convoy to pass through before closing it behind them.

A short distance later, the dirt road emptied onto a larger US high-way, where the convoy faded into the American heartland.

DAWN'S first light was just breaking over nearby hilltops as they pulled into the mountain compound that was their destination.

Guards opened the automatic gates, waving them into a modern gated community of luxury homes. They finally pulled up to a large estate— it was a private house the size of a resort hotel.

"Hello, Leyla, I'm Senator Ahmadi," a distinguished-looking young woman greeted as she held out her hand. "It's nice to meet you in person finally."

Sammu-Ramat Ahmadi was the first-term senator from Nevada. Her presence at this remote retreat was unsurprising, given her sympathetic background. Several years prior, she had been the welfare secretary in President Sheen's administration and was a close friend of Athaliah's. She had arranged for these resort-like accommodations. The recently completed luxury compound was her creation — funded with Federal money and by the generous people of Nevada, albeit without their knowledge.

"You must be tired from your travels. We can talk later if you wish — after you've rested," the Senator offered. A sly smile crossed her face. "I think you'll approve of what you find here... your eminence." The Senator pressed her hands together, touching her fingertips to her forehead, and bowed.

A SHORT WHILE LATER, Leyla stood on the balcony of her palatial penthouse suite, smiling as she surveyed the scene. Her carefully positioned vantage point overlooked it all. A large park-like garden filled the center of the community before her, full of rich vegetation with flowing streams and waterfalls.

Surrounding the park in a large circle were various temples and places of worship — Hindu and Buddhist temples beside Shinto, Baha'i, Sikh, and Zoroastrian. There were houses of prayer for Jainism, Confucianism, Islam, and others. At the far end of the circle opposite her residence were various modern-looking churches. Her eyes flashed with a yellow glow as she looked at their crosses and statues of Saints — her nostrils flared as she carefully sensed the air, detecting no power from their spiritually vacant halls. Her eyes brightened even hotter as she gazed at the Star and Menorah on a lone Jewish temple in the distance.

Directly beside the hotel was a structure that dwarfed the rest—a large glass cathedral with jutting spires that caught the sun and sent beams of light reflecting everywhere. It was the new Temple of Enlightenment, symbolic of the ecumenical joining of all religions, the emerging One-World Church.

Leyla's eyes were drawn back to the lush circular park as she smiled sinisterly. A broad pathway led from the cathedral to the center of its impressive gardens. There, positioned prominently at the hub of all the temples and churches around it, was a larger-than-life statue of the goddess Anath.

SAN FRANCISCO -- MARCH...
Eleven months ago

"TODAY'S CHURCH must include all people!" the man known as Aurora proclaimed to a cheering crowd. "The days of outdated rules and traditions are over; God accepts all faiths — there are as many roads to Heaven as there are people."

He turned and raised an arm toward the woman on stage to his right... "In this new age of unity, it is my pleasure to introduce a new friend of mine, a prophetess in her own right — her movement seeks to unite all religions. Please welcome her eminence, Leyla Athaliah Majedah."

Leyla accepted his outstretched hand and raised it in the air victoriously, lifting her other hand and basking in the crowd's applause.

"It is my pleasure and privilege to join all of you!" she shouted. Looking at Aurora, she acknowledged his comments with a nod of agreement... "A new day is dawning in America and the world! A day of unity. We invite all people to come just as they are and worship however they choose. No one can tell you what to be or how you must identify. Join us and be free to do as you choose with your life — to find your own reality!

"In our movement, all religions are welcome. We are the true religion that unifies all — we are *Unum Amor*, the One Love!"

The crowd exploded with shouts and cheers. Even the reporters and television crews applauded enthusiastically as thousands of new converts joined this burgeoning movement. They embraced the new *enlightenment* as their eyes became shrouded in a deep spiritual darkness.

MADRID, SPAIN -- APRIL...
Ten months ago

THE GROWTH of the *Unum Amor* movement was spreading rapidly across America and the world. Along with its embrace of all religions, it brought a plethora of false messiahs, some of whom were performing amazing miracles.

Jesús Diez was one of those self-proclaimed messiahs. His electrifying smile was on display as he sat for an internationally broadcast interview. The setting was in a beautiful garden surrounded by cultivated flowers and shrubbery.

Q. "MR. DIEZ, you prefer to be called Jesús, is that right?"
    A. "Si... yes, please. That is my name."

Q. "YOU BELIEVE yourself to be a manifestation of Christ, returned. How do you explain the fact that several people are making that same claim? Which one of you, if any, is the true messiah?"
    A. "It is obvious that God is reaching out to all people everywhere. It only makes sense that we would be manifested in many forms to relate to many cultures in their own way. This is inevitable."

. . .

Q. "WHY NOW? What has changed to cause so many of these... manifestations, as you call them?"

A. "The day has come for the world to come together. It is God's will for people everywhere to join together in worship. All religions must come together."

Q. "DOES that mean you support the *Unum Amor* movement?"

A. "Of course. There is one true love that embraces all people; *Unum Amor* is the greatest demonstration of this. We wish for all people to join together to seek their own view of God, no matter how they worship."

Q. "ARE YOU GOD?"

A. "I am the manifestation of God's love come to earth."

Q. "WHY SHOULD people believe what you say?"

A. "Believe the works that I do; they speak for me."

Q. "WORKS... YOU MEAN MIRACLES?"

A. "Behold..."

He waved his hand toward the beautiful azalea bushes beside him, causing them to instantly burst into flame. There were gasps of alarm as the heat of the raging flames was felt from ten feet away. While they burned, he reached into the fire and plucked one of the beautiful flowers, presenting it to his interviewer unburned. With another wave of his hand, he extinguished the flames to reveal a bush now covered with twice as many gorgeous flowers as before.

Washington DC -- May...

Nine months ago

THE EXPLOSIVE GROWTH of *Unum Amor* caught the attention of political leaders. Politicians rushed to align themselves with the new movement as the November elections neared.

It wasn't merely a philosophical alignment. Massive donations flowed to the new World Church movement, giving Leyla and the movement's leaders growing political power as they generously funded the campaigns of their chosen politicians.

The coordination behind their new Super PAC[1] was impressive. It operated as if it had been planned for years—of course, it had been; Senator Ahmadi and her staff had carefully seen to that. The party affiliations of their selected candidates were not important. What they all bore in common was an uncommon loyalty to *the movement.*

Presidential election years always garnered the most attention, and this year was no different. The current president, Joshua Godard, was finishing his second term and could not run again. This was the year for someone new to assume the office. President Godard was a strong advocate of religious freedom, but the spirit now sweeping the nation emphasized a different view of that freedom. Calls for unity and acceptance had begun to devolve once more into demands for compliance with popular values that often conflicted with Biblical values. The *Unum Amor* movement embodied those populist values better than any.

The presidential candidate, backed by Unum Amor, was a relative newcomer. Elvio Nero had just been elected for his first term as governor of New Mexico the year before. His run for president was surprising, but then, nothing was typical about his candidacy. He was mysteriously unopposed in his party's primary and now seemed unbeatable in the general election. Those tailwinds, along with the blizzard of political advertising being run in his favor — not to mention massive investments in 'voter incentives,' seemed to guarantee a likely victory in November.

Governor Nero emerged from a meeting on Capital Hill with his party's Congressional caucus to a forest of microphones. A contingent of friendly Senators and Congressmen stood supportively behind him as he was joined by his running mate, Senator Tamara Bravo. He flashed a brilliant smile and then spoke to the cameras, offering impromptu remarks.

"WHEN I ANNOUNCED MY CANDIDACY, I promised the American people that mine would be a positive and unifying campaign without the negative attacks we have all grown tired of. I have kept to that promise. Unity is something that I care about deeply.

"I believe that we have a historic opportunity — such as we have never known in our lifetime, a chance to heal the bitter divisions in our country. We are on the verge of unifying our nation in a way we have never seen. America is ready for a new day of unity. The beautiful *Unum Amor* movement has shown that the country is hungry for unity and acceptance. It is time to cast off our differences and burdensome traditions, time to eliminate once and for all the outdated beliefs that divide us.

"Join us in fulfilling this vision! This November, a vote for me is a vote for unity!"

⌘

20

INFLAMED

"It has taken us generations of untiring effort... But finally, victory is within our grasp."

BROWNSVILLE, BROOKLYN -- LATE MAY...
Nine months ago

Rad smashed a bottle onto the sidewalk in a fit of rage, pulling a pistol from the back of his waistband in the same motion. He waved it toward the car that was speeding away down the street and screamed a stream of vicious threats.

Badrick ran out through the Mission doorway, waving his hands. "Rad... put that gun away, mon! What ya be doin'?"

"Those were the guys that shot at us—those...!" He went on, releasing a blizzard of noxious curses. Then he turned to Jay Jay and Scamp: " They've been hauntin' us long enough. I swear they're going down—they're going down hard!"

Rad looked at his gun in disgust, shoving it into his belt. "We're takin' 'em down," he vowed angrily.

Badrick yelled after him as he stormed off, trying to talk sense into him. But Rad was oblivious in his fit of rage.

"Should we chase after them?" One of the Mission workers asked.

"Too dangerous," Badrick answered regretfully. "He's in an evil way. We need to be praying' fer that boy. That'd be de best we can do fer him now."

SANTA FE, NEW MEXICO -- JUNE...
Eight months ago

ELVIO NERO WELCOMED Senator Ahmadi to the New Mexico statehouse.

"To what do we owe the pleasure of your visit, Senator Ahmadi?" he said in greeting. His welcome was heartfelt. His election as governor had been largely due to the Senator's powerful Super PAC, and now his rapid rise toward the presidency was mainly due to that same support.

His vice presidential running mate, Senator Tamara Bravo, stood beside him, giving their visitor a familiar hug. The two Senators were not strangers. Their political alliance was well known, as was their closer-than-usual personal involvement.

"So formal," Senator Ahmadi feigned. "In case you've forgotten, my name is Sammu-Ramat. Please call me Sammu, or just Sam, if you like. You have a great admirer in Leyla Majedah," she added.

"Of *Unum Amor ,*" Elvio acknowledged happily. "Yes, she is a friend of our campaign."

"Indeed she is," Sammu replied, sharing a knowing glance with Tamara. "As you may know, she is a large contributor to our Political Action Committee. She is pleased to see how well you are doing in the polls."

"I'm humbled," the governor said politely, although humility was honestly not a familiar trait to him.

"I'm here somewhat on her behalf," Sammu continued. That is, I happen to share her enthusiasm for the causes she holds most dear. In light of her great generosity in supporting our committee, I felt it worthwhile to convey a message from her to you personally."

"A message…," Elvio noted in surprise. "It must be quite special for you to have traveled all the way here to New Mexico to deliver it."

"Yes, I would say that it is."

After a moment of awkward silence, Elvio discerned that her message required more privacy. "We can speak more freely in my office. Please, follow me."

The three of them made the short walk across the Statehouse lobby into a private elevator, riding it to the Governor's office suite. "See that we are not disturbed," Nero instructed his secretary. He held his office door open as the two Senators entered and closed it behind them.

"Please make yourselves comfortable," he offered, extending his hand toward an opulent leather couch and several large armchairs. Sammu quickly selected the highest chair, which offered a commanding view and sat in it stiffly. Her movements and demeanor echoed the actions of an ancient queen familiar with power. Her choice surprised Nero, who had anticipated sitting in that seat himself. Tamara took a seat in the stuffed chair beside her fellow Senator. Nero eyed the empty couch, which sat several inches lower, deciding to remain standing.

"I must admit, I am quite curious what could be so important as to interrupt your duties in Washington."

Sammu glanced at her friend knowingly and then smiled at Elvio. "Given your strong standing in the polls, Her Excellency, Ms. Majedah is looking for certain assurances regarding your position on important matters that the next President will undoubtedly face."

Nero's shoulders lifted and fell questioningly. "What matters, in particular?"

"Ah, there are so many… you are familiar with the goals of *Unum Amor* ?"

"Well, yes…. Unity is a cornerstone of my campaign."

"Yes," Sammu agreed, "*Unum Amor* seeks to unite all the world's religions. This can only be achieved by fighting against the prejudices of those with divisive beliefs.

"We also seek a world where humanity lives in harmony with nature and the planet is cherished."

"Climate change has been a major part of my platform, I agree," Nero avowed.

"We must also expand and accelerate the move to a global currency and a unified economic system. We seek ultimate unity among all nations."

"Yeah, who doesn't? That seems like a tall order these days," Nero said, attempting to joke.

The Senator grew serious, and her voice lowered in a commanding tone that surprised him. "The next President must understand clearly that these goals are the means to an end. The only way to truly unify all people is by convincing and encouraging them, forcefully if necessary — controlling them if you will. Opposition to these ends must be eradicated for the sake of future generations. Only when all people aspire to these same ideals will we have perfect unity."

"And perfect control," Nero added, grasping the fact. Sammu smiled with a cold and calculating look.

"You now understand… The true purpose behind all of these measures is for ensuring orderly control of the masses — for the good of all, of course."

Nero felt a rush as he considered the power he would have as President over such masses. With a sly smile, he quipped, "I suppose some would see the irony in using the American Presidency to achieve such control… with all our American ideals of freedom and self-determination."

"People have not been free for a very long time, even in America; that is nothing new," Sammu offered. "It is simply a matter of who they serve."

Nero nodded at her point, pondering it silently for a moment. "A goal of global unity — global control — is quite ambitious. What makes you think it's achievable?"

"It has been achieved before — the Babylonians, Persians, Greeks, and Romans each accomplished it through military conquests. We prefer a more creative and enticing method that uses influence and subtle indoctrination to convince people. People love to join popular movements."

"Who would be the leader of such a global... movement, as you have called it?" Nero asked, confident that it would likely be the leader of the free world—the American President.

Sammu read Nero's conclusion in his eyes, her eyes narrowing as she answered. "The American President will be a key and indispensable ally; we are talking about a syndicate of nations, after all. The US will represent a key constituency. However, its ultimate control will rest in a new international leader. Is that a problem?"

The phrase: *key and indispensable* reverberated in his mind. The thought of having such influence on a global level was intoxicating. Perhaps, he secretly schemed, he could even ascend to become the new group's leader himself.

"No problem at all," he asserted eagerly. He turned to look through the large floor-to-ceiling windows beside him, considering what he was hearing. The news of such a far-reaching global conspiracy should have been shocking, yet it seemed to explain global events in a way that hadn't occurred to him before. The fact that he was now being included in this elite group of in-the-know officials only added to the thrill of it.

That thought led to another that he hadn't fully considered. As it occurred to him, he turned to Sammu.

"How long have you been part of this... who else is involved?" he asked her.

She shared a glance with Senator Bravo. Nero discerned that their exchange revealed a deeper connection between them.

"You?" Nero asked his running mate in surprise. "How long have you known?"

"Officially... I'm hearing it now, the same as you. Let's say I've had some previous exposure to the upper echelons of *Unum Amor*," Tamara answered with a sly smile.

Nero turned back to Sammu. "Exactly what is the role of *Unum Amor* in all of this?"

"*Unum Amor* is a recently adopted name for a much older movement," she explained. "In fact, it is older than the kingdoms I mentioned, including Babylon."

"Talk about a long game," Nero jabbed, unable to help sounding derogatory. "That's either an incredible degree of planning or a sad commentary on the movement's effectiveness."

"You might be surprised at how effective it has been. Merely look at the latest generation of emerging leaders from today's universities; our efforts have shaped them from the time they were in elementary school. We have rewritten their history books and robbed them of moral guidance. Confused them with relativistic definitions of good and evil and filled their minds with hatred and contempt. Now, they have become a blank canvas for our final creative act... the inflamed mass hysteria that will drive them to abandon their freedom and rally behind a single global leader.

"IN ALL OF HISTORY, America was the greatest challenge our cause had known. Now, most of America's leaders have become corrupt and self-serving, using lies and division to secure their power and enrich themselves. They have corrupted justice, encouraging lawlessness. They don't even care that they have turned justice and fairness into bitter poison, using their laws against their rivals while bribing the people — creating overwhelming debt that has bankrupted the nation.

"IT HAS TAKEN us generations of untiring effort, that is true. But finally, victory is within our grasp."

———————————

GENEVA SWITZERLAND -- JULY...
Seven months ago

THE ITALIAN PRIME MINISTER, Donato Mari, wiped a bead of sweat from his brow as he emerged from the World Bank's headquarters. He was accompanied by his Treasury Secretary and a contingent of senior staff.

It was no secret that his country's economy was in shambles, much like the rest of the world. His delegation had successfully 'won' a desperately needed bailout from the International Monetary Fund, albeit in exchange for deep concessions. It had been at the cost of Italy's national sovereignty. The country's domestic affairs would now be operating under the watchful eye of the IMF's newly appointed Magistrate of International Affairs... a man with extensive experience on the world stage, who nonetheless remained a mystery to most — known simply by the name Bahal.

While the bailout would be described to the Italian people as a win, Prime Minister Mari knew it was anything but that. He could still feel Bahal's gaze bearing down on him as they shook hands.

There was something deeply troubling about the man that Mari couldn't quite put his finger on. However, he was certain of one thing: Bahal would not be an easy master.

He had only to look to the experience of Spain's Prime Minister, Cabrera, for evidence of this. Donato's friend, Johar Cabrera, had not been seen in public for days following a published statement he made that was vaguely critical of the new Magistrate. Donato knew that it was not just public events from which his friend had been absent; he had not been seen by personal staff or his family either. A fact that his country's new masters were carefully concealing.

Donato nodded uncomfortably to the teams of heavily armed IMF security guards who now escorted his small motorcade. He watched them board their black SUVs to accompany him as his group prepared to depart.

⌘

21

ANGELS HEARD ON HIGH

"I will give you a new heart, and a new spirit I will put within you. And I will remove the heart of stone from your flesh and give you a heart of flesh."
~ Ezekiel 36:26

CENTER SPRINGS -- JULY...
Seven months ago

The winds of revival that began stirring again a year earlier continued to increase in intensity. It was starting to feel like the services at the new Living Springs Church were once again at the epicenter of a global move of God that was shaking the world.

It wasn't surprising that the outpouring began with the youth groups. It was among the High School and College kids that the wind of the Spirit was first felt. Their unrestrained worship and burgeoning faith soon swept through the church and then the schools, taking root in their homes and families. It stirred memories of experiences at the old tent grounds.

"Hey, Dad," little Maddy Johnson asked her father, "Is it true that everyone saw angels at a church service here once?" Maddy and her friends, Beth and Kaley, sat wide-eyed as they listened. The girls hadn't seen those events themselves—they had been at home in their beds, barely three years old, on that remarkable New Year's Eve. They'd recently overheard some of the older kids at church talking about it.

Her question stirred one of her father's most vivid and astonishing memories. "Yes, it is true," Chuck Johnson answered. "I'll never forget that night for as long as I live."

"What happened?"

"Well, it's hard to describe, really…. It was unbelievable! There weren't just a few angels — there were thousands! The sky was filled with them for as far as we could see. I'll never forget how they raised their bright swords above their heads and cheered after defeating the terrible attack."

"Attack? Who attacked them?" Maddy asked curiously.

Chuck recalled the sight of the hideous demon creatures and Hell Hounds who invaded the tent grounds that night, quickly deciding not to describe them to the young girls.

"The important thing is that the angels won," he offered instead. "I remember how they shouted together in a cry of victory that shook the ground underneath us. Everyone joined them in shouts of praises to God — it was incredible!"

"Wow… I wish I could have seen it," Maddy said wistfully. Her friends agreed.

Chuck had a sudden thought. "Well, you *can* see it… there was video of it."

The girls' eyes lit with excitement. He retrieved his tablet and searched for *Center Springs, angels,* and *New Year's Eve.* Soon, dozens of news reports appeared. He chose a clip from the local TV station, WCST, and carefully skipped past the scenes of battling demons, then shared it on the room's large TV screen.

The girls stared with their mouths open at the sight of skies full of bright angelic hosts. They could see someone who looked like a High School kid standing amidst the huge angelic warriors.

"That's Jimmy... Mr. Moretti," Kaley exclaimed. "He's with the angels!" They watched the scene enthralled as Jimmy turned and saluted the bright hosts and then suddenly disappeared. The microphone he was holding dropped to the ground with a thud.

"What just happened? Where did he go?"

Mr. Johnson rubbed his head as he tried to explain... "Yeah... he did that sometimes."

LITTLE MADDY and her friends couldn't stop talking about angels for the rest of the week. Every day, they pretended to be angels battling imaginary enemies with their plastic swords. They even took turns pretending to disappear by ducking behind a couch or pulling a blanket over their head.

They ran excitedly into Sunday school class on Sunday morning, anxious to tell their friends about the amazing event.

"Yes, that was an amazing night," their teacher, Shirley Owens, readily agreed. "I don't think any of us were the same after that. It changed our lives."

"We saw Jimmy — Mr. M — with the angels!" Maddy declared. "We saw him disappear!"

"That's right," Shirley admitted. "It was incredible!"

"He disappeared?" Billy Greca asked. "What do you mean?"

"He just kinda vanished," Maddy explained. "The mic he was holding just fell on the ground when he was gone."

"Miss Owens, is that really true?" One of the other boys challenged.

"Yes, it is. Jimmy did that a few times back then."

"How?"

"Well, no one knows, exactly. It was something that God did."

"Why'd He do that?"

"It's a little complicated. God was protecting him from some bad people who were after him."

"Is that who the angels were fighting?" Maddy asked. "My dad said the angels fought a big battle. They cheered real loud when they won."

"Wow, yes, they did!" Shirley agreed, suddenly reliving the astonishing events in her mind.

"I want to see angels…" Joey Snyder said wistfully.

As soon as church ended, Jimmy found himself surrounded by kids from Miss Owen's Sunday School class. They shouted a flurry of questions as they anxiously tugged on his shirttail.

"Mr. M! …Tell us about the angels!" "…Why were bad people chasing you?" "…Did you go to Heaven when you disappeared?"

Anna smiled at the sudden swarm of young admirers, amused by how the kids caught him off guard with their questions. Jimmy honestly didn't know which event they were asking about; it could have been any one of many.

Maddy clarified, relishing her role as the best-informed expert on the subject among her peers. "My dad showed me the video of New Year's Eve when all the angels came to church."

Jimmy shifted VJ in his arms and caught Anna's smile, matching it with his own. "Angels!" he acknowledged happily. "Did you know that angels are all around you?"

"They are…?" Billy replied in an awestruck voice.

"Yup," Jimmy confirmed, dropping to one knee and jostling VJ on the other. He lowered his voice mysteriously, "Usually, they're invisible, but sometimes God lets us see them."

"What are they doing?" Beth asked in a near whisper as if hearing a secret.

"Well, that depends," Jimmy said. "The Bible tells us that angels are ministering spirits… that means they're here to help us."

"How do they do that?"

"Oh, they can do lots of things. They're very strong, for one thing."

"They are?"

"Sure. One angel can sweep away a whole army," Jimmy explained, recalling how he'd seen Ardent clear legions of demons from the sky with a wave of his arm. He didn't attempt to describe that scene to the children.

"Is that what they were doing? Did an army attack the church?" Joey asked, sounding thrilled by the idea.

"Well, not an army exactly. But there were some bad... enemies there who wanted to hurt people. The angels stopped them."

"Wow, cool!" Billy exclaimed.

"I still don't get it..." Kaley wondered aloud. "How did you disappear? Where'd you go?"

Jimmy shared a glance with Anna, and she lifted her eyebrows with a smile, anxious to hear how he would explain this one.

"It's pretty unusual for that to happen, I guess that's true. But it's not really complicated; it happened to people in the Bible, too. A guy named Phillip was transported like that, and Enoch and Elijah were transported like that to Heaven. The Apostle Paul and Jesus' disciple John visited Heaven like that, too, and so did Daniel and Isaiah."

"Did you go to Heaven when you disappeared?" Kaley asked. She grew quiet as she searched his eyes. "Mommy says that my Grandma is in Heaven now."

Her question brought a sudden rush of memories of times when he actually did visit that amazing place. The memory of his meetings with Kelly, his dad, and then his mom sent thrills through his soul. However, the event the kids were asking about was not one of those times.

"No... to be honest, I was just transported home that night... to there." He pointed across the open field toward the farmhouse and barn in the distance.

"Wow, that must be kinda like Heaven..."

"Yeah," Jimmy agreed, glancing at Anna with a smile... "You're right — it kinda is."

NORTHERN ISRAEL-- AUGUST...
Six months ago

CALEB BERGMAN, field commander for Israeli forces on the northern border, gazed into the distance with a worried look on his face. He lifted his binoculars and scanned the distant horizon again, then turned to his second in command, Major Davidson. "How is morale among our troops?"

"Morale is high," the Major assured him. "They know what is at stake — they're prepared to fight for their families and homes. They'll give it everything they've got."

"Let's pray that is enough," Caleb replied quietly. His unguarded comment was unusual for him; the Commander ordinarily reflected the epitome of confidence and military protocol. That was growing more difficult each day. The sight of what his forces were now facing honestly made his knees weak. The distant valley seemed to be covered as far as he could see with a vast army of mechanized infantry. To make matters worse, his intelligence resources reported that even more were on their way from Iran and points north.

The US carrier strike force that remained offshore in the Mediterranean was a small assurance compared with such a large threat. Caleb also knew that the political landscape in Washington was changing. Who knew if those US forces would even defend Israel when the time came?

IT WAS nightfall as students from a small yeshiva school beside the Sea of Galilee met for evening prayers. Tonight, the synagogue where they met was filled with people from the local community — a solemn reverence permeated the air among them. Even the small children understood the threat that loomed mere miles away.

Rabbi Malachi led the packed assembly of families in a selected reading. His heart was heavy with concern for those gathered there. He'd known most of them for all their lives. His spirit was noticeably contrite as he opened the ancient scriptures for the evening's reading. He wiped a tear from the corner of his eye as he paused in silent prayer, then looked over their faces.

"It seems appropriate for tonight's reading to be taken from the writings of the prophet Ezekiel. Hear the word of the Lord..."

> *Though you don't deserve what I'm going to do for you, I will*
>   *lead you home to bring honor to my name*
> *and to show foreign nations that I am holy. Then, they will*
>   *know that I am the Lord God. I have spoken.*
> *I will gather you from the foreign nations and bring you*
>   *home.*
> *I will sprinkle you with clean water, and you will be clean*
>   *and acceptable to me. I will wash away everything that*
>   *makes you unclean, and I will remove your disgusting*
>   *idols.*
> *I will take away your stubborn heart and give you a new heart*
>   *and a desire to be faithful. You will have only pure*
>   *thoughts,*
> *because I will put my Spirit in you and make you eager to*
>   *obey my laws and teachings.*
> *You will once again live in the land I gave your ancestors; you*
>   *will be my people, and I will be your God.*
> *I will protect you from anything that makes you unclean. Your*
>   *fields will overflow with grain, and no one will starve.*
> *Your trees will be filled with fruit, and crops will grow in your*
>   *fields, so that you will never again feel ashamed for not*
>   *having enough food.*
> *You will remember your evil ways and hate yourselves for*
>   *what you've done...*
> *After I have made you clean, I will let you rebuild your ruined*
>   *towns and let you live in them.*
> *Your land will be plowed again, and nobody will be able to see*
>   *that it was once barren.*
> *Instead, they will say that it looks as beautiful as the garden of*

*Eden. They won't see towns lying in ruins, but they will see
your strong cities filled with people.*
*Then the nearby nations that survive will know that I am the
one who rebuilt the ruined places and replanted the barren
fields. I, the Lord, make this promise.*
*I will once again answer your prayers, and I will let your
nation grow until you are like a large flock of sheep.*
*The towns that now lie in ruins will be filled with people, just
as Jerusalem was once filled with sheep to be offered as
sacrifices during a festival. Then you will know that I am
the LORD.[1]"*

THE RABBI LOOKED up from his reading and spoke with a sincerity
that everyone present could feel. It moved many of them to tears.

"I have known many of you since we were young together and
many more of you since your birth. It has been a great honor to have
been your Rabbi for almost sixty years. Together, we have rejoiced at
weddings and bar mitz·vahs and mourned and sat shiva for loved ones
who departed."

The Rabbi's hand shook slightly as he laid it on the lectern, grip-
ping it for support.

"We stand tonight on the verge of the greatest threat in my lifetime. Yet we know that God has promised to be our shield and
protector. What more can we do but ask for God's help in this time of
trouble? Let us humbly pray for the Lord's great mercy!"

Every head was bowed low as he began to pray the ancient
Hebrew prayers in an earnest entreaty.

Outside, the crowd that overflowed the small synagogue had also
joined in earnestly praying.

SUDDENLY, one of the small children tugged on her mother's arm. The
young girl pointed toward the northern sky...

"Momma, they're here — they've come. I asked God to send them — there they are."

Her mother seemed confused as she followed the girl's gaze, and then her mouth dropped open in startled awe. She, in turn, shook the woman beside her, who responded equally dumbfounded and gasped aloud, drawing the attention of others.

Soon, all those gathered outside stood staring at the sight with looks of awe and astonishment.

"COME AND SEE!" Someone shouted to those inside the synagogue, interrupting their prayers. "You have to see what's happening!"

The gasps and rumbling of the crowds outside drew others to come and see. Soon, streams of people were making their way outside. The mesmerized throngs cleared a path for more as they emerged, unable to draw their eyes away from the sight they were beholding.

The Rabbi was the last to join them, following the people's gazes to look upward toward the north. The sight made his knees shake, and he grabbed a man's arm beside him to steady himself.

THE DARK EVENING skies were filled with bright, glowing lights. They could clearly see what they were. For as far as they could see, the skies were full of angels!

⌘

22

DOCTRINES OF DEMONS

"God's Spirit clearly says that in the last days, many people will turn from their faith. They will be fooled by evil spirits and by teachings that come from demons."
~ 1 Timothy 4:1

THE NEVADA DESERT — EARLY SEPTEMBER
Five months ago

"Nero is a risk to us," Leyla noted with concern as she switched off the televised debate. She stood beside Senator Ahmadi at the palatial mountain retreat that she now called home. Nero had done exceptionally well in the debate they'd just watched, skewering his opponent in a potent assault.

"He seems strong and popular; he could be emboldened to defy us. We would be better served by someone weak and easily manipulated."

Senator Ahmadi smiled and calmly assured her... "He can be manipulated just as easily. He is young, and his thirst for personal power and glory is too strong to resist. He understands what is at stake if he fails us."

"Us?" Leyla questioned threateningly.

Sammu grew fearful as she apologized, "I meant, if he fails *you*, of course."

"Do not underestimate our enemy," Leyla warned. "Don't forget what happened to President Sheen at the hands of the Moretti boy... or the terrible fate of our beloved Athaliah."

Sammu's face hardened in an angry scowl at the thought of it. She had been there herself on the platform in the Rose Garden on that terrible day when lightning destroyed Athaliah, her friend and mentor. She still bristled at the memory.

"That was the greatest travesty of justice," she breathed through gritted teeth. "The boy should have been arrested for murder. Instead, Godard invited him to the Whitehouse as a national hero."

"Perhaps with a new President, we will have an opportunity to correct that injustice," Leyla offered. "We must be patient, however; it must be carefully planned. The boy has many friends who will protect him; we must wait until the time is right."

"Yes, your eminence," Sammu conceded with a bow of her head. Her face remained twisted in a sinister scowl; she was already devising plans to make that a reality.

LEYLA WALKED ONTO THE TERRACE, enjoying a night breeze as she looked down at the lush compound below. Sammu followed, obeying Leyla's unspoken invitation.

"The events in Israel are unsettling," Leyla complained. "We have known of the enemy's forces there for ages, but now He has allowed common people to see them. There are increasing reports of it from throughout the region."

"Yes, but not everyone can see them," Sammu noted. "Our campaign to paint the reports as unreliable is yielding fruit. Our AI-generated deep fakes have filled social media and news programs, making it virtually impossible to distinguish between the truth and our lies. Most here in the West now dismiss the sightings as fake or merely the rants of religious zealots."

"That is excellent work," Leyla approved. "Nonetheless, the sightings represent a new undertaking by our enemy," she worried. "He is preparing something; I fear He could turn the tables on our allies' forces. Such a victory would bring Him great glory, undoubtedly emboldening faith throughout the earth. It would set back our cause once again. We are too close for that to be allowed!"

Sammu conceded Leyla's point. "Perhaps you could discuss the matter with the new Magistrate of International Affairs," she carefully suggested.

"Yes, you're right," Leyla agreed as she considered Sammu's point. "It is time to visit our old friend, Bahal. I would like you to accompany me. See to the arrangements at once."

"Yes, your eminence."

GENEVA, SWITZERLAND...
Several Days later

BAHAL SAT stone-faced behind his large desk as he listened to the German chancellor seated before him. The Chancellor, Jensen Krause, was unaccustomed to groveling. It was normally he to whom others groveled.

Like President Godard, Krause had opposed the new international currency, which the German legislature nonetheless approved over-whelmingly.

"I must remind you that Germany held a surplus in its accounts before converting to the new currency," he argued. "We were not a debtor nation. We will not stand for such a violation of our sovereignty!"

"The terms to which your government has agreed are quite clear," Bahal said sternly. "The exchange rate was what it was; I have no control of that. If your country is now experiencing a period of hyperinflation in the cost of goods, it is none of my doing."

"That's a lie!" Krause argued angrily. "It is not the cost of goods that has changed, but the value of the Earthcoin. "The IMF enriches itself by minting more currency for its own use. That is what is flooding our markets. You are thieves!"

Bahal stood to his feet and glared at the Chancellor, who was shocked by a sudden flash of fire in his eyes. "That is a grave accusation," Bahal said sternly. "I will not tolerate having the World Bank's reputation excoriated in this way."

Two large guards stepped closer to where the Chancellor was sitting, but Bahal waved them away. He lifted a tablet device from his desk and scanned its screen as his eyes narrowed. His gaze remained on the screen as he spoke without looking at Krause...

"I see that you hold a rather large personal fortune yourself," Bahal said as he read the amount of the Premier's personal holdings aloud. Krause swallowed uncomfortably at Bahal's thinly veiled threat. He knew that the assets in those accounts could be invalidated or deleted with a simple altering of the IMF's computer records. Bahal had the power to cause such a change with a stroke of his hand.

"Y-You wouldn't dare!" He challenged nervously.

"Of course not!" Bahal lied. "Accidents do happen from time to time, however. It would be a terrible tragedy, would it not?"

Bahal settled back into his seat and leaned forward with a hardened expression. "It would be an even greater tragedy if your country's accounts were likewise affected. Especially if certain amounts were discovered to have been siphoned off into a secret account... perhaps one with your name on it. Should such facts be discovered by the media, it would be quite scandalous, I imagine... I believe the term is embezzlement."

"How dare you!" Krause objected. "No one would believe such a thing. I have never... I would never!"

"Yes, but bank records never lie," Bahal said smugly. He sat back in his seat, touching the tips of his fingers together. "Now, what was it you were saying about thieves?"

"This is outrageous! You have not heard the last from us on this," Krause vowed.

Bahal ignored the Chancellor's charge, standing as he motioned toward the door. "If you will excuse me, I have other matters to attend to."

The guards approached and waited for Krause to stand. He stood, red-faced with anger, and pulled his arm away as one of them touched his elbow to escort him out.

———

BAHAL'S ARRIVAL thirty minutes later at the Geneva Ritz-Carlton's famous *Michelin-three-star* restaurant created the usual buzz. When he entered, the head chef and a small entourage of wait staff met him at the door.

"Your private dining room is ready, sir. Your guests have already arrived," Chef Miriam Gallo welcomed him with a smile. She offered an air kiss beside his cheek while he did the same, and then she extended her arm toward the back in welcome. The stylish restaurant's head waiter led the way, while another followed alongside him with her notepad. "Your usual from the bar, sir?"

"Yes, thank you, my dear," he replied, clearly relishing the attention.

Leyla and Sammu stood to greet him as he entered the large private dining room.

"It is so good to see you, my dear," he said to Leyla as he greeted her. Telltale flashes in their eyes hinted at a sinister comradery. He turned to Sammu, who accompanied Leyla; she greeted him nervously.

"It's good to see you again, Minister Ebezej," Sammu said as she offered him her hand.

"You must call me Bahal, please," he encouraged, kissing her trembling hand in welcome. "You were a loyal friend to my daughter; I am most grateful."

He looked at them both with a welcoming gesture. "I trust that the hotel's accommodations are to your liking?"

"The grand suite is beautiful," Leyla praised as they agreed. "It is very generous of you. We couldn't be more pleased."

A team of waiters held each of their chairs as they sat down together, while another arrived immediately with Bahal's drink, a glass of his favorite Frapin Cuvee 1888 Cognac. A vintage so rare that it remained under lock and key, reserved for him alone.

"May I propose a toast," Bahal said as he lifted his glass. "To a new world of peace and unity!" Leyla and Sammu raised their wine glasses in solidarity as they wholeheartedly agreed.

The group made small talk while waiting for the restaurant staff to leave them. Once they were alone, Leyla spoke softly. "We have come to seek your counsel. The ...sightings... in Israel are somewhat disturbing. What do you think they may portend?"

Bahal acknowledged her question with a slight dip of his head, considering it carefully. "Their presence is nothing new, of course," he admitted. "It is rare, however, for them to show themselves to so many. As I'm sure you know, it is not the first such occurrence in recent years."

"Yes, but why is it happening?" Leyla probed. "Do you think they will involve themselves in an attack against the northern alliance?"

Bahal smiled knowingly. "Our enemy values these human lives too much for a direct physical attack against them, even those of the north. He will seek to sway them with manifestations and warnings first."

HE PAUSED and considered the point. "This presents an opportunity for us. The sightings are no doubt frightening to many people throughout the world; it should not be difficult to instill in them a fear and distrust of the forces of light. Indeed, it will be easier than ever to convince the masses that these forces are their enemy."

Bahal felt pleased with himself for the brilliant idea. "Yes, it can be used quite effectively," he repeated as he pondered the thought. He looked to the women, explaining his idea further. "Thanks to our successful efforts over the past century, most of the populace already confuse darkness and light. They have no bearing with which to judge between truth and lies or good and evil. It will not be difficult now to turn them against the light."

He looked to Leyla with a sinister grin. "You are in a unique position to accomplish this, my dear. *Unum Amor* is the perfect venue to lead them away from the enemy's light."

Leyla smiled as she understood. "Yes, I see Anath's brilliance in leading us to this point. She has obviously been anticipating such a move on the enemy's part."

"As have all of our master's princes," Bahal added. He leaned closer, taking his guests into his confidence... "A great battle with the enemy is indeed coming. We must work to turn all the world to oppose Him."

CENTER SPRINGS...
That same night

JIMMY REAPPEARED in the root cellar, standing beside the old wooden folding chair on which he'd spent so many hours praying.

The meeting he'd just overheard in that Geneva restaurant wasn't surprising but disturbed him nonetheless. It was true that most of the world's people could no longer distinguish between good and evil. He could see how easily Bahal's plan would sway people.

The glow of Chozeq's folding wings brightened the old cellar as he appeared. Jimmy looked to him with concern, readily seeking his wise friend's counsel. He spoke the question that burned in his heart.

"I hate to say it, but Bahal is right; people can be easily manipulated to confuse good and evil. It seems like the whole world has lost its way. How can we prevent their plan from succeeding?"

Chozeq answered reassuringly. "Many still have not bowed their knee to the Ba'als. It is the church's work to lead men and women to the truth. Bahal knows this himself."

"That's why he's using Leyla's false church, I know," Jimmy conceded. "But how do we overcome their influence? It has infiltrated everything—it's everywhere."

"Do not underestimate the Spirit's power in turning human hearts. The true church may be weak, but her very weakness makes her strong.

"Indeed, ye should never be disheartened because of the apparent feebleness of Christ's Church no matter how great is the work or the enemies she must face. God Himself is her strength, her glory, and her hope, and to despair of her would be to deny the power and faithfulness of God Himself.[1]

"Remember that the sufficiency of believers is not of themselves but of God. The mission will be realized, not by them, but by the Spirit of God through them. They might seem altogether helpless and inadequate, but a living fountain of oil is prepared to furnish them with inexhaustible supplies of strength and Heavenly power.[2]

"Take heart; it is God Himself who sustains His church. None of the gates of Hell shall prevail against her!"

⌘

23

DECEPTION

"You have wearied the Lord with your words.
"How have we wearied him?" you ask.
By saying, "All who do evil are good in the eyes of the Lord, and he is pleased
with them..."
~ Malachi 2:17

The strange religious movements in San Francisco, Kolkata, and Madrid continued to grow as more people became convinced that their chosen prophets held the answers to the world's problems.

Unum Amor embraced these movements as 'legitimate religious manifestations'—Leyla was all too happy to reinforce their deceptive influence, using them to strengthen her own power.

NEVADA DESERT COMPOUND — EARLY OCTOBER...
Four months ago

LEYLA STOOD BENEATH A FULL MOON, wearing her high priestess robes and headdress. The young priestesses of Anath sat on the ground in a semicircle around her, enclosing the area in front of Anath's larger-than-life statue. Just behind where Leyla stood, a candlelit pentagram was traced in swine's blood in the center of their formation.

Leyla closed her eyes and raised her hands toward Anath's image. "Great goddess Anath... goddess of love and war... life and death. We call to you; come to us. Lend us your aid in drawing the spirits of your prophets to us here. Those spirits who are sent to deceive the nations."

Leyla turned toward the pentagram and spread her arms wide. Her eyes snapped open, appearing like the eyes of a large predatory cat, yellow and glowing ominously. Her voice thundered as she cried out in an ancient language — a language that human ears could not understand.

From the midst of the pentagram, a hissing sound was heard, then another, and soon a third. Three hideous forms rose from the ground, like snakes stalking prey. With glowing eyes, their scale-covered bodies morphed and thickened, rising higher until they assumed their complete forms — bat-like with enormous leathery wings, standing like giants, nearly nine feet tall. They nodded in a slight bowing gesture toward Leyla — in truth, the deference they showed was not to Leyla but to the dark, queenly spirit that possessed her.

"OUR MASTER COMMANDS US," her voice thundered unnaturally... "Speak as one. Deceive... Deceive the nations."

Then her eyes narrowed as she spoke confidentially to her sinister comrades, explaining the purpose for which they had been called.

"The enemy's hosts have begun to show themselves to many. Speak against them — make the people fear them. We are commanded to stir the people to fight... they must defy the hosts of light!"

"The master is wise…" the demon called Aurora agreed in a monstrous voice. "It will be done."

His cohorts nodded in agreement, their sly smiles demonstrating their pleasure in complying.

SAN FRANCISCO, CALIFORNIA…
Several days later

THE 'PROPHET OF MISSION BAY' walked onto the stage at his largest rally yet. The dazed looks in people's eyes and the strong smell of burning cannabis hinted at the audience's state of mind. The crowds that filled the large concert hall chanted his name, repeating it over and over like a mantra.

"How're ya all doing, brothers and sisters?" he shouted over the microphone. The audience responded with a rumbling cheer that shook the building. "How many are glad to be in the Prophet's house?" he yelled, wild-eyed. The crowd exploded again in wild cheers. Then they broke into another spontaneous chant, repeatedly yelling… "Aurora… Aurora…"

He waved his hands up and down in a gesture, encouraging them to shout it louder. Then, he turned to the band on stage and signaled for them to play. The blasting rock music added to the wild atmosphere, whipping the crowd into a frenzy. He wagged his head and jumped up and down, encouraging the audience to do the same, rejoicing in the eruption of frenzied chaos.

The wild frenzy continued for some time until the music eventually ended in a dramatic crescendo. Aurora stood alone in the spotlight with a microphone in his hand as the exhausted crowds finally focused their attention on him again.

"This is what I call doin' church!" He shouted, drawing another cheer. "The difference here is that we don't ask you to change or give up the things you love. You can be whatever you want to be…, do whatever you want to do…. My god is big enough to accept what you are and let you stay that way — he wants you to feel good, not be good." He grinned wide as the crowds cheered and applauded, then punched his fist in the air and shouted, "Turn it on, people!"

Just then, his head fell backward, his sweat-drenched hair partly covering his face. The audience recognized it as the familiar signal that he was having one of his 'prophetic' visions. Everyone grew quiet as they waited in rapt attention. After standing with his head thrown back for a full minute, he lifted the mic and spoke into it in a deep voice... the demon Aurora's voice, his eyes still closed and his head back...

"Enemies are coming... not of this world — inhuman enemies. They will seek to overthrow and subjugate you. Beware! They have great power, filling the skies with glowing light. Beware, people! Beware!"

His head snapped forward dramatically as his eyes stared ahead in a trance-like glaze, completely black.

"Fight against them...," he nearly growled — this time in a monstrous-sounding voice. "Fight those who serve them. Resist those who reject our way. Resist those who seek to divide you by saying that only their way is right. You must band together in defiance against them. All people of earth, you must fight together as one against your great common enemy!"

KOLKATA, INDIA...
The following day

KALA MEHMOOD KAUSALYA... now known simply as Kala by most of the world, sat in a lotus position among a large throng of worshipers. Since turning water into wine on Christmas day nearly a year ago, he had not ceased to astound and enthrall the world with his miracles.

He sat surrounded by several hundred meditating pilgrims. The open-air temple hummed with the buzz of their repeated mantra, Kala... Kala... Kala. A thousand others surrounded them, straining for a glimpse of the self-proclaimed reincarnation of Christ. Thousands more filled the streets around them in a chaotic scene of busy traffic and teeming masses.

As the day approached noon, a rumbling suddenly began — it emanated from beneath the platform where Kala was sitting, drawing the attention of those nearby. Their gazes turned to gasps as they saw Kala begin to rise into the air. The platform did not rise — only he did. The gasps of those nearby were quickly joined by more cries from the surrounding crowds as he was seen hovering above the heads of everyone else. Traffic in the streets came to a halt as crowds swarmed closer to see the sight that everyone was talking about. Hundreds of cell phones were aimed at the scene, recording the amazing event for online posts that would soon flood the world's information networks.

As a hush finally settled over the crowd, Kala's eyes opened suddenly, staring blankly ahead in a glazed trance. His voice thundered unnaturally, echoing from the nearby buildings.

"My people... hear my warning! Beware the creatures who make lights in the skies and walk among you unseen. Beware their great power. They come to bring you harm and not good. They seek to enslave you. Hear me! You must rise against them as one people. Fight them as soldiers of my army — I am with you! All people of earth, you must fight together as one against your great common enemy!"

MADRID, SPAIN...
The next morning

JESÚS DIEZ WALKED along the Avenue de la Ciudad.de Plasencia in central Madrid, approaching the Cathedral de Santa Maria and the Royal Palace of Madrid. With his long hair and beard and wearing first-century robes, he looked as much like Jesus of Nazareth as possible.

He was surrounded by crowds that followed and pressed closer to him. They shouted prayers and praises while many strained to get nearer, begging for healing. Jesús touched some of them as he passed by, making them swoon and drop to the ground in trances with enraptured expressions on their faces.

He drew nearer to the steps of the cathedral where a man lay, crippled and unwashed, apparently homeless and destitute. The man's back and limbs were cruelly bent, and his face was wrenched in agony. No one would ever suspect that he'd been walking normally until the night before, when a mysterious black mist suddenly engulfed him in the place he now lay, leaving him twisted in excruciating pain.

Jesús Diez waved for the crowds to stay back as he climbed the stairs toward the suffering man. Reaching down, he took the man's hand just as a thick black mist lifted from the man's chest, freeing him from his crippling torment. The man knelt, weeping as he thanked Jesús and kissed his hand.

From his perch at the top of the cathedral steps, Jesús Diez turned to the crowds and cried out in a loud voice. His words were carried with unnatural force, being easily heard by all who could see him in the vast throng.

"I have come here to the beautiful Cathedral of the Blessed Mary, my beloved mother, to bring you an important message. It is a message for all the world. Dangerous messengers have come among you. They reveal themselves in glowing lights, like a great invading army. Beware their power. They have come to fight against all that we desire as good. They are enemies of my work.

There are those living among you who are allied with them — these misguided souls must be helped to see their error or else be counted as enemies of our cause. We seek peace throughout the Earth. We must not allow these powers to destroy that peace. All people of Earth, you must fight together as one against your great common enemy!"

CENTER SPRINGS...

JIMMY WATCHED the news reports that swirled across all the media and flooded online posts everywhere. It was clear to him that Leyla was behind these closely orchestrated messages. She was following Bahal's instructions.

The deceiving demons even used the same words in each of their closings, a point that had not gone unnoticed in widespread news reports. The supernatural manifestations that accompanied each of the demons' pronouncements remarkably made them appear even more credible.

The world was soon locked in a frenzy as increasing panic took hold. Within days, governments around the globe called special meetings of their legislatures to discuss a response. US Senators demanded that the US Space Force deploy a meaningful response to this 'alien invasion.'

US INVESTIGATORS DIDN'T TAKE LONG to arrive at the farmhouse door. Who better to suspect of an angel alliance than someone who'd been seen with angels? The video footage of the events from several years prior at the tent grounds and the Glass Cathedral still filled the internet, not to mention the more recent events in Harbor City. If they knew how often Jimmy still saw those powerful guardians, they'd have been even quicker to arrest him.

The tension in the room was rising rapidly as a pair of agents interviewed Jimmy. With growing concern, Anna slipped into the kitchen and called her mom, letting her know what was happening. The worry in Anna's voice conveyed the situation's urgency even better than her words could.

Lena immediately pulled in Mike, listening to Anna's worried account on the speakerphone. Mike used his phone to call Sheriff Flanagan right away.

. . .

THINGS HAD ESCALATED to a point where Jimmy was being led to the agents' car in handcuffs when the Sheriff and a pair of his deputies pulled their three patrol cars into the driveway with lights flashing, blocking the agents' exit. What followed was a flurry of phone calls....

The investigators immediately called their supervisors.

Sheriff Flanagan called his friend Frank DeMassi at the FBI.

The agents' supervisors called in their Director.

Agent DeMassi quickly escalated it to the Whitehouse staff, and, to everyone's shock, the President immediately joined the call.

President Godard put an end to the agents' ill-conceived mission and ensured that no one else would be caught up in it, promising reprimands of the leaders involved.

Jimmy sat handcuffed in the investigators' back seat as he gratefully thanked the President, whose voice carried over the car's speakerphone.

"These are interesting times we're living in; there's no doubt of that," President Godard said. "You take care of yourself and that family of yours, Jimmy."

"Yes, sir. Thank you, sir!"

The agents apologized with embarrassed looks as they unlocked Jimmy's handcuffs and released him.

MIKE AND LENA were waiting at the end of the driveway and ran closer as the standoff broke up. Lena wrapped Anna and the baby in an anxious hug as Mike hugged Jimmy, slapping him on the back. He turned to the Sheriff with a grateful nod.

"Thanks, Connor. You were all over this... Nice goin'."

Connor smiled. "No Sweat...," he said, deliberately using one of

Mike's familiar expressions." He placed his hand on Jimmy's shoulder. "I've got to admit, I had no idea when I called DeMassi that we'd be talking to the President. This guy has some serious connections."

"You talked to the President!?" Mike responded in surprise. "Oh man... ya gotta tell us all about it!"

Connor tipped his hat and accepted Jimmy's thanks before driving off while Mike and Jimmy followed their wives inside, talking excitedly.

⌘

24

RESTLESS

"God shall send them a strong delusion, that they should believe a lie:"
~ 2 Thessalonians 2:8-11

Election Night — November...
Three months ago

Anna switched off the TV and leaned her head against Jimmy's shoulder. Even though it was early in the evening, the election had already been called, and the Nero / Bravo ticket had won.

"How can we be back to this again?" she said sadly. "Can't people see that his brand of unity is the same as Athaliah's?"

"They can't," Jimmy acknowledged with a shake of his head. "It's a delusion." He picked up his Bible from the coffee table and opened it to Second Thessalonians, finding the verses he sought in chapter two. He pointed to them as he read to her aloud...

"And then shall that Wicked one be revealed, whom the Lord

shall consume with the spirit of his mouth, and shall
destroy with the brightness of his coming:
Even him, whose coming is after the working of Satan with all
power and signs and lying wonders,
And with all deceit of unrighteousness in them that perish;
because they received not the love of the truth, that they
might be saved.
And for this cause God shall send them a strong delusion, that
they should believe a lie[1]:"

Anna held onto Jimmy's arm and looked at him with concern. "Do you think Nero is him... the Antichrist?"

Jimmy placed his hand on hers and shook his head... "No, it's not him. But the time is getting closer; the delusion is growing — it's already blinding people."

IT WAS midnight when Jimmy climbed out of bed, unable to sleep. The day's events still troubled him — the circumstances of Nero's win felt ominously similar to Devlon Sheen's win eight years earlier. No assassination was needed this time; Nero's opponent never had a chance. The delusion was already strong in the country and rapidly growing stronger. It surprised Jimmy how quickly it seemed to have come over everyone.

It brought to his mind the firestorm that appeared at his mom's memorial service. He knew that the tremendous revival it foretold would be followed by cold darkness — a darkness that would finally extinguish the revival's fire.

Jimmy looked over at Anna, confirming that she was sound asleep. He slipped out of bed and grabbed his warm flannel robe, pulling it on over his pajamas, feeling drawn to his *prayer closet*—the root cellar. He no longer spent his days there in hiding but still found comfort there on many nights—nights like this one.

.   .   .

THE CELLAR'S familiar worn carpet felt comfortable, bringing memories of extraordinary times there, not to mention incredible travels. Thoughts of the entries in his journal ran through his mind, raising the question that most burned in him.

"Lord, you said that my journal would be for others. Is my time nearly finished here? How much longer?"

The question didn't bring fear. He was honestly ready for whatever came next, whether it meant imprisonment, death, or the Rapture; it didn't really matter. If the past eight years had taught him anything, it was that God could be trusted.

As he prayed, a deep sense of comfort pervaded his soul. He could feel the Spirit's presence surrounding him in a loving embrace, bringing a sudden joy to his heart. He began to feel an anxious anticipation well up within him as the Spirit conveyed a sense that, indeed, something new *was* coming... it wouldn't be much longer.

He lost track of time as he prayed, eventually realizing that much of the night had passed. Climbing from his knees, he sat in the chair quietly, feeling a subtle stirring within him—a familiar sense that something was about to happen.

IN THE NEXT MOMENT, Jimmy's surroundings grew unexpectedly darker. The bright lamplight in the root cellar was replaced by a much dimmer light reflecting from a place behind him. He realized that the room where he now sat was sparsely furnished, with a smell of burning candles and firewood in the air.

He turned to look behind him and recognized William Tennent kneeling beside his bed in the light of a single candle. He quickly noticed another voice coming from the next room that was weak and hoarse-sounding; he recognized it as John's. He was praying too — weeping. Jimmy could hear him wrestling with God over a deep heaviness that seemed to burden his soul like a mountain of weight. As he listened, he heard John lifting people in prayer by name, one after another, in heartfelt intercession.

After a time, his cries died out, and Jimmy understood both men to be finally sleeping.

ALMOST IMMEDIATELY, his surroundings changed again, and Jimmy found himself outside. The day was clear, with a bright sun and gentle breeze; fresh buds on the leafless trees revealed that it was early springtime. However, the thing that caught Jimmy's eye the most was the sight of William and John walking. William supported his brother, with John's arm draped over his shoulders. John's faltering steps were weak, and his face was thin with obvious illness. John coughed several times into his closed fist with a rough and deep cough that disclosed lungs stricken with disease.

The brothers were dressed in Sunday suits and were making their way to the new church that Jimmy had seen them building on his last visit. Others were arriving as well, all well-dressed in their finest clothes.

"Happy Easter morning to ye Reverend Tennent," one of them greeted. "It's so good to see thee up and about for this fine morning."

John smiled broadly and returned the greeting. "I was glad when they said unto me, let us go unto the house of the Lord!" he offered in a quiet voice. His words were followed by a painful attack of coughing, which he quickly shook off and smiled once again.

William helped him inside, where he was seated in the first row. The small one-room church had no organ or piano, but the congregation sang a cappella from their Hymnals...

'When I survey the wondrous cross On which the Prince of
    Glory died,
My richest gain I count but loss, And pour contempt on all my
    pride...[2]'

John sat with his eyes closed, tears streaking his face. When the singing ended, he leaned toward his brother, asking for his help to stand. William supported him as he stood and faced the congregation, his face still wet with tears. He cleared his throat carefully and looked over their faces, seeing those for whom he'd spent so many nights praying. The church was silent with rapt attention.

"I WOULD NOT HAVE you think the worse of the ways of holiness because you see me in such agonies of distress, for I know there is a crown of glory in heaven for me, which I shall shortly wear."

Several women dabbed their eyes with handkerchiefs as tears welled. It had been months since they'd seen John, and they felt shaken at seeing his feeble state.

John continued. "I am truly grateful to my brother William for his care of the pulpit whilst I have been ill these six months past. Indeed, for his care of me as well." William looked to the floor humbly. He was fighting to keep a stoic face.

"I feel blessed indeed for God's gracious work in this church. I was greatly humbled that He had chosen to use a flawed and barely adequate vessel such as me to work so marvelous a work. It has been my greatest joy…" His words were interrupted by another bout of violent coughing as he covered his face with a handkerchief. A slight hint of blood could be spotted on the cloth as he quickly hid it.

"I do not fear nor dread the path that He has laid for me," he said as he struggled to quiet his coughing. "I look earnestly to the rest that He has graciously procured for me.

"If I may be so bold as to quote the words of King David as he drew near to his departure from this life…" John opened his Bible to the place marked and read aloud with all the meager volume that he could muster…

> "The Spirit of the Lord spoke by me, And His word was on my tongue. The God of Israel said [it], The Rock of Israel spoke [it] to me: 'He who rules over men must be just, Ruling in the fear of God. And he shall be like the light of the morning when the sun rises, A morning without clouds,

Like the tender grass springing out of the earth, By clear
shining after rain.'
"Although my house is not so with God, Yet He has made with
me an everlasting covenant, Ordered in all things and
secure. For this is all my salvation and all my desire...[3]*"*

Several openly wept as John finished while the affirming cries of 'Aye' and 'Amen' rose throughout the congregation.

JIMMY WAS QUICKLY CARRIED to a new scene at John's bedside. Jimmy sensed that days had passed, and John was clearly in the throes of his final moments. The morning's light was breaking outside the window. John struggled to call for his brother, barely able to gasp out the words before succumbing to a violent fit of coughing.

He looked into William's eyes urgently as he came to him. "I long so for the Heavenly sights you told me of. Pray with me that I may finally be freed to that blessed rest!"

William understood the longing in his brother's soul; he had not ceased to feel it himself since those glorious days when he had returned from the brink of eternity. He had relived their emotion a dozen times in the past few weeks as John begged him to recount them for him time and again. Still, it was difficult for him to pray for his brother's request — to pray for his death.

The brothers prayed together in an uninterrupted vigil until around eight o'clock when John suddenly opened his eyes with an expression of rapturous wonder, and they began to flood with tears. He grasped William's hand firmly and spoke in a firm voice that belied his body's frail state.

"Farewell, my brethren, farewell father and mother; farewell world, with all thy vain delights. Welcome, God and Father—welcome, sweet Lord Jesus! Welcome death—welcome eternity...![4]"

Then, with a low voice and eyes that no longer beheld anything around him, he faintly said, "Yes, Lord Jesus, come closer, Lord... Jesus!"

With those words, he immediately sank back into his bed and fell asleep in Christ.

JIMMY BARELY HAD time to digest the stirring emotional impact of that scene when another abrupt change in surroundings washed over him in a wave of bright light. The sudden change of scene didn't surprise him, but the new venue did. He was at a large city park where a crowd of more than twenty thousand people were gathered.

Jimmy could see Reverend Edwards praying with several who knelt among a gathering of weeping souls being led to the Lord. The move of the Spirit was powerful in their midst.

Besides Edwards, he saw George Whitefield there as well. Jimmy noticed a printed bulletin announcing Whitefield's evangelistic series at Boston Common, Massachusetts. The date was October 12, 1740. Reaching to pick it up, he saw that it passed through his hand, confirming that his travel here was not temporal — he was invisible, just as he had been with John and William Tennent. He felt a sense of relief, noting that he was still dressed in his pajamas and a bathrobe.

Looking around, he smiled at the sight of the Heavenly messengers who ministered to people throughout the crowd. Their glowing wings and joyous expressions thrilled his soul. As he watched, he felt a familiar hand grip his shoulder and turned to see Chozeq, who offered a nod of welcome.

The look in Jimmy's eye asked the question that he didn't need to speak aloud — wondering at the purpose of their visit here.

CHOZEQ LIFTED his hand with a wave, and they immediately stood in the small living room of Edwards' parsonage. The glow of a low fire, hot with embers, hinted of the late hour as Edwards and Whitefield sat beside it, engaged in a lively conversation.

"Our young friend described today's meeting well, wouldn't you say?" Whitefield offered.

"Indeed he did," Edwards agreed. "Say ye that he first told of it long ago?"

"Aye, years past," Whitefield confirmed.

"He's been a welcome guide to me as well these years passed," Edwards noted warmly. "It stirred my soul when ye spoke of him. I thought it to be only I who saw him here." He leaned forward in deep thought. "What thinkest thou... is he man or angel?"

"An honest query indeed," Whitefield pondered. "He seems more likely a man than not. His manner of conveyance is unusual, surely."

Edwards' eyebrows lifted higher at his friend's remark. "Indeed! What man is there who vanishes thusly into thin air?"

"Perhaps a man who is carried whithersoever God wills. Remember what was written of Phillip, who is said to have done the same in the book of Acts," Whitefield suggested.

Edwards stroked his chin as he considered the point. "Yea, as did our Lord after his appearance on the road to Emmaus. Glorious things the Lord is doing in these days."

"Aye, a faithful saying that is," Whitefield agreed.

The men stared silently into the fire for a moment as they each breathed a thankful prayer.

"How long are ye able to remain?" Edwards asked hopefully.

Whitefield contemplated the question... "It would seem that the Lord is working; perhaps I'll stay and work several days more if there is no objection?"

"No, none," Edwards assured him. "I welcome it. The Lord is truly working, without question. Thy ministry here is a great blessing."

"It is the Lord who has helped us both," Whitefield agreed thankfully. "I worry, though, for those who have been saved in these few days and the recent years. Workers are needed to shepherd them. We must pray for God to raise up pastors for his flock."

"Schools are needed to train them," Edwards added.

"Aye, that is surely true. The universities in England are no option for most here. I dare say that their teaching would be little help in any event. What they know of revival is sorely wanting." Whitefield lamented.

"Now, there's a job that our young friend could well assist with," Edwards offered, looking as if the idea had just sprung into his mind.

"Well, I would dare to agree. However, such an endeavor would require him to remain in one place. It wouldn't do to have him disappearing into thin air while in the middle of a lecture."

Both men laughed at Whitefield's joke. Unbeknownst to them, Jimmy found it pretty amusing as well.

———————

JIMMY WAS STILL SMILING as he found himself back in his old root cellar. He made his way up to the kitchen, closing the cellar hatch behind him. The clock on the mantle was approaching three o'clock, as he stifled a yawn... he might still be able to catch an hour or two of sleep before starting the day.

⌘

25

HARVEST

"For they have sown the wind, and they shall reap the whirlwind…"
~ *Hosea 8:7*

CENTER SPRINGS — LATE NOVEMBER…
Three months ago

P ete pulled the combine into the barnyard and checked the hopper; it was filled to the brim with a healthy crop. There would be plenty of corn to sell, and they would still have enough to feed the cattle and supply the food pantry for another year.

Jimmy was busy plucking their Thanksgiving turkey—a job Anna gratefully deferred to him. Thanksgiving was still two days away, but it wasn't too early for them both to be busy preparing. They'd invited a large group for dinner, including Mike and Lena, Pete and Angela, Pete's dad, Big Jay, PJ and Baibina, Nyle and Caden Koller, and Chrissy and Sean Daniels, who worked full-time at the food pantry. Jimmy couldn't wait.

"That's a healthy-lookin' bird," Pete commented as he watched the action.

"Well, he's not exactly in good health anymore," Jimmy joked. "But this old-timer was a good 25-pounder. I suppose we'll be feeling pretty good after eating it."

"It'll be awesome," Pete agreed. "Angela is makin' a couple o' apple and pumpkin pies, and my dad's bringin' his famous stuffing. We'll have plenty o' corn on the cob. The sweet potatoes are lookin' pretty good, too."

"Sweet!" Jimmy approved. "Anna's mom is bringing her special cranberry sauce, and Mike is making all the pasta. And don't forget all that ice cream we made — it's the old Van Clief recipe," Jimmy bragged.

"Oh man, that's the best," Pete agreed. "I'm ready right now!"

Jimmy carried the cleaned turkey to the kitchen's large refrigerator and washed his hands. The news broadcast on TV caught their attention. It showed scenes of the increasing unrest in the country, reflecting the growing turmoil worldwide. The world's governments were tightening control, using more deployments of UN Peace Force troops, but the more they tightened, the more their control seemed to slip away.

Scenes of rioting were increasingly common everywhere. They brought back memories of the unrest during the terrible drought seven years earlier during President Sheen's administration. Jimmy and Pete were both reminded of the devastation in cities throughout the country, especially in Brooklyn and immediately thought of Rad.

"HARD TO BELIEVE it's been seven years already since his grandmother died," Pete said somberly. "A lot has happened to the kid since then."

"Yeah, you're right," Jimmy agreed. "Heard anything lately about how he's doing?"

"Not since back in the Spring. Badrick said he was in rough shape then. He wasn't a bad kid; hope he hasn't done anything stupid."

Jimmy thought about the future scenes he'd been shown, including the night Rad stabs PJ and the day his friends are killed. He kept the heart-wrenching memories to himself but couldn't hide the sorrow in his voice as he considered the amount of tragedy still to befall him.

"We have to keep him in prayer. God has him in His sights, but it'll be a rough road."

Pete looked at Jimmy, sensing that his friend knew more than he was sharing. He didn't probe—he knew better. "Roger that," he replied sadly, agreeing to pray.

———

ON THANKSGIVING DAY, the Bed-Stuy Mission was filled with hungry locals. They came in shifts for dinners, which were served every two hours from noon until 8:00 PM. Badrick made a point of texting Pete with pictures of the feast, thanking him for their generous donation of provisions. Pete shared it with Jimmy and then rang Badrick's phone in reply...

"You're doing God's work; thanks for all you do," Pete commended him as he answered.

"We're bein' truly grateful for th' feast that ya sent us, mon. We'll be expectin' more 'den a hundred families an' it's truely enough t' feed 'em all."

"Any chance that Radison and his friends will stop by?" Pete asked.

"I'm hopin' for it! We sent d'word to 'em two or three times fer good measure."

"Thanks," Pete said appreciatively. "Let me know how it goes, will ya?"

"Surely I will, mon. A Blessed Thanksgivin' to ya."

"Likewise, man."

IT WAS early afternoon when Pete received another text from Badrick with a picture of Radison and his friends enjoying their Thanksgiving dinner together. He showed it to Jimmy and PJ, who led the three of them in prayer together for the struggling kids.

THEIR OWN THANKSGIVING dinner was even better than Jimmy and Pete had imagined. The table was loaded from end to end with the most delicious bounty they'd ever seen. Mike and Lena outdid themselves with seafood and pasta dishes, and everyone else brought their own specialty, from Pete's Dad's delicious stuffing and Angela's sweet potatoes to Sean Daniel's candied yams. Baibina brought plenty of her delicious Brazilian pastries to go with the wide selection of pies and ice cream. Jimmy was happy to see lots of Lena's homemade cranberry sauce, and Anna did a superb job with the turkey and mashed potatoes.

The men sat around after dinner in a semi-comatose state of satisfaction, watching football while the toddlers napped nearby. The women retired to the kitchen, laughing together in spirited conversation.

IT WAS HALFTIME when a news bulletin interrupted the game. More angel sightings had been recorded over northern Israel; this time, they were visible to mainstream media reporters covering the tensions along the border.

The field reporter sounded breathless as he introduced news footage showing clear images of the bright hosts filling the sky as they stopped a massive missile offensive in mid-air. Some of the missiles detonated in the sky and many more had been miraculously turned around and sent back to their launching points, wiping out a massive swath of the offensive's ground-based arsenal.

Nyle, Mike, and Pete were on the edge of their seats as they watched the report. Seeing angel armies was nothing new to Jimmy, but he couldn't help enjoying his friend's thrilled reactions.

"Whoa!" Pete exclaimed. "This is incredible... it's just like something right outta the Bible, man!"

PJ sat quietly beside them with a somber expression.

"What are you thinking?" Jimmy asked him quietly.

"Just guessing how the world is going to react to this."

Nyle soberly nodded in agreement.

PJ was right in anticipating the world's reaction. News commentators immediately condemned the angels' response as frightening and dangerous and began to call it a new escalation in the *sky aliens'* actions. There was fear and speculation about where they would strike next.

Anna and the others joined the men in the living room, watching the coverage sadly. All of them shook their heads as they listened to the news analysis, honestly dumbfounded by the degree of delusion it demonstrated.

OVER THE FOLLOWING WEEK, the news offered an endless barrage of condemnation of the *'alien forces'* that now constantly appeared in the skies over Galilee and along the Lebanese border.

Interviews were shown with Kala and Jesús Diez, and posts were rebroadcast from Mark Ostenhizer's video podcast—the man called Aurora. All three railed against the threat and warned of terrifying destruction at the angels' hands. Their words caused widespread terror throughout the world.

Leyla added to this relentless condemnation in her public statements, saying that the angels' actions did not reflect the love and unifying spirit of *Unum Amor* . She ended her remarks by repeating the deceiving spirits' line encouraging: 'all people of earth to fight together as one against their great common enemy!'

RUSSIAN-LED forces naively sent jets to attack the Heavenly army. Their attacks were fruitless, of course. Even the US Space Force secretly searched for anything that could affect them. The angels remained invisible to radar and other sensing tech and, unsurprisingly, were impervious to earthly weapons.

It wasn't long before several news analysts brought up the infamous events involving angels that occurred in Center Springs and Washington, DC, in recent years. Jimmy's prominent involvement in those events had certainly not been a secret. The pressure was growing for authorities to 'question him.'

Jimmy had already turned down interviews with Caden Koller at WCST and Vanessa Filmer on America Tonight. Although he couldn't have hoped for more friendly interviewers than both of them, he knew he couldn't share his experiences. Chozeq's old charge to *'tell no one'* echoed prominently in his mind. Besides, the risk wasn't just to himself anymore; he had Anna and VJ to think of.

To be honest, Jimmy was bracing himself. He guessed that once Nero took office, the restraint being imposed by President Godard would end. He knew it wouldn't be possible to hide at the farmhouse this time; his location was too well known. Hiding in the Secret Passage might work temporarily, but that was certainly not a solution. The fact that he now had a family to worry about naturally added to his concern. It became a regular subject of prayer in their daily devotions as he and Anna sought the Lord over it.

DECEMBER...
Two months ago

PRESIDENT GODARD CELEBRATED the Holidays as usual with huge displays of trees and lights and a life-sized nativity on the White House lawn.

His annual Christmas ball for disabled children invited hundreds of special needs kids and parents from across the country, along with artists and celebrities who supported the cause. Over the past several years, the televised event had become a phenomenal success, drawing millions of dollars in private charity to support deserving causes.

Nonetheless, many people sensed an apprehensive feeling in this year's event. There was no telling whether President-elect Nero would continue the tradition. Even if he did, no one expected the same spirit of celebration for the Holiday.

In fact, most professing Christians worried that the country would return to the policies of the prior administration, remembering how Athaliah had banned Christian expression in all its forms. Given the current state of the world, some Pastors wondered aloud whether this might be the last Christmas they'd ever celebrate, half expecting to either be imprisoned or raptured within the next year.

Jimmy didn't know when the Rapture would come but had a pretty good idea from some of his travels that a lot remained to happen first. Yet, there was no denying that events were happening rapidly. He had to admit imprisonment seemed like a real possibility once again.

One thing that still nagged him was that so many of the events recorded in his journal seemed to be approaching so quickly. He couldn't help remembering that his journal was meant for someone else— *after he is gone.*

JIMMY WAS JOLTED from his thoughts by Anna's nudge...

"Are you watching this?" She asked, catching his distracted look.

He followed her gaze to see VJ enthusiastically ripping the wrapping paper from his first-ever Christmas present. He watched his son's face light up with a wide smile as he found the toy inside. It suddenly occurred to Jimmy why parents loved Christmas so much; watching the magic in his own child's eyes was like experiencing it again himself for the first time.

He felt Anna nuzzle against his arm happily, sensing that she was feeling the same thing. They sat quietly and watched VJ play, trying to make the moment last as long as possible.

Soon, VJ was ready for breakfast, and the fireplace was ready for another log. Anna scooped up their son while Jimmy took care of the fire. A short while later, he was happily working at the griddle. His mom's Christmas morning breakfast tradition of French Toast and bacon had become Jimmy's favorite.

MIKE AND LENA soon arrived with armfuls of presents.

"That breakfast smells awesome," Mike praised as he hung up their coats. "You ain't lost yer touch, kid."

"That's high praise coming from a famous restauranteur," Jimmy joked.

"You ain't kiddin'. You can come cook breakfast at the restaurant anytime."

"Does that mean you're planning to open before noon?"

"Hmm... maybe we could compromise and do 11:00; we'll call it *brunch* like all the other fancy restaurants," Mike offered. Lena rolled her eyes and smiled, hugging Anna as she anxiously accepted VJ from her arms and then sat down, jostling him on her knee.

THE COUPLES SAT TOGETHER hours later after a beautiful day of gift-sharing and a fantastic Christmas dinner. Lena happily snuggled her grandson as he napped in her arms. They made it a point not to turn on the TV, opting for an evening of conversation and Christmas music.

Despite their relaxed smiles, they each wrestled with the same concerns about the coming year. They remembered all too well the events of those days — now almost eight years ago when the country was turned upside down, and Jimmy was in the middle of it all. Even though he'd been out of the spotlight for several years, they couldn't help wondering if he'd soon be in the center of it again.

A winter wind rattled the window panes as Jimmy got up to put another log on the fire.

"Want to help me put him in his crib?" Anna asked her mom sentimentally. She loved watching how Lena cherished their little boy in her arms. Lena nodded with a smile, and the women headed upstairs together.

"THINGS ARE GETTIN' pretty crazy out there again," Mike said quietly as soon as he and Jimmy were alone.

Jimmy poked the fire, positioning the log he'd just added. He certainly couldn't disagree — if anything, Mike's comment was a huge understatement. Mike could see that Jimmy agreed and wasn't surprised he didn't answer. He suspected Jimmy knew more about what was coming than he let on.

"It's obvious that the country is shiftin' again," Mike continued. Nero gives me the creeps, the same way Sheen did." He paused, considering his next question: "If it goes the way Sheen took things, do ya think God'll give the country another chance this time?"

Jimmy was quiet for a moment as he settled back into his seat. "Only God knows what's coming for sure. But I think it's a lot bigger than America this time. When you look at all that's happening with Israel, along with *Unum Amor* and those so-called messiahs, plus the mad rush toward a single currency and a world alliance between countries, it's pretty clear that things are much worse this time. The world is on a collision course with everything the Bible says about the last days. It's not just one president defying God this time — now it's the whole world.

"Everyone is obsessed with blame and hate and is basing their hopes on empty promises. They're sowing nothing but wind... and will reap the whirlwind."

Mike bent forward and hung his head. Jimmy's words gave him a chill.

"How much time do ya think is left?"

"I don't know..." Jimmy said as he exhaled a deep breath. "I'm hoping to stay out of the spotlight this time, for Anna and VJ's sake."

"Ya think that's possible? Ya ain't exactly been unnoticed lately."

"We're in God's hands. All we can do is pray— maybe He'll hide us again."

Mike nodded his head, agreeing that he'd be praying for that for sure. In their heart of hearts, however, neither of them really believed that would happen. They both felt it — God had no intention of hiding Jimmy from the spotlight.

⌘

26

TROUBLE

...it was like a deep sleep had descended on the country.

WASHINGTON DC — JANUARY... INAUGURATION DAY
One month ago

Jimmy couldn't help feeling a sense of déjà vu as he watched Nero's inauguration ceremony. The parallels with the start of Devlon Sheen's presidency eight years prior were almost eerie.

Over the TV broadcast, he could see the dark forces gathered overhead. This time, President Godard and his wife were notably alone, the only ones on stage flanked by angelic guardians. The Congress seemed void of believers now that the remaining few had retired or been voted from office. In a reflection of the godless tone of the day, Nero used a copy of the Constitution rather than a Bible for his swearing-in, just as Sheen had done.

At least Jimmy wasn't in hiding this time. Life almost seemed normal despite a chorus of events that signaled the world's growing labor pains. People were going along with their lives as if nothing at all had changed — it was like a deep sleep had descended on the country. '*A strong delusion*,' Jimmy repeated to himself ominously.

Meanwhile, nations teetered on the brink of war while famine swept the globe and armies continued to mass in the Middle East. The World Bank's new EarthCoin had already replaced the US Dollar as the globe's fiat currency, and the United States was now the world's largest debtor nation. China's military had far surpassed the US in size and capability. The changes in global power were happening so quickly that it was almost surreal.

Elvio Nero stepped to the podium for his acceptance speech, thanking his colleagues on stage and the American people for his humbling good fortune. It would likely be the last time that humility would characterize the man.

"I STAND BEFORE YOU TODAY, a humbled man, grateful for your trust in me to lead this great nation. As I have said throughout my campaign, this is a new age of unity in the world. I pledge, first and foremost, to make unity the guiding principle of my administration. We must move past the differences that have divided us and accept the *common* values we hold dear. It is time once again for us to unite against divisive beliefs!"

...The crowds erupted in thundering applause...

"My administration will work hand-in-hand with the international community to meet the world's most difficult challenges. Vice President Bravo and I will work tirelessly to see that the United States does its part to foster peace and neutrality while fighting against outdated dogmas.

"In light of this, I have charged the Vice President with spearheading a new program of national unity that will be a model for the world. Heavy-handed tactics are not needed. Instead, a welcoming and inclusive approach will bring people together in this quest.

"We will work with our religious communities and leaders to achieve this vision. In this effort, I am pleased to announce a joint initiative with *Unum Amor* to usher in this new day with the greatest respect for our individual and shared beliefs. We know it is their goal, as it is the desire of all people, to create a world that is joined together in peaceful harmony.

"HERE WE GO...," Jimmy said, half under his breath. A flurry of images swirled in his mind — of coming events he'd seen and recorded in his journal over the past few years.

Anna looked over from her place beside him on the couch. She sensed that his words were more than a worried expression. "Can't people see that this is heading right back to how things were under Athaliah?" she worried. "You were right... it is a strong delusion."

"People are desperate for some sense of safety as the world melts down," Jimmy related. "They'll grasp at anything that promises it. It's like they're grabbing a live wire to keep from falling, only to find that the wire is more deadly than the fall."

BROWNSVILLE, BROOKLYN...
Two days later

PJ PARKED on the street a few doors down from Rad's hangout. This was his fifth visit in the past three months, and he couldn't help but notice that each meeting was a little more unpredictable and dangerous. It seemed that Rad was becoming more hardened and bitter with each passing week. PJ breathed a prayer for the boy as well as for his own safety before switching off the engine.

A stiff winter wind took his breath away as he stepped from the car. The basement door opened quickly after he buzzed, and he held out the large cardboard box he carried full of hot food from the Mission.

"Thought you guys could use a hot meal," he explained, offering it to Nacio, one of Rad's friends. The boy grabbed it eagerly and pulled out a warm roll, taking a hungry bite as the others converged around him.

While the others grabbed containers of food from the box and tore them open, PJ turned to Rad. "How are you doing?"

Rad shrugged. "Never been better...," he lied sarcastically. He looked at his shoes then slowly raised his eyes to meet PJ's, nodding his head toward the food. "Thanks for that. It's been kinda cold for walkin' cross town."

"No problem," PJ answered sincerely. He looked around the room for a place to sit — its three chairs were occupied, and the dingy mattresses scattered around the floor didn't look very inviting. He leaned against the wall and pushed his hands into his pockets, making a mental note to bring them some soap and cleaning supplies the next time he came.

"Pete was asking about you; he says hi," PJ offered.

Rad nodded awkwardly without answering. He glanced at the food, obviously hungry.

"Go ahead, get some," PJ encouraged.

Nacio, Scamp, and Jay-Jay were busy eating from the containers in their laps. Rad grabbed his own from the open box. "Want some?" he said to PJ, almost as an afterthought.

"No thanks, I'm good," PJ assured him. He studied Rad's face, trying to gauge the boy's mood. He seemed calmer than usual, but PJ knew from experience that Rad could change in a heartbeat.

This wasn't just a social call. PJ had pretty intense news to deliver, and he wanted to be sure Rad was in as steady a state of mind as possible. He figured it would be better received on a full stomach, at a minimum. He made small talk as Rad ate.

"This is sure some cold spell we're having...," he said, mimicking a shiver.

"That's fer sure," Rad agreed with his mouth full.

"Seems warm in here, though," PJ noted thankfully.

"Yeah, the only decent thing 'bout this place — we're right next t' the furnace," Rad nodded toward the open door to the building's furnace room beside them.

. . .

THE INNOCUOUS CONVERSATION continued for the next twenty minutes; PJ talked about the weather, the election, the news, sports... anything he could think of while the boys finished their dinner. He finally signaled that he had to leave, nodding for Rad to follow him to the door. He lowered his voice to avoid being over-heard by the others, hesitating for a moment before sharing what he had to say....

"I WANTED to let you know — I got a call from the prison... Stockslock. Your dad's been given an execution date; it's next month."

He studied Rad's face for his reaction but couldn't detect anything; it looked like he was numb but with just enough acknowledgment to show he'd heard what PJ said. PJ glanced at the floor uncomfortably, then back at Rad. "I know he'd love to see you before... then. I can take you there if you want."

Rad didn't respond; he pretended he hadn't heard anything. "Thanks for th' food...."

"Rad, you should see him," PJ urged. "You'll regret it if you don't."

"SHUT UP! LEAVE ME ALONE!" Rad shouted in an explosion of anger.

PJ raised his hands in a gesture of surrender. "OK, OK, sorry, I'm sorry." He opened the door and stepped one foot out before turning again... "Call me if you change..."

"**GET OUT!**" Rad yelled through a barrage of expletives, cutting PJ off mid-sentence.

CENTER SPRINGS...
Later that afternoon

JIMMY SAT behind the microphone for his weekly Blaze podcast. No longer in the old root cellar where the podcast got its start, he now sat in a state-of-the-art recording studio at the Living Springs Church.

Josh, the sound engineer, was no longer just a high school kid with raw talent — he was now a graduate of one of the country's premier engineering schools. With the help of Nyle Koller's resources and network expertise, they'd built the humble Blaze podcast into a small broadcasting network in its own right.

Josh pointed to Jimmy with a signal that he was on the air.

"Thanks for joining this week's podcast. We have a lot to talk about today.

"As you know, if you've been listening in recent weeks, the Nero Administration is instituting a lot of *new* policies that look a lot like the *old* policies of eight years ago. Most of you probably recognize the recent *unity* initiative as nothing more than a thinly veiled repeat of the previous Unity Enforcement Agency that President Sheen finally disbanded.

"This time, these efforts are being wrapped in the guise of religious tolerance through a close association with the *Unum Amor* movement. This week, President Nero announced a mandate for government agencies to adhere to *Unum Amor 's* proclamations. Companies are being pressured to do the same. Some major religious denominations have embraced this new World Church movement. Many of the world's governments seem to be trying to outdo one another to get on board.

"I want to spend time today examining this movement from the perspective of Bible prophecy. Fasten your seatbelts; this could get a little bumpy.

"From a Biblical standpoint, the *Unum Amor* movement resembles the false church described in Revelation chapter 17."

Jimmy went on for the next thirty minutes to explore Revelation's account, describing how the false World Church will align with the coming Antichrist and will be responsible for the persecution and martyred deaths of thousands of Believers. As he came to the end, he explained the context of his message.

"I realize this has been a heavy topic today. I wish I could report that the sunshine of revival we've experienced for the past few years will continue forever. Unfortunately, that is not what the Bible describes or what the Lord has laid on my heart.

"We can see the signs all around us. The Globalist movement toward a single world order and a global currency is now in its final stages. The situation in the Middle East is growing more dangerous by the day.

"It may only be a matter of time before believers who resist calls for *Unum Amor 's* brand of unity are singled out and charged with intolerance. That will just be the beginning. The Lord's Return may be imminent, or some may be called to suffer for Him before that day. May God give His church a powerful endowment of strength and an anointing of grace for the days to come.

"In closing, I'd like to ask all of you listening from around the world to join me in praying for that very thing."

> "Lord, the coming events are an open page to you. You have known them from eternity past, and through the ages, your prophets have provided glimpses of them to us. What you have shown us can be frightening; we can't deny it. But we know you have promised to *protect us from the hour of trial, which is to come upon the whole world, to try those who dwell on the earth.*[1]

"Please give us strength and the wisdom to do what is
needed in the approaching days... as we await Your
coming."

LATER THAT NIGHT

JIMMY KNELT ALONE TO PRAY, once again finding solace in the old root
cellar. PJ's news about Chase's execution date was a little jarring.

"Next month?" He remembered repeating in surprise when he
heard the date. All of the events he had foreseen of that night rushed
suddenly through his mind. For some reason, he had still assumed it
would be further in the future.

PJ's description of how things had gone with Rad weighed on his
heart. Jimmy knew that Rad would soon get much worse; it was all he
could do to keep himself from warning his friend and mentor about
the night that was coming — the night when PJ would be stabbed.

Events were happening so fast now that it made Jimmy's head
spin. It wasn't just Chase's execution date that seemed to approach so
suddenly out of nowhere. The whole combination of world events
seemed to be accelerating rapidly.

JIMMY KNELT beside his old wooden chair, lifting in prayer each of
those whose fates weighed on his heart.

When he finally finished, he sat quietly, still burdened by an urgent
cry within his spirit — there was something he was being called to do,
something urgent and monumentally important. Yet, he wasn't able to
discern what it was.

His meetings with Edwards, Whitefield, and the Tennents
continued to puzzle him. He truly enjoyed his times with them, yet he
still didn't feel as if he had contributed anything to their work. It was
a mystery to him why God would ask him to focus his attention there
— so long in the past, when events right now were more dire than at

any time in the earth's history. After all, he was living in *the End of Days*.

Briefly closing his eyes, he breathed another prayer for help with the puzzle.

THE SUDDEN FEELING of a bright sun on his face and the sound of a neighing horse made him open his eyes. To his surprise, he was sitting on a stoop beside a small dirt road. The approaching horse was pulling a wagon that came to a stop as it reached him.

"Well, praises be. I wondered if we'd see thee again," the wagon's driver called out. "Jim is thy name, is it not?"

Jimmy recognized William Tennent, smiling as he stood to greet him. "Yes, that's right. It's good to see you, William."

"It surprises me that ye remember my name. We met only once, as I recall, and that nearly ten years passed."

"In that case, I'm more surprised you remember *my* name," Jimmy noted honestly.

"When a man vanishes from sight before one's eyes, it tends to make a memorable impression. I've since learned from others who have made your acquaintance that you have shown a habit of disappearing thusly. Both Jonathan Edwards and George Whitefield have spoken of it."

"I suppose I can see why that could be a topic for conversation," Jimmy admitted. "I'd rather it not be too well known."

"Worry not; it has only been spoken of among ourselves. We fear that others who have not witnessed the feat would simply think us mad."

Jimmy felt relieved. Being well-known in his own day was difficult enough without being a famous curiosity here, too. He simply nodded that he understood: "I appreciate that."

"Dare I ask what brings thee here to this desolate place?"

Jimmy looked around at the deep woods that surrounded them. It was true there were no buildings nearby — probably none within miles, but he wouldn't describe the place with its rich foliage as desolate. "I kind of like it here," he said honestly. "I think you may know better than I do what brings me here. What is it that you've been struggling with lately?"

Reverend Tennent slid over to make room for Jimmy on the wagon, waiting for him to climb in before driving on. "Well, if my struggles are of interest, then we can take our pick," he joked. After considering the question more seriously, he seemed to zero in on one thing in particular.

"As I believe you know, God has blessed His work richly these past few years. There has been a great awakening of His church throughout the colonies. I am not alone in fearing that it shall all be for naught if more Pastors are not soon equipped to lead His flock."

Jimmy remembered the conversation he'd heard Edwards and Whitefield having on the same topic. "Have Edwards and Whitefield mentioned it?" Jimmy asked carefully.

"Well, yes, most surely. Also others... Jonathan Dickinson, Ebenezer Pemberton, Aaron Burr, Pierson, Blair, and Witherspoon, to name several more. We have been greatly in prayer, seeking God over the forming of a new college to equip those He calls to ministry."

"What is needed is not a common school of learning," William said adamantly. "It is not to be like the seminaries in England. We desire to raise up prophets and not mere clergymen. It will take an act of God Himself to fulfill such a vision."

William looked at Jimmy intently, revealing the deep faith that burned in his soul over it as he continued to explain.

"JIM, thy own words to us gave the promise that I hold steadfastly in my heart. Ye said that God would send a Great Awakening in the land, and He has done so. Yet we have already seen losses among the servants of God, my dear brother John among them. To make it a lasting work, we must raise up more God-filled ministers to continue it. And He shall do it — I know He shall. With merely the faintest mustard seed of faith, it shall be done!"

William looked to the skies and spread his hands in the air expressively, "If need be, God will part the very forces of darkness like He parted the sea. It is His own work, and it shall be done!"

He paused as if a sudden thought had entered his mind.

"I DON'T SUPPOSE ye would be interested in joining the effort? An instructor such as thou wouldst surely bring great insight regarding the ways of the Spirit in leading a man of God."

"Me? Seriously?" Jimmy was about to claim that he knew nothing about equipping prophets but felt a sudden rebuke in his spirit. How could he deny the miraculous works that God had done through him, not to mention his travels through time? His very presence here confirmed that.

"That is... I mean... I'm not sure that I can. It's more complicated than you could imagine." He thought about other ways to help, finally suggesting: "Have you considered Reverend Edwards? He would be a great president for such a school."

"Edwards? I hadn't considered it, but ye make a magnificent point. He would be an excellent president indeed."

AS THEY RODE TOGETHER, they spoke at length about Tennent's vision for the school. Jimmy offered ideas for the curriculum, using his own recent college experience as a guide. Tennent was most interested in Jimmy's insights into what Tennent called 'untraditional ministry.' Jimmy eventually understood him to be talking about following the moving of the Spirit. Tennent listened in rapt attention as Jimmy described his own experiences with the great outpourings at the tent meetings and manifestations of healing. The authenticity and vibrancy of Jimmy's faith stirred Tennent even more than his words, causing his own faith to swell as they talked.

Finally arriving at the church where they'd first met, Jimmy recognized its finished state from his vision of John's last Easter service there. Its construction had been completed years earlier. Reverend

Tennent climbed from the wagon and unharnessed the horse, leading it to a nearby rail and watering trough.

"I can offer you a tour of the church..." he said to Jimmy over his shoulder. But as he turned back toward him, he found the wagon empty — Jimmy was nowhere to be found.

⌘

27

HEAVENLY LEGIONS

"If need be, God will part the very forces of darkness like He parted the sea."

MOMENTS LATER...

Jimmy had just begun to climb from William Tennent's wagon when a bright flash instantly transformed his surroundings. The serenity of Tennent's eighteenth-century church-in-the-woods was suddenly replaced by a shocking scene of battle-field carnage. He ducked for cover as an explosion tore through a nearby structure, sending debris in all directions.

The air was filled with dirt, smoke, and the stench of exploding sulfur and munitions. It rang with a cacophony of battlefield sounds, with massive explosions and bullets whizzing past. Jimmy dove to the ground and covered his head in a disoriented fog of confusion and surprise, scraping his face as he skidded through the debris.

He'd seen battlefield scenes in his travels before, but never as a live participant. The trace of blood on his hand made it clear that this experience was very much alive. He shivered from the cold as he lifted his head to look around, noticing soldiers waving to him from a bunker a short distance away. They were calling for him to come.

With explosions and bullets flying all around him, the soldiers' refuge looked like as good a place to hide as any. He scrambled toward it, somehow reaching it alive.

He was still making sense of the scene as he looked at the men, realizing they were speaking to him — he couldn't understand a word they said.

"I only speak English," he said, pointing at his ear.

"American," one of them said in recognition. "Are you a settler here or Press Corp?"

Jimmy noticed their uniforms for the first time; they were IDF... Israeli Defense Forces. His mind raced for an answer... "A traveler... a visitor — I'm just here visiting."

"You've picked a farkakte *(lousy)* time for a tourist visit," one of them said. He eyed Jimmy suspiciously. "Where's your coat?"

Jimmy looked down at his T-shirt and trousers and crossed his arms, shivering from the cold. "I-I don't have one... it's... I left it."

One of them threw him a heavy army-issue overcoat. It was filthy, but at least it was warm. He pulled it on and zippered it gratefully. "Thanks," he offered.

He scanned his surroundings for any clue about where he was or even what year it was. Asking the soldiers either of those questions would be sure to raise suspicions. He noticed the men were wearing small receivers in their ears and could see something attached to their helmets that looked like computerized night vision scopes. That ruled out the distant past; it implied that the setting was current or in the near future.

The man who'd thrown him the coat barked orders at several of the men, who quickly rushed outside and took up positions. That's when Jimmy looked at the sky overhead for the first time. A battle raged in the air, but it wasn't fighter jets — it wasn't human at all. It was a clash of forces larger than anything he'd ever seen, and in Jimmy's case, that was really saying something.

The angelic hosts that filled the skies had formed a perimeter of defense around the stranded troops. The black hordes that filled the skies beyond them nearly blocked out the sun with their numbers. Jimmy looked at the soldiers to gauge their reactions — it was apparent that they couldn't see the overwhelming spiritual onslaught that raged overhead. Their focus was on the very tangible tanks and armored infantry that drew ominously nearer by the minute.

As tempting as it was to be terrified, Jimmy felt an unusual calm. He suddenly remembered words that Chozeq had once said to him:

> *'You hold the protection of all the legions of Heaven. You have omnipotence as your guardian, and God will sooner empty heaven of angels than leave a saint without defense.'*

Feeling an irresistible urge to stand, Jimmy turned toward the doorway and stepped outside. He could hear the battalion commander yelling for him to stay down, along with the sound of bullets flying past him. His focus was on the skies above as a prayer filled his consciousness — a cry for God's deliverance.

Once outside, he looked behind him at the skies to the south and east, watching as they filled with unnumbered legions of Heavenly hosts. Then, the air shook with the thundering cry of an archangel as all of the bright hosts thrust their swords forward in a unified assault, filling the skies with fiery beams of light that cut through the demon hordes. As the ghostly black devils scattered, a massive barrage of enemy artillery filled the skies in their place - sending missiles and glowing artillery shells racing toward Jimmy's position.

Jimmy's natural instinct should have been to run for cover, but instead, he suddenly heard William Tennent's heartfelt words rush through his thoughts with immense gravity...

> *'If need be, God will part the very forces of darkness like He parted the sea.'*

Jimmy felt an overwhelming urge to raise his hands in the air, closing his eyes as he breathed a desperate prayer. The battalion commander and his men stared in disbelief as the approaching missiles and shells suddenly parted in mid-air, striking the ground far to either side and behind them.

More astonishing still, when the dust cleared, it became apparent that the enemy tanks and armored vehicles that had fired the barrage were gone! The battlefield that had been filled with them moments earlier was red with scattered pools of molten steel, while massive numbers of troops stood shocked and defenseless, their weapons rendered suddenly useless.

It was then that Jimmy realized where he stood. Turning, he saw the cityscape of an ancient city in the distance. Rising in its center was a raised mount that he recognized — he could see the ancient wall beneath it, the sacred Wailing Wall. On the mount's open heights, Jimmy saw the most shocking sight of all.

The golden *Dome of the Rock* and Al-Aqsa Mosque were in flames! They had been struck by several of the missiles that Israel's enemies fired. As Jimmy watched, he saw the Mosque and massive dome collapse, completely destroyed.

IDF forces were quickly converging on the now-disarmed invaders as Israeli jets raced past overhead. Jimmy looked to the glowing armies above and pressed his fist to his chest in a salute, offering his thanks; he smiled as they saluted back and then disappeared in flashes of light.

Finally, it was Jimmy's turn to leave. He looked back at the Battalion Commander and his men, who were staring at him open-mouthed in astonishment. He nodded to them and smiled, then vanished in an instant, leaving his borrowed coat to fall empty to the ground.

WHEN JIMMY REAPPEARED in the old root cellar, the first thing he did was fall on his knees in thankful relief. Whatever unnatural boldness he'd felt on the battlefield was replaced by the realization of what had just happened. His heart was racing wildly.

His near panic slowly gave way to cries of thanksgiving and joyful praises. It was a while before he'd calmed down enough to consider the strange combination of the night's travels. It was a fair bet that the events he'd seen in Israel had not happened yet.

For the sake of curiosity, he opened his laptop and did a quick search of news reports. As he expected, there were no reports of armies converging on Jerusalem or the Dome of the Rock being destroyed. Not yet, anyway.

THE MORNING'S first light was peaking around the window shades when Anna stirred from sleep. Jimmy was still sleeping soundly beside her.

"What happened to you?" Anna said in surprise when she saw him.

"Huh?" Jimmy said, still half asleep.

"Your face is scratched, and it looks like your ear is cut."

Jimmy touched his ear to investigate.

"Your knuckles are all scraped up, too! Were you in a fight last night? Where were you?"

Jimmy did his best to think fast. He'd never had to explain an injury from one of his travels before.

"Well, I fell... I slipped and got hurt falling," he explained. That was true, to a point — he just left out the part about being on an Israeli battlefield.

"Oh my gosh... how — what happened?"

"It was nothing... I just tripped. It's nothing - I'm not hurt. It's no big deal." He glanced at the clock, looking for an excuse to change the subject. "Oh man, look at the time! I was supposed to help Pete outside." With that, he quickly jumped out of bed and headed for the bathroom to shower.

PETE HAD the same question as Anna when Jimmy met him. It occurred to Jimmy that he would need a better story if he wanted to explain how he got hurt, but every scenario he could think of quickly led to the same uncomfortable impasse. He finally decided to deflect the question.

"Wounded in the war," he said simply.

Pete shrugged and kept walking. "I hear ya," he said, letting it drop.

JIMMY COULDN'T GET the night's shocking experiences out of his head for the rest of the week. The battlefield events had been stunning, without a doubt. Yet, as odd as it seemed, it was his conversation with William Tennent that replayed in his mind the most.

"I don't suppose ye would be interested in joining the effort?"

William's words rang in Jimmy's mind incessantly. Maybe that was what God wanted him to help them with — establishing the new school. But he certainly couldn't be part of it full-time — that was obviously out of the question.

After wrestling with the confusing puzzle for days, he finally resolved to leave it unresolved. It stood to reason that God would reveal the answer when the time was right. Until then, he would do what he could to help his unlikely friends. That is, if he ever saw them again.

⌘

28

PERSUADED

"Just speak the truth and let the seeds fall."

NORTHAMPTON, MASSACHUSETTS — JUNE 1741...

Jonathan Edwards sat in his small office alone, wrestling with Tennent's offer to lead the new college that they were planning. The offer was not unwelcome; his love for learning and higher education had been defining factors in his life, and he certainly shared Tennent's burden for raising up ministers. On the other hand, his own parish in Northampton needed shepherding as well. His struggle with the decision had occupied his thoughts endlessly for the past several days.

He decided to take a walk to clear his head. The day was bright and cloudless, with a gentle breeze that carried the scent of apple blossoms and wildflowers. Small birds splashed in the puddles left by an overnight shower and feasted on worms drawn to the surface by the rain. In the distance, he watched a whitetail doe grazing in the tall grass with her two young fawns. Everything about the scene reminded him of God's provision and blessing.

He drew a deep breath of the clear air and exhaled, releasing the tension around his shoulders, breathing a thankful prayer for the beautiful day. The empty road led through deep woods, typical for most roads in this part of the country, away from the larger cities. He loved to walk this one and did it often, following it to a nearby creek. He had just settled onto his favorite rock beside the gurgling stream when a familiar voice called to him.

"REVEREND EDWARDS...!"

He looked up in surprise to see Jimmy drawing nearer. They had met here before on several occasions, though it had been more than a year for Edwards since their last meeting.

"Master Jim!" Edwards waved in greeting. "'Tis a welcome surprise. Hast thou been at Northampton very long? What brings thee here?"

"I just arrived," Jimmy answered honestly. The flash that had delivered him there moments earlier was characteristically unplanned. "I'm here to see you, apparently."

Edwards bobbed his head as if he wasn't surprised by the answer. He offered his hand as Jimmy drew near, welcoming him with a firm shake. "I believe I owe thee thanks for recommending me to William Tennent."

"Have you decided?" Jimmy probed with a smile.

"Not as yet. It is a great honor and truly a work to which I feel called. Yet I worry for the work here in Northampton."

Jimmy nodded in understanding as he considered Edwards' comment. After a brief pause, an idea came to mind.

"If you're worried about your replacement, it seems like the perfect opportunity for a trial run."

"I beg your pardon... a trial run?"

"For training someone to replace you. It's the perfect chance to raise up a minister right here. You could use it to work out the college program, develop the curriculum, and try out your ideas. I'm guessing it will be a few years before they're ready to open the college, right?"

"Well, yes, I suppose that's true."

"Then it looks like God has given you ample time to transition your pastoral duties—more than typical, I'd suppose."

"Are ye suggesting an apprenticeship?"

"I guess that's one way of looking at it," Jimmy agreed. "I'm sure many aspiring ministers would be grateful for the chance to work under you as their mentor. You'll likely have several candidates to choose from."

As Edwards considered the suggestion, it looked as if a lightbulb was coming on—at least, that was Jimmy's impression—he realized as soon as he thought of it that Edwards would be confused by the lightbulb analogy, having never seen one.

"I believe ye have made an excellent point," he finally said. "An excellent point indeed."

He slapped his knees with both hands and moved on to another question.

"What of thee? Reverend Tennent told me of his offer to thee as well. What might convince thee to join the faculty of the new college?"

Jimmy seemed caught off guard by the question; he thought he'd put that idea to rest when Tennent first brought it up.

"That's a more complicated question than you might suspect. I don't think it's an option; I'm not exactly from around here."

"Ye needn't fear that; the college will not be here in Massachusetts. Tennent plans to establish it in New Jersey. Ye have been there already, I believe?"

Jimmy had to chuckle at that. He'd spent his entire life in New Jersey, as a matter of fact, albeit a few hundred years removed. He knew he couldn't explain that to Edwards. "It's not quite that simple."

"Why is it not? Is it a replacement for thy current duties ye require? Perhaps the training of an apprentice is in order for thee as well."

Edwards' words struck a chord as Jimmy heard them, although perhaps not for the reason Edwards intended. Jimmy was reminded once more of what Chozeq had said — words he'd recorded in his journal: *"It will be for a revelation to this final age of man at the appointed time – in the time of His choosing."* He'd been praying over their unspoken meaning for months. Remembering once again that his travels were recorded for others — it was meant for someone else after he was gone.

"An apprentice…, well, maybe," he finally answered in a distracted voice. He refocused on his current conversation with Edwards, letting those other thoughts go for now. "I suppose we have a few years to figure everything out. Who knows what God has in store by then."

Jimmy wandered along the creek bank distractedly, then picked up a smooth piece of shale and skipped it across the water. He finally took a seat on the ground cross-legged, deep in thought.

EDWARDS KEPT QUIET, allowing his young friend some time with his thoughts. He knew what it was to struggle with important questions himself.

As he watched the rippling water, his thoughts slowly drifted to his first meeting with Jimmy on that snowy afternoon seven years prior. It brought the memory of his vision of Hell's terrible inferno. That vision had remained with Edwards for all the years since. The burden he felt for warning people about it had only grown stronger. He bowed his head and silently prayed for wisdom to reach more of those who needed to hear that message. A tear glistened on his cheek as his soul was powerfully moved by it once again.

Jimmy eventually noticed Edwards' anguish, perceiving it had nothing to do with the college. He had a pretty good idea of what might be bothering him — he had witnessed that vision of lost souls. The two of them had discussed it several times since then, in visits that had occurred over years for Edwards but took place over mere months for Jimmy.

. . .

JIMMY CLIMBED to his feet and sat beside his friend, leaning forward — elbows on his knees as he rubbed his hands together.

"That burden can be a heavy one... I know," he shared sympathetically.

"It grows greater still," Edwards lamented. "The faces are oft times different, but their terror is not."

Jimmy stared at his hands and nodded that he understood. After a short silence, he glanced over at him. "Did you ever write that sermon you talked about? The one about Hell?"

"Many times have I begun it. I fear that people would be offended by it or think it too much drama for the church."

"Too much drama?" Jimmy repeated with a smile. "Have you heard Whitefield preach?"

Edwards smiled and nodded that he had a point. "He is surely effective with it. Perhaps the more drama there is, the better."

Jimmy broke another long silence, clearing his throat. "You have a lot more experience with preaching sermons than I do," he confessed, "but it seems to me the most important thing is to convey what God has laid on your heart. Let the Spirit do the work in people's hearts and minds. If the message is from God's heart, it will find its way to those He intends it for. Just speak the truth and let the seeds fall."

"The sower..." Edwards noted, agreeing as he considered the parable. He placed a hand on Jimmy's shoulder and patted it. "As usual, ye've been a help to me; I perceive thou art God sent, my friend."

"I'm glad I can play a small part — God does the real work," Jimmy said with a humble shrug, smiling back.

Edwards climbed off the rock and bent to collect his walking stick from the ground, speaking with his back to his friend. "I pray that the part God gives thee next is on my faculty," he joked.

He straightened with a smile and turned back to Jimmy, once again finding him already gone.

CENTER SPRINGS — LATE-JANUARY...
Three weeks ago

JIMMY SAT AT HIS LAPTOP, reading the articles he'd gathered in his research. After all the talk about William Tennent's college, he'd decided to find out what he could about it. What he found nearly floored him.

Not only would the fledgling school survive, but it would become one of the premier institutions in the world — now known as *Princeton University.*

Jimmy found in his research that the school would open its doors in 1746—about five years after his creekside meeting with Edwards. It would initially be named The College of New Jersey and located in the city of Elizabeth, then moved a year later to Newark and finally to Princeton in 1756.

In a testament to its early influence, Jimmy read that its campus would serve as the seat of the New Jersey legislature during the American Revolution. Several of its early graduates would go on to make important contributions to the young nation, including John Witherspoon, a signer of the Declaration of Independence, and James Madison, the country's 4th President.

Jimmy read that Edwards would not serve initially as its president but would take the post four years later, in 1750. It would be Edwards who presides over the school's move to Princeton.

While studying Edwards' tenure, Jimmy learned some disturbing news. In 1758, Just two years after the move, his friend would fall ill with a fatal case of smallpox.

Jimmy wished he hadn't come across that information. He feared any chance that he might let such a detail slip prematurely. As he thought of it, he realized his worry revealed a presumption that he would see Edwards again. As he pondered it, in fact, there was no doubt in his mind that his involvement with Edwards, Whitefield, and the Tennents was not done.

Who knows, maybe he'd end up taking that faculty post after all, he joked to himself.

⌘

AN ANGRY GOD

"Their foot shall slide in due time."
~ Deuteronomy 32:35,

ENFIELD, CONNECTICUT — JULY 8, 1741...

J onathan Edwards wiped tears from his eyes as he laid down his pen and reread the sermon he'd just written. Across the top of the page was the sermon title that had been impressed upon him: 'Sinners in the Hands of an Angry God.'

He shuddered and breathed a prayer for God's help in delivering it. He was shaken by the power of its vivid imagery and strong language and felt doubtful whether he could deliver such a message. Yet the burning conviction in his spirit drove him. He needed to warn people of the dangers of hell's horrors and their need to be saved from it! The sermon was as powerful and dramatic a call to repentance as he had ever given.

By now, Edwards had become a well-known figure in the revivals that were spreading throughout the colonies. Despite this, he wondered whether this sermon was too much for a guest speaker to deliver to his hosts. The Congregational Church in Enfield to which he'd been invited was surely not a den of iniquity deserving of such a message. Yet Edwards knew that sinners needed to hear what God had laid upon his heart — not just the worst of sinners, but *all* sinners.

EDWARDS COULD NOT SMILE as he rose to the pulpit. His heart, and even his stomach, churned in turmoil over the deep anguish that pressed upon him. He opened his Bible and announced the verse that was the topic of his message: Deuteronomy 32:35, allowing a moment for those who wished to look it up to do so.

He cleared his throat and let his eyes roam over the large congregation. The sizable church was filled to capacity. Concern for their eternal fates consumed him, causing him to close his eyes as he earnestly prayed for God's help. Without further delay or introduction, he read the short verse aloud....

"Their foot shall slide in due time."

He drew a deep breath and began in a loud voice...

"In this verse is threatened God's vengeance on His own visible people, who lived under the means of grace; but who, notwithstanding all God's wonderful works towards them, remained void of counsel, having no understanding in them. Under all the cultivations of Heaven, they brought forth bitter and poisonous fruit....

"The expression I have chosen for my text, *Their foot shall slide in due time*, implies... that they are exposed to **sudden** unexpected destruction. As he that walks in slippery places is every moment liable to fall, he cannot foresee one moment whether he shall stand or fall the next; and when he does fall, he falls at once without warning, Which is also expressed in Psalm 73:18 and 19.

'Surely thou didst set them in slippery places; thou castedst

them down into destruction: How are they brought into
desolation as in a moment!'

"Here, it is implied that they are liable to fall by themselves
without being thrown down by the hand of another....

"That the reason why they have not fallen already and do not fall
now is only that God's appointed time has not come. For it is said that
when that due time, or appointed time, comes, **their foot shall slide**.
Then they shall be left to fall, as they are inclined by their own weight.
God will not hold them up in these slippery places any longer but will
let them go, and then, at that very instant, they shall fall into destruction, as he that stands on such slippery declining ground, on the edge
of a pit, he cannot stand alone, when he is let go he immediately falls
and is lost.

"The observation from the words I would now insist upon is this.
— *'There is nothing that keeps wicked men at any one moment out of hell but
the mere pleasure of God.'* — By the mere pleasure of God, I mean his
sovereign pleasure, his arbitrary will, restrained by no obligation,
hindered by no manner of difficulty, any more than if nothing else but
God's mere will had in the slightest degree, or in any respect whatso-
ever, any hand in the preservation of wicked men for one moment.[1]

———————

EDWARDS PREACHED for an hour as the faces of many in the
congregation grew more distressed. His earnest pleas grew more and
more urgent the longer he preached until he was nearly shouting—
like a man racing to warn riders that a bridge was out over a raging
flood.

———————

"...So it is not because God is unmindful of their wickedness and does
not resent it that he does not let loose his hand and cut them off!" he
cried. "The wrath of God burns against them; their damnation does

not slumber; the pit is prepared, the fire is made ready, the furnace is now hot, ready to receive them; the flames now rage and glow! The glittering sword is whet and held over them, and the pit hath opened its mouth under them!

"The devil stands ready to fall upon them and seize them as his own, at what moment God shall permit him. They belong to him; he has their souls in his possession, and under his dominion.... The devils watch them; they are ever by them at their right hand; they stand waiting for them like greedy hungry lions that see their prey and expect to have it but are for the present kept back. If God should withdraw his hand, by which they are restrained, they would fly upon their poor souls in one moment. The old serpent is gaping for them; hell opens its mouth wide to receive them, and if God should permit it, they would be hastily swallowed up and lost!²"

As HE CONTINUED to preach under an irresistible anointing, many were deeply affected by the message. Some people fainted, while others cried out in fear; tears covered many of their faces. The presence of God's Spirit became so powerful that every soul clung to each word that Edwards uttered in near panic.

"...THIS that you have heard is the case of **everyone who is out of Christ**. That world of misery, that lake of burning brimstone, is extended abroad under you. There is the dreadful pit of the glowing flames of the wrath of God; there is hell's wide, gaping mouth open; and you have nothing to stand upon, nor anything to take hold of; **there is nothing between you and hell but the air....**

"Your wickedness makes you as it were heavy as lead, and to tend downwards with great weight and pressure towards hell; and if God should let you go, you would immediately sink and swiftly descend and plunge into the bottomless gulf; and your healthy constitution, and your own care and prudence, and best contrivance, and all your righteousness, would have no more influence to uphold you and keep you out of hell than a spider's web would have to stop a falling rock.

"...There are the black clouds of God's wrath now hanging directly over your heads, full of the dreadful storm, and big with thunder; and were it not for the restraining hand of God, it would immediately burst forth upon you!

"The wrath of God is like great waters that are dammed for the present; they increase more and more and rise higher and higher until an outlet is given; and the longer the stream is stopped, the more rapid and mighty its course is when it is let loose.

It is true that judgment against your evil works has not been executed hitherto; the floods of God's vengeance have been withheld, but your guilt in the meantime is constantly increasing, and you are every day treasuring up more wrath; the waters are continually rising, and waxing more and more mighty; and there is nothing but the mere pleasure of God, that holds the waters back, that are unwilling to be stopped, and press hard to go forward. If God should only withdraw his hand from the floodgate, it would immediately fly open, and the fiery floods of the fierceness and wrath of God would rush forth with inconceivable fury and come upon you with omnipotent power. If your strength were ten thousand times greater than it is, yea, ten thousand times greater than the strength of the stoutest, sturdiest devil in hell, it would be nothing to withstand or endure it!

"...Thus all you that never passed under a great change of heart, by the mighty power of the Spirit of God upon your souls; all you that were never born again, and made new creatures, and raised from being dead in sin to a state of new light and life, are in the hands of an angry God!

"...Now God stands ready to pity you; this is a day of mercy; you may cry now with some encouragement of obtaining mercy. But when once the day of mercy is passed, your most lamentable and dolorous cries and shrieks will be in vain; you will be wholly lost and thrown away of God as to any regard to your welfare.

. . .

"AND NOW YOU have an extraordinary opportunity, a day wherein Christ has thrown the door of mercy wide open and stands in calling and crying with a loud voice to poor sinners; a day wherein many are flocking to him and pressing into the kingdom of God. Many are daily coming from the east, west, north, and south; many that were very lately in the same miserable condition that you are in are now in a happy state, with their hearts filled with love for him who has loved them, and washed them from their sins in his blood, and rejoicing in the hope of the glory of God. How awful is it to be left behind on such a day!

"...Therefore, let everyone who is out of Christ now awake and fly from the wrath to come. The wrath of Almighty God is now undoubtedly hanging over a great part of this congregation. Let every one fly out of Sodom: **Haste and escape for your lives**, look not behind you, escape to the mountain, **lest you be consumed!**"[3]

A GREAT STIRRING filled the church like the rush of a mighty wind as people stood and wailed. Many rushed to the altar, dropping to their knees and weeping aloud. It was a day that stunned everyone who heard of it — when more than 250 in that congregation gave their hearts to Christ at once.

⌘

30

FALLING PIECES

'He wondered if God might say, yes.'

CENTER SPRINGS — LATE JANUARY...
Two weeks ago

"It's positive," Anna said with a thrilled smile as she held out the pregnancy test for Jimmy to see. Jimmy placed his hands on his head as his eyes grew wide, and then he grabbed his wife and hugged her excitedly.

Stepping back, he ran his hands through his hair distractedly. "A new baby and a two-year-old... that won't be crazy."

Anna smiled and hung her forearms on his shoulders. "It's been done before, believe it or not."

Jimmy's face creased in a mock-worried expression, "I guess I'd better take my endurance training regimen up a notch."

"Yeah, ya better," Anna laughed.

He looked more serious, "We'd better make an appointment with Dr. Crenshaw."

"I already did... I'm seeing her tomorrow," Anna informed him, three steps ahead as usual.

It was late in the afternoon the following day when PJ rang the doorbell.

"Thanks for coming," Jimmy welcomed him. They soon settled together around the kitchen table, making small talk; Jimmy served hot coffee, and PJ used his mug to warm his cold hands.

"We have some news we wanted to ask you to pray with us about," Jimmy began. "Anna just got back from the doctor...." He glanced at her smiling face and then back at PJ... "she's expecting."

"That's awesome news!" PJ congratulated.

"Thanks," Anna said sincerely. "We have a long way to go; it's still early. That's why we don't want to tell anyone yet — anyone else, that is. My mom and Mike know about it; they're the only ones."

"I appreciate your trust in me. I promise not to tell a soul," PJ assured them. He sensed that there was something more. "Is there anything in particular that you want to pray about?"

Anna looked at Jimmy, and they exchanged a concerned glance. "Everything's fine, the baby is healthy, and I'm fine," she assured him. "We just have a different feeling about this pregnancy," they looked at each other again, and Jimmy took hold of her hand... "we both do," she added.

"It's not an ominous feeling or anything bad," Jimmy quickly added. "We just want to ask God to keep Anna and the baby strong ... and safe."

PJ knew not to dismiss one of Jimmy's premonitions, especially one about his own child. He quietly nodded and looked at both of them, then leaned forward and took their hands while they held each other's.

" Lord, thank you for this blessed news. Children are a heritage of the Lord, and we give you praise for this new child.

"We ask for your strong hand of protection on Anna and the baby. Keep them safe from harm from any dangers or unforeseen threats that may arise. We know you are our strong tower, our rock and shield.

"May this child come to love you and to know your love. May he be strong in faith and held in your hand all the days of his life. Use him in remarkable ways to turn many hearts toward you.

"We commend him to your care, along with little VJ, Anna, and Jimmy. We know that, whatever happens, you are faithful and good, and you care for your own with a strong arm and a tender hand. We pray your blessings upon them in the days to come."

"AMEN..." they all said together in agreement.

"Him... *or her...*" Anna added with a smile as they finished.

"Double Amen," Jimmy agreed with a laugh.

"SPEAKING OF VJ, there he goes now," Anna said in response to their young son's cries from upstairs.

She excused herself and headed up to nurse him.

PJ turned to Jimmy as she left the room, speaking quietly as he changed the subject. "I'm concerned about Rad. It might be his life's greatest regret if he doesn't talk to his father before the execution."

The mention of that coming night, now so near, sent a small jolt through Jimmy. He did his best to push away the thoughts of what he'd seen and recorded in his journal about it. PJ sensed his reaction.

"What is it? What have you seen?" PJ probed.

Chozeq's familiar charge echoed for the hundredth time in Jimmy's head: *'Tell no one....'*

"Sorry..., I still can't believe Chase is being executed," he offered in explanation. It was actually the execution's rapidly approaching *date* that rattled him, but he couldn't reveal that to PJ.

"I'd like to visit Chase myself," Jimmy said honestly.

"I'll be there on Friday for my weekly visit. You can come along if you'd like."

"Thanks. Maybe Pete could try talking to Rad," Jimmy suggested as the thought struck him.

"Not a bad idea. He needs to be careful, though; Rad's not the same these days — he's pretty bitter," PJ warned. Jimmy didn't need the warning; he already had a pretty good idea of what Rad was capable of.

"I can take Pete up there tomorrow if that works for him," PJ offered.

"Sure, I'll confirm with Pete. He'll probably want to leave after the cows are milked."

"Right," PJ smiled, looking at the small pitcher of cream on the table. "After all this time, I still have trouble picturing you guys as farmers."

LATER THAT EVENING, Jimmy and Anna watched the evening news. It showed the usual scenes of war and famine, which had become increasingly commonplace.

The night's major headline was that Congress passed a national **moratorium on death penalties**. President Nero was shown signing the bill, to great fanfare as the reporter described the scene....

The new law takes effect at the end of the month, Too late for a few unfortunate death row inmates whose executions are scheduled before then.

Jimmy's thoughts immediately returned to Chase. The events surrounding the night he is executed had rushed closer; they were suddenly only days away.

JIMMY WAS WRESTLING with the mix of emotions caused by that news when an image on the screen seized his attention even more profoundly. He leaned forward attentively and grabbed the remote, raising the volume higher....

The Iraqi National Museum in Baghdad reported that an attempted robbery was foiled last night when museum guards apprehended a team of internationally known burglars.

Their target appears to have been several ancient artifacts, including the amulet pictured here, which was at the center of dramatic events in Washington DC several years ago. That incident, you may remember, involved the attempted murder of a newborn infant along with dramatic *manifestations* that injured then-President Sheen of the United States. Experts are still unable to explain those events.

The museum has confirmed that the pendant remains safe and secure under the protection of robust security measures.

"Is that..." Anna began to ask.

"...The amulet of Baal Grimoire," Jimmy answered her unfinished question. His mind was suddenly filled with scenes from the night at Bahal's Glass Cathedral when Jimmy banished Moloch, the ancient demon prince. This triggered another scene that he couldn't mention —where he learned of Bahal's plans to steal that same amulet again in the future. It was a safe bet that Bahal was behind this attempt.

"That night was pretty scary—all that stuff at the Glass Cathedral," Anna said, shuddering.

"It was pretty amazing," Jimmy replied, feeling a thrill as he considered those events. He could imagine what his new friend Jonathan Edwards would have said if he'd been there to see that. The thought made him laugh to himself. Anna rolled her eyes, assuming that her husband was reveling in memories of his macho heroics — which he was.

The Township of Old Freehold, New Jersey —
August 30, 1741...

AFTER PREACHING HIS POWERFUL SERMON, 'Sinners in the Hands of an Angry God,' in Enfield and again at his own church in Northampton, Edwards was called upon to deliver it again a month later at William Tennent's church in Freehold, New Jersey. Each time he preached it, the effect upon his audience was equally powerful. In Freehold, the people were particularly moved. Many cried out while others flung themselves upon the altar, weeping loudly in repentance.

THE NEXT DAY, Edwards sat with Reverend Tennent and a pair of rare visitors. Although rarely all together in the same place, the four men had come to consider each other dear friends. Jimmy was humbled to be among them and especially honored to be considered a friend by these giants of the faith. Sitting there with them was a wonder on many levels, time travel notwithstanding.

William Tennent recounted the prior night's events, which Edwards humbly declined to describe himself.

"I dare say, George, it was a sermon to rival any of your own," William recounted admiringly to Whitefield. "Many in the audience were powerfully moved, and I am grateful to say that there were many in attendance who are not in a regular habit of attending the church; they seemed to be greatly affected as well."

"Well, I will say it was quite a fervent gathering," Edwards admitted. "The crowds were becoming a bit corybantic, I'm afraid."

Jimmy looked at Edwards, slightly confused, prompting Whitefield to lean nearer and speak in his ear, "The people were a bit wild 'n frenzied," he explained with a smile.

Whitefield looked back to Edwards, assuring him it was nothing to be concerned about.

"I have witnessed such things many times; it is nothing less than a move of God upon the soul.

"Back in England, the church clergy thought it a shameful thing for people to be so moved; they all but drove me from the country for it. Doubtless, there are some in large crowds who merely are carried away with the emotion of it all, I'll admit. But those who condemn it altogether cast aside the wheat along with the chaff."

"I agree," Jimmy added. "If you'd seen some of the things I have, you'd hardly believe it. I expect that Heaven will be a little — how did you say it...? — corybantic. Think of the multitudes from every nation, tribe, and tongue falling on their faces and casting golden crowns before the throne in worship. That doesn't seem very 'calm and stayed' to me."

Whitefield slapped him on the back with a broad smile, "Amen!"

William felt a warm thrill in his soul as he remembered his own experience among Heaven's worshiping throngs; Jimmy could see the hint of it in his friend's eyes as he considered his own memory of it.

Edwards conceded Whitefield's point with a smile. He pointed toward Jimmy as he looked to Tennent, "Speaking of crowns to be earned, I suspect we might still convince Jim here to consider that faculty position."

Whitefield and Tennent looked at Jimmy with a subtle tilt of their heads, expressing their curiosity.

Jimmy could feel his face redden slightly. The prospects for him to ever assume such a role were slim, to say the least. Now, even more so, after hearing Anna's news about their newly expected child.

"I... I don't think that's ever going to happen. That is, I mean, it's a wonderful invitation... one that I would be grateful to take if I could. It's just... there are complications."

Whitefield leaned forward and gripped his knees with an ardent gaze toward each of them, "Then let us pray for God's intervention to remove such encumbrances."

With that, he began to lead the men in earnest prayer. Jimmy closed his eyes to join them, surprised and admittedly uncomfortable over the subject of their request to God. Given the caliber of faith these particular men possessed, he had to admit that he wondered if God might say yes.

⌘

31

PREPARE

"But you are not in darkness, brothers, for that day to surprise you like a thief."
~ *1 Thessalonians 5:1-6*

STOCKSLOCK PENITENTIARY — EARLY FEBRUARY...
Ten Days Ago

"It was half-past ten in the morning as PJ and Jimmy entered the prison chapel. Chase waited alone for them there; the regular Friday chapel meeting didn't start until 11:00. Other inmates would begin filing in around five minutes before that.

They found Chase kneeling at the chapel's bare altar — a low, elevated platform with no altar rail. He had a peaceful expression when he turned and stood to welcome them.

"Jim, it's great to see you, my friend," he said in greeting, wrapping his arm over Jimmy's shoulders as they shook hands. "I appreciate ya comin' out, I really do."

Jimmy hadn't visited Chase in over a year — probably longer. He was struck by how much older he looked; in fact, it was exactly how he looked in Jimmy's vision of *that* night. The truth of it added to the tangibility of what was happening. In all of the travels recorded in his journal, it had become clear that the night of Chase's execution would mark the beginning of a flurry of events that will send the world racing toward the End of the Age. The speed with which those events were now gathering was sobering.

"Pete went with me to see Rad," PJ revealed carefully, sensitive to how much Chase wanted to see his son one last time. "He agreed to come on the 15th. We'll arrive in the late afternoon. Warden Grey arranged for you to have dinner together in one of the small dining rooms; you'll be able to talk there in private."

The 15th was the date of the execution. PJ had arranged for Chase to spend his last few hours with his son.

Chase wiped a grateful tear from the corner of his eye and grabbed PJ in a heartfelt embrace. "That means an awful lot, brother... ain't words enough t' say thanks."

He reached into the pocket of his prison overalls and pulled out an envelope. Jimmy recognized it, and his throat suddenly tightened.

"I wrote this letter for Radison. I'd appreciate it if you could wait till after... you know, then give it to him."

"You have my word," PJ promised.

IT WASN'T LONG BEFORE MORE men arrived for the chapel service. The number of men attending PJ's Friday meetings hadn't diminished since the Firestorm and revival that swept the prison eight years ago.

While PJ was leading the meeting, Chase privately leaned closer to Jimmy....

"Can I talk to ya... in the back?"

"S-sure," Jimmy answered uncertainly. He followed Chase along the outside wall to the back of the chapel. Chase waited beside the back wall for Jimmy to join him.

"There's somethin' I gotta ask ya... I think you're the only one who can maybe answer it. I didn't wanna say it in front of anybody else."

"OK, sure. I'll help if I can," Jimmy promised.

"It's about a dream," Chase explained. "It started about a month ago when I had it two or three times, but for the past week, I've been havin' it every night.

"It's always the same... It starts out beautiful. I'm in a golden city — it shines like the sun! There's a feeling like warm sunlight on my shoulders, and I feel a comfortable breeze on my face that smells like fruit blossoms and clean, pure air, like nothin' I ever knew before, especially here. I'm looking out on a scene that's indescribable, with crystal clear rivers and lush forests that look like they stretch on forever.

"As I'm standin' there, I hear a loud blast of music — like trumpets announcing a king, ya know? Then, everything is dark all-a-sudden, followed by a bright flash of light, and the next thing I know, I'm flyin' up into the sky, and there are people with me — thousands at first, and then it grows to millions in the blink of an eye.

"I start to recognize people I know — guys from here at the prison, even guys I know aren't alive anymore. That's when it gets to the confusin' part. As I'm meetin' people, I come face to face with this guy who's older. He's old-fashioned-looking, dressed like Washington and Franklin; I can tell he's from the olden days. Then the guy hugs me, and it becomes clear who he is... he's you."

JIMMY FOLLOWED THE SCENE CLEARLY, confident that it was a dream about the Rapture. He was about to explain that Chase was probably experiencing it from the perspective of one of the resurrected saints— those who are 'dead in Christ' who rise first. But the last thing Chase says unexpectedly hits Jimmy between the eyes. *'He's old-fashioned looking... he's you.'* Those words repeated in his head as new questions swirled in his mind.

As his thoughts began to clear again, he heard Chase still talking to him. "Man, I've read enough about the Rapture to know that that's what it was," he explains. "But the part about you being so much older and from back in time really threw me. What d'ya think it means?"

"Well, for one thing, it means we're both there at the Last Trumpet call — that's good," Jimmy joked. He hesitated before giving a more serious answer... "Chase, I think God gave you that dream as a message for *me*. I can't explain it any better than that right now. But just know it's a message I needed more than you could imagine. Thanks for sharing it!"

Jimmy gave him a hug and a slap on the back.

"Yup, that's the hug!" Chase said with a smile, recalling how they hugged in his dream.

BEFORE THEY HEADED BACK to their seats, Jimmy motioned for Chase to wait. "Chase, I want to let you know that God has His hand on Radison. He has a plan for him. I know you've wanted to see him find the Lord more than anything. I can tell you this... keep trusting God; it'll happen in His timing... you may not get to see it, but it *will* happen."

A tear welled in Chase's eye. He held onto Jimmy as he quietly thanked him, "Thanks for that word, man... thanks."

WASHINGTON DC...
Eight Days Ago

PRESIDENT NERO STOOD behind a forest of microphones as he addressed reporters at the White House. A group of elementary and High School students stood behind him, along with a large contingent of teachers and school administrators.

"My administration takes seriously the unity of our nation. There is no challenge more important to me than the unity of our citizens. In pursuit of this goal, I am announcing a new initiative in all of the country's public schools: we are introducing a new curriculum that fosters inclusion and acceptance among people of all faiths and ideologies. Students will be taught to reject divisive prejudices and hold to a common faith in the goodness of humanity. We seek a worldwide unity of all faiths, upholding the rights of people everywhere to worship as they choose without pressure or coercion. Those who reject this premise and continue to teach otherwise will be called to account."

Anna shook her head as she watched the President on TV.

"Talk about coercion... what does he think his own initiative will do if not coerce people into bowing to his ideas?"

"That's the whole point," Jimmy noted. "They want to demonize others for doing the very thing they're doing themselves. It's classic."

"It's sad," Anna bemoaned. "I thought the country had learned something from everything that happened under Athaliah. It seems like we're heading right back down the same path."

"We've had a reprieve for the past few years," Jimmy shared, "but we're still in the last days. I have a feeling things are going to get worse from here."

Anna looked at Jimmy, studying his eyes briefly before conceding his point. "I just worry about VJ and our new baby. What will the world be like for them?"

Jimmy didn't answer — struggling instead with a flurry of images from countless travels and premonitions. He just took Anna's hand and held it between his. The prayer that he silently breathed wasn't just for themselves — it was for Anna's mom and Uncle Mike, Pete and Angela and their baby daughter, Caden and Nyle, PJ and Baibina, and countless others. Dark days were approaching — maybe the darkest ever known.

WASHINGTON DC...
Six Days Ago

LEYLA ATHALIAH MAJEDAH was escorted into the President's Cabinet room with all the pomp and esteem of a foreign dignitary. She was dressed in flowing robes with a tall collar that rose at the back of her head and was flanked by Senator Sammu-Ramat Ahmadi, and several of her trusted Priestesses. Members of her personal security detail took their posts beside the door.

President Nero welcomed her, offering her the floor for remarks.

"Thank you for your kind invitation, Mr. President," Leyla began with a grateful nod. "As you know, your predecessor overlooked a terrible injustice seven years ago when he did not prosecute the one responsible for the former First Lady's murder. The danger of that oversight has now been brought into grave clarity by the recent events in the Middle East. We have seen what these alien powers are capable of.

"James Moretti's known involvement with otherworldly beings is a risk to this nation and the world. It is our assessment that he must be detained and properly interrogated in the interests of international harmony and national security. It is most important that an example be set for any others who may be sympathetic with the alien beings."

President Nero nodded that he understood, accepting Leyla's

remarks as though they were orders rather than requests. He turned to his Attorney General.

"Launch an investigation at once, but do it quietly. We don't want to repeat the mistake of letting Mr. Moretti slip away into hiding this time. I want a report in one week outlining all we know about him and recommendations for action."

Leyla glanced at Sammu, whose eyes narrowed as she gave a sly smile and nodded appreciatively.

THE LIVING SPRINGS CHURCH, CENTER SPRINGS...
Sunday morning, Four Days Ago

THERE WAS ALWAYS excitement in the air whenever it was Jimmy's turn to preach, not because he was particularly eloquent but because unusual things tended to happen whenever he was in the pulpit. This time, the feeling that weighed on Jimmy wasn't excitement; it might be better described as concern. He was beginning to understand how Jonathan Edwards felt under his relentless burden to warn people about Hell.

The warning in his heart wasn't about Hell, but it was just as urgent. It was about being ready for the Lord's coming at a time when it had become palpably imminent. He hadn't shaken the dream that Chase shared with him.

He usually opened every message with informal remarks — often a joke or a personal story. It was uncharacteristic for him when he approached the podium this time and immediately began to read the scripture text for his message, skipping any introductory remarks. The verses were displayed on the church's large screen as he read them aloud:

Now, concerning the times and the seasons, brothers, you have
no need to have anything written to you. For you your-
selves are fully aware that the day of the Lord will come

like a thief in the night. While people are saying, "There is
peace and security," then sudden destruction will come
upon them as labor pains come upon a pregnant woman,
and they will not escape.
   But you are not in darkness, brothers, for that day to surprise
you like a thief. For you are all children of light, children
of the day. We are not of the night or of the darkness. So
then let us not sleep, as others do, but let us keep awake
and be sober.
1 Thessalonians 5:1-6

He stood looking at his notes for a moment, but the notes were not the only thing on his mind — he was contemplating a range of images along with the burning message that blazed in his spirit. The congregation could feel his passion even in the silence, and anticipation grew stronger by the moment. He quietly walked away from the podium and stepped down from the platform, standing directly in front of the audience.

"Seven years ago, our country experienced a brush with evil that brought us to the brink of history — not just the history of our country but human history. We were delivered from those days by God's mercy and due to the prayers of millions around the globe. For seven years, we have seen a reprieve from the days of trouble.

"As we sit here today, however, it is becoming increasingly clear that this reprieve is ending. The days of golden harvests and revival are drawing to a close. The implications of this could not be more profound for the church — and, by extension, for the world.

"All of you are close friends. We've been through a lot together."

He looked across the audience with a burning conviction, imploring them to listen carefully...

"FRIENDS... the coming of the Lord is at hand!

There were a few subtle gasps from some who were surprised by the declaration, combined with scattered shouts of praise and amen.

"I don't say that lightly, and I'm not date-setting or trying to make any new prediction. The Bible has given us all the predictions needed. Jesus urged us to be awake — to look at the seasons! Paul told the Thessalonians that the church would not be surprised by Christ's coming if they *stayed awake*. God does not intend for His church to encounter His coming like a thief — it's the unbelieving world that will see His coming that way, not the church."

He turned and pointed at the scripture verses still displayed, reading verse four:

> 'You are not in darkness, brothers, for that day to surprise you
> like a thief...'

"What was the Apostle Paul saying? He was saying that the church would have every opportunity to anticipate Christ's coming by looking at the signs. The Rapture will not be a Heavenly *surprise attack*, as if the church is a conquest that Jesus wants to overthrow. The Rapture is not a lottery for a few lucky winners.

"Think about it — it is the Lord's call to His marriage feast... the Marriage Supper of the Lamb. It will be the greatest day of rejoicing in all of eternity! He *wants* His bride to be ready, and He has given us all we need in order to know when to look up. The signs of His coming are given to us so we'll have the best possible chance of being ready.

"What are the signs?"

A LIST FLASHED onto the auditorium's large screen, a line at a time as Jimmy referred to them:

- - **"The dry bones reborn** — Israel's return to nationhood after eighteen hundred years. Check that off; it's done!
- - "Increased **earthquakes**... Check.
- - "People will be bewildered by **roaring seas and storms**... Check.

- - "**Wars** and rumors of wars… Check.
- - "**Famines**… Check.
- - "**False Christs and False Prophets** with cults that lead people astray… Check, check, check.
- - "**Evil** shall **increase**…
- - "**Many will hate** and devour one another…
- - "The **love** of many will **wax cold**…
- - "**Deception and delusion** will come over the world's population…
- - "**Believers** will be **hated** and persecuted…
- - "The **Gospel is preached** throughout the **entire world**…

"All of these things have happened or are happening now.

"IN ADDITION TO THESE, we can also see prophetically significant events looming on the horizon:

- - "The coming together of the **World's Governments** under one banner,
- - "A global currency that allows **control over commerce**,
- - "Armies massing against **Israel**.

"It sounds like the evening news, doesn't it? Friends, it's time to look up — our redemption is drawing nigh!

JIMMY CONTINUED to preach for the next forty minutes, expounding on prophetic texts throughout scripture and tying them to current events. He didn't have to mention any of his travels or the things recorded in his journal — he had a feeling that those would be revealed soon enough. Plenty of evidence was already mounting that people could see for themselves in their everyday lives. By the time he finished, most of the church was gathered around the altar, recommitting themselves, powerfully moved to tears, either for themselves or with burdens for others who still needed Christ.

PJ and Reverend Wilkes joined Jimmy to pray with those who had come forward. Jenna, one of the girls in the youth group, was kneeling with tears streaking her face as Jimmy placed his hand on her shoulder.

The moment he touched her, she looked up at him through wet eyes that burned with urgency. The words she spoke struck him powerfully—like a declaration from God's own heart. From the way they seized his spirit, Jimmy knew with an inward certainty that her words were a message from the Holy Spirit—a message just for him….

> *"Prepare! Prepare to leave! Your work is great in the calling to which you are sent. Don't be afraid; your family will be safe where I am sending you. You will be leaving soon! You must prepare!"*

⌘

32

INITIATION

"Don't be afraid; your family will be safe in the place I am sending you."

Center Springs...
Sunday afternoon, later the same day

Jimmy was quiet as he sat on the floor beside Anna in their farmhouse living room. A cold wind whistled in the chimney as he laid another log on the fire. Anna could see that something was on his mind and knew him well enough to understand that it wouldn't do any good to try getting him to share it. She reasoned that it likely had something to do with his work with the church or with PJ at the City Mission.

In fact, he struggled with how to share with her the confusing jumble of clues he'd been getting. For almost ten years now, he'd been faithful to his vow not to share anything about his travels with anyone —not even her. But Jenna's words at the altar still burned in his heart: *'Your family will be safe in the place I am sending you.'*

The implication was hard for him to understand — it implied that wherever he was being sent, Anna would be going with him. Somehow, he knew without a doubt that it would not be a temporary assignment. He felt an undeniable conviction that this would not be like his other travels. Ultimately, wherever they were going would be a permanent move — at some point, they wouldn't be coming back.

He distractedly closed his eyes and rested a hand on the bridge of his nose as he silently breathed a prayer for help. Anna recognized the familiar gesture and could sense the depth of his struggle, feeling a burden growing in her own heart as well. Although she didn't know what she was praying for, she took hold of Jimmy's hand and closed her eyes, joining him in prayer.

Jimmy accepted her hand gratefully and was about to lead them in prayer together, but she beat him to it, praying with an urgency that had begun to well up in her soul.

> "Lord, you guide our steps and enlighten our path.
> You're the God who cares for us and is moved by our
> distress and weakness. We trust you because you
> have always shown yourself trustworthy.
> "We ask you to show us your will. Enlighten the path before
> us today and make our hearts strong to follow it."

As she prayed, the sudden sound of goats bleating interrupted her words. Along with a sense that their surroundings had brightened — they felt the warmth of sunshine engulfing them. The change was so sudden that it startled her. She opened her eyes and looked around wide-eyed, completely astonished.

Jimmy was accustomed to sudden changes like this, but Anna had never experienced anything like it before. What astonished Jimmy was that she was experiencing it along with him.

Anna was breathless. "Wh-where...? Those aren't our goats. I-it's summer. What's happening?"

A loud voice in the distance caught Jimmy's attention — it was a voice he'd recognize anywhere, George Whitefield's voice. He turned around, following the sound, and realized they were seated at the edge of a vast crowd that covered the gradually sloping hillside above them. Whitefield was at the top of the hill, almost half a mile away. The crowd was spellbound as he bellowed and gestured like a trained actor on a stage, except his words carried a powerful spiritual anointing like few they'd ever heard.

JIMMY GRABBED Anna's hand and rose to his feet, tugging her along beside him as he began to make his way closer. He led her through the enthralled crowds, weaving among many who were deeply moved with tears streaking their faces. Anna was as confused by the crowds as she was by the sunshine; the people were dressed in historic-era clothes as if they were all in some enormous costume party. She recognized their outfits from pictures and movies but couldn't imagine where they'd gotten a wardrobe large enough to dress them all — there were thousands of them.

By the time they neared the top, Anna was as enthralled as everyone else by Whitefield's sermon. She stared at the famous preacher as Jimmy led her around behind the small platform that served as his pulpit. Whitefield noticed his younger friend and gave Jim a wink as they passed him.

The sermon continued for nearly an hour longer, and then the throngs of convicted souls who flooded around them for prayer remained for an hour beyond that. Jimmy joined in praying with as many as he could, leading great numbers of them to the Lord with Anna at his side.

When the press of desperate souls finally waned, Whitefield came alongside them and slapped Jimmy on the back in a warm greeting. "You're a blessed sight, Lad. Thank ye for thy help in prayin' for these dear souls."

"Glad to help. Your message was brilliant."

"Ah. Well then, the Lord's brilliance has done it," Whitefield said humbly. He looked at Anna and held out his hand in greeting.

"Oh, right. This is Anna... my wife," Jimmy introduced.

"Mrs. Moretti, it is the greatest pleasure to meet thee at last. I can see why Jim is inclined to leave us so quickly. It is no surprise that he would desire to return at once to thy company."

Anna was speechless. They were speaking as if they knew each other — as if nothing about this astonishing scene was the least bit unusual. She imagined she must be dreaming.

"She's just a little overcome with all of this," Jimmy offered in explanation, placing his arm around her supportively. "Anna, meet Reverend Whitefield... George Whitefield."

Anna's mouth dropped open as she heard his name. Before she could ask a question, they heard another voice call out...

"Twas a wondrous crowd; such a marvelous work the Lord is doing!"

"Reverend Tennent, it's good to see you," Jimmy said as he offered his hand to the approaching man.

"Such formality! Call me William if ye please. Thou art a friend and no stranger, Jim."

Jimmy introduced Anna, who appeared even more overwhelmed by each thing she saw. Reverend Tennent greeted her with a friendly smile and a gracious nod and then spread his arms toward all of them.

"Ye must all lunch with us. Come!" He placed his hand on Jimmy's shoulder and added, "Me thinks we have catching up to do with thee lad." He gave Whitefield a wink as he said it, prompting the preacher to let loose a hearty laugh.

"Tis true indeed," Whitefield agreed. "As I recall, thy departure from our last meeting was characteristically abrupt."

"Come...," Tennent repeated in invitation, "...we can discuss it over a warm meal."

Tennent and Whitefield walked ahead, quickly engrossed in conversation. Anna tugged Jimmy's arm to slow their pace.

. . .

"Jimmy, where are we? What is this? How do you know these men? Are they really who they say... how could that be?"

Jimmy sympathized with her distress, remembering how fearful and confused he felt the first time he traveled himself. He spoke softly in her ear to avoid being overheard.

"I can't explain it right now, but I will, I promise. Just trust that it's something God is doing; God has a purpose in it. Don't say anything about where we're from, especially what year it is. As far as they know, we belong in this time and place."

"We belong...?" Anna repeated in confusion. "What year do you think it is?"

Jimmy scanned their surroundings and momentarily studied Whitefield and Tennent, gauging their ages. "I'm guessing it's around 1741 or '42," he answered.

Anna's eyes widened. "Seventeen-forty-what?!" She exclaimed in a loud voice.

Jimmy shushed her and looked sheepishly at Whitefield and Tennent, who had turned to look at them. "Sorry, we were just discussing a family matter. Everything's fine."

The men chuckled and continued with their conversation.

Jimmy spoke softly to Anna, looking her in the eyes. "Believe me, I understand how confusing this must seem. I promise I'll explain everything the best I can as soon as we're back home. Please trust me, trust the Lord!"

Anna's eyes widened again as a new thought struck her. "VJ...! He's home alone!"

Jimmy sighed, realizing things were getting harder to explain by the minute. The fact that VJ was not with them was what convinced him they'd be returning home — this was not the permanent move he'd been struggling with. He decided to level with her the best he could, even if it meant violating Chozeq's charge. She was right here with him, after all. At least for the moment, she was a traveler, too.

"Anna," he said tenderly, leaning closer. "Do you remember those times when you were holding my hand or leaning on my shoulder and felt something strange? You said it felt like I was gone for a second."

The panic in her expression softened a little. A whole series of those moments came to her mind; it had happened more often than she could count over their years together. She remembered that it seemed like he was gone and then back again in a split second. She slowly nodded her head as it dawned on her.

Jimmy nodded in confirmation as he saw her piecing it together. "I was traveling at those times… just like this right now. Some of those travels lasted for whole days, but it was like no time at all had passed when I got back.

"VJ will be fine — he'll be right where we left him; it'll be like we never even left."

"This is what you…?" she said as it struck her. "All those times? Why didn't you tell me?"

Jimmy held back a laugh. "Would you have believed me?" He squeezed her hand gently to reassure her of what he was saying. "There's more I need to tell you about this, but I can't right now. Please trust me?"

She nodded, still feeling dizzy from it all. He waited a minute for her to collect herself, then nodded toward the widening gap between them and the others. She drew a deep breath and put on a brave face; then, they raced together to rejoin them.

THE TENNENTS' home was a comfortable farmhouse on a large plot of land. It was owned by the church, but William and his wife Catharine operated it as their own as their means of support.

Anna was introduced to Mrs. Tennent and offered to help her in the kitchen. "Please call me Catharine. Mrs. Tennent makes me feel old," she offered with a friendly smile. "William is quite impressed with your husband," she said as they worked together. "What do you think of his invitation to join the new college?"

"New college?" Anna replied, caught off guard. "I'm… not sure."

"Still praying about it, I see. William is perfectly obsessed with it;

he prays for it most every day. It is a large decision for both of you, no doubt. I can see clearly why you need time to consider it."

She gave Anna a friendly smile. "Having husbands in the ministry is surely an adventure at times, isn't it."

"Yes, you have no idea," Anna replied distractedly.

"Is it my understanding that you have a child?" Catharine asked warmly. It was a favorite topic of hers.

"Yes, a son. He's nineteen months old." Anna went on without thinking, adding, "...and one on the way." She placed a hand on her stomach.

Catharine put down the utensils she was holding and placed her hands on Anna's shoulders. "Oh! That's wonderful, my dear, simply wonderful! Congratulations!"

Anna smiled, feeling comfortably at home with the kind-hearted woman. "Thanks," she beamed with a smile.

Mrs. Tennent returned to pealing her potatoes, and Anna returned to slicing carrots as their conversation turned to stories of the Tennent children. It soon became apparent that Catharine was a marvelous storyteller.

THE MEN WERE ENGAGED in a serious conversation in the home's small parlor.

"Not a day has passed since our last meeting when I have not prayed for God's arranging to bring thee here," Tennent revealed.

"To that, I can attest," Whitefield joined in. "He has us both praying for the same."

Jimmy looked at the two of them uncomfortably. "It's still more complicated than you could imagine. Even if we *could* make such a move here, there's Anna's mother and my uncle, and my ministry, of course.

"Besides, where would we live? We wouldn't know the first thing about living in... well, here."

"I understand thy concern, truly I do," Tennent shared. "The decision to uproot one's family from their familiar home is a difficult one. It is a calling that men in ministry are often called to do."

"Aye, I can attest to that for a certainty," Whitefield agreed soberly. "But surely ye are accustomed to traveling. Thy recent travels throughout these colonies have been as extensive as mine."

Jimmy felt guilty at the comparison. He hadn't been called to make sacrifices that were anything like the ones Whitefield had made. Jimmy hadn't given up any of his own life at all. His recent words to Anna rang in his ears: *'It was like I never even left.'* He sat quietly, tormented by the thought.

Anna was smiling and laughing as she emerged just then with Mrs. Tennent from the kitchen. She was obviously enjoying their conversation a great deal.

The seriousness of the men's conversation changed swiftly as the women joined them, turning to talk of farming, festivals, and local customs. In fact, Anna seemed more at home in their unlikely surroundings than Jimmy, despite all of his previous visits.

Jimmy quietly admired his wife's comfortable expression—she was genuinely enjoying herself. He wondered whether she'd feel the same if their move here became permanent. He breathed a silent prayer for God's help in this crazy situation. It seemed like it must be the hundredth time he'd prayed about it in recent days. Unfortunately for Jimmy, each time he prayed about it, the situation grew more complicated.

⌘

33

THE STRANGER

"Trust in the Lord, and get ready for the adventure of your life."

CENTER SPRINGS...
Later Sunday Afternoon, Four Days Ago

Jimmy and Anna said goodbye to Whitefield and the Tennents after their lunch. Just as Jimmy had predicted, they found themselves back in their living room as soon as they were out of sight of the Tennent's farmhouse. The fireplace crackled with the freshly placed log that Jimmy had just added before they left. As expected, it was as though no time at all had passed.

Anna's eyes flashed with excitement. "WOW! That was *aMazing!*" she exclaimed, barely able to contain her enthusiasm. "I can't believe you've been doing that for all this time! Where else have you gone? Is it always to the seventeen hundreds?"

Jimmy considered his reply carefully. He'd never discussed his travels with anyone except Amos, a traveler himself. He had to admit that what happened today with Anna now made her one as well.

"It's called traveling," he began carefully. "Remember that Journal from Amos? He was a traveler too; that's how he saw all those things about the drought and the events that happened a few years ago."

"Wait, Amos traveled like that to the future?" Anna said as the thought hit her. Did you meet him? Have you done that, too? Have you seen the future?"

Jimmy reluctantly nodded yes. The pace of her questions accelerated.

"Yes, what...," she clarified, "yes, you met him, or yes, you've seen the future?"

"Both," he answered carefully.

"Wow! What did you see?"

Jimmy looked at her silently for a moment, looking for a way to slow her down.

"Look, I know how exciting this is for you," he said, taking hold of both her hands. "But I'm not sure what I can share right now. Please understand."

Anna grew quiet as she looked into his eyes, sensing that some of what he'd seen still troubled him. She sat thinking for a minute and then spoke more softly. "Reverend Tennent really wants you to take that job at the college. Catharine said he prays for it every day. Do you think that's even possible — could you be there all the time like that?"

Jimmy didn't answer; he looked down at their joined hands, afraid to make eye contact.

"I suppose if God wants you there, He can do it — He can do anything," Anna offered on her own. She paused as another thought came to her, quietly asking... "Is that what you were praying about earlier this afternoon... before we... traveled?"

He nodded yes.

ANNA WAS quiet for a moment longer, then looked at him... "Why me? Why did God send *me* with you this time?"

Later That Night

Anna's final question replayed in Jimmy's mind as he lay in bed, unable to sleep. The only answer that made sense was the one he already felt in his soul. God was preparing Anna for the thing that Jenna prophesied. He no longer wondered where they'd be going — it seemed obvious now, but he struggled with everything that needed to be prepared. What would become of the farm? Who should he tell about the secret passage and the provisions? What about his Journal — who was that supposed to go to?

He considered a future meeting he'd foreseen with Radison — how would that happen if he was already gone?

That thought reminded him of Chase's execution date, which was fast approaching... it was now only three days away. He pondered the dream that Chase described during his recent visit to the prison. Events since then confirmed his theory of why Chase had seen both of them in resurrected bodies. It seemed unbelievable to think that he and Anna could be home with the Lord for *hundreds of years* by the time that dream is fulfilled.

The verses from First Thessalonians chapter four replayed in his mind... *'The dead in Christ will rise first...'* it stirred his soul as he thought of it.

All of these swirling thoughts made it impossible to sleep. He quietly climbed out of bed and made his way downstairs. The fireplace was dark, but a few small embers still glowed in its warm ashes behind the fireplace screen. He sat in the dark room replaying the afternoon's events until he was exhausted by them, exhausted but still unable to sleep.

The cold living room made him shiver. He grabbed a scarf from the coat rack and wrapped it around his neck, rubbing his arms to warm himself. Soon, he was in the kitchen placing the teakettle on the stove. He usually didn't drink Anna's herbal tea but tried some this time, hoping it could help him sleep.

. . .

A SHORT WHILE LATER, he sat at the old kitchen table, grateful for the hot mug in his hands. His eyes closed in prayer in a familiar reflex as his heart readily sought the Lord in the room's quiet.

A voice suddenly broke the silence — it sounded like his father's. Jimmy opened his eyes quickly and was startled to see a familiar-looking man standing across the room from him. The man was dressed in eighteenth-century attire, wearing a linen shirt with frills and a waistcoat that was short in the front and long in the back. He was likely in his mid-to-late 70s; his gray hair was tied behind his head.

Jimmy had never seen this traveler before; he didn't recognize him from any of his travels until now. The stranger stepped nearer and took a seat opposite Jimmy at the table.

Although the old man's voice was like his father's, he looked more like he could be someone's grandfather.

"It's a tumultuous time, I know," the stranger began saying as he was taking a seat. "In a way, I envy you at this time in life. Savor each moment; cherish the time you have left here with your friends and those you love."

"Do you know how much time is left?" Jimmy asked, half expecting him to decline an answer.

The man paused for a moment as if debating what to say. He looked at Jimmy earnestly as he continued — emphasizing the importance of his message with the fire in his gaze.

"Be vigilant on the night that Chase is executed. That day is the keystone of your entire life. It connects and influences everything that happens before and after it. It's not by chance that it's the night you were shown when you first met Chozeq. Be sure and have things ready by then."

"That's three days from now," Jimmy noted nervously.

The stranger acknowledged his words with a simple nod. The look in his eyes was mostly business.

"Listen carefully," he said seriously. "When you go, be sure to bring your journal with you. There's more that needs to be recorded in it, a great deal more. When the time comes, it'll be PJ who it's entrusted to.

You'll need to retrieve it from the place where it's now hidden and put it where he's sure to find it."

"Now hidden?" Jimmy questioned. "It's in the root cellar, inside the secret door."

"That's the current copy of it, the one you need to bring with you. You'll find the final copy hidden deeper in the secret passage. It's under the staircase that leads to the old church; count twenty steps up from the bottom. That step is a slab that'll move if you pry it open. Underneath it is where you'll find the journal."

"The steps..." Jimmy repeated thoughtfully. "Are you the one who carved them?"

"I had a lot of help," he admitted. "Amos is the one responsible for the chest with provisions. The rest of it was prepared before he got there."

"You know Amos?" Jimmy asked with some surprise. "Are you the traveler who came before him?"

The stranger shrugged with a smile, "Before... after... I guess you can say it's both."

Jimmy was confused by his answer but figured he was just being evasive.

"What about the farm?" he asked.

"You'll need to deed the property to those you chose. The same is true for your trust fund — it'll be sorely needed after you're gone. Ward O'Malley will be a great help with the paperwork."

Jimmy was amazed at how well the stranger seemed to know important details about his life. "What other advice can you give? Will Anna and the kids be OK? Will they be safe and happy there?"

"They'll be happiest when you're with them; keep that in mind. Their lives are your greatest earthly treasure, as yours is theirs."

As he spoke those words, Jimmy sensed the genuine emotion in them. He stared at the man across the table as it suddenly dawned on him who the man was.

"You... you're ME."

The older man nodded in a humble gesture of admission. "We're going to do fine. Trust in the Lord, and get ready for the adventure of your life."

With that, Jimmy watched his older self fade from sight.

MONDAY MORNING, THREE DAYS AGO

JIMMY HADN'T SLEPT much but managed to catch a few hours before dawn. Anna let him sleep in while she took VJ downstairs for his breakfast.

"Gwood... mornin'..." Jimmy said through a yawn as he entered the kitchen a short while later.

"Restless night?" Anna asked understandingly. "I saw you weren't in bed; that was around midnight."

Jimmy poured a cup of coffee and kissed her good morning.

"Yeah. Couldn't sleep. I came down here and made some tea." He debated whether to tell her about his extraordinary overnight meeting, unable to make up his mind.

ANNA LOOKED him in the eyes. "When do you think we'll leave?" she asked, seemingly out of the blue.

"What?" Her question honestly threw him.

"God wants you there, I know it. I'm going too — wherever you go, I'm going there too," she said adamantly.

Jimmy leaned forward, speaking carefully. "The move could be permanent... I mean, it *is*... it'll be permanent this time. There won't be any more coming back."

Anna looked at him with a bold determination that barely masked the fear in her eyes. "I know. I've been feeling that too," she said, growing emotional as tears welled...

"I'm not letting you go without me... I'm not letting you go!"

Her tears began to run down her cheeks as she grew more impassioned... she stood suddenly and touched his shoulder imploringly...

"...Don't you dare go without us! ...Don't you dare!"

Jimmy took her in his arms and held her tightly as she buried her face against his shoulder and shook with sobs.

LATER MONDAY MORNING

"HI, UNCLE WARD," Jimmy said into the phone as Ward O'Malley answered. It was 9:00 AM West Coast time. "I need your help with some legal stuff. I need to change the trustee for the Christian Defense Fund; I want it to be you and Pastor Rodriguez."

Ward seemed caught off-guard by the request. "Are you sure you want to be removed? That's a lot of money."

"It's the Lord's money, not mine. It never was mine to begin with. Besides, you've always known better than me the best way to use it for the defense work. It needs to keep being used for that. I have a feeling things will be getting crazy again soon — it'll be needed more than ever."

Ward reluctantly agreed to the request, but nagging questions remained about why Jimmy was asking for the change. He finally stopped probing after the fifth or sixth try.

"There are a few other things," Jimmy said after they finally moved on. "We want to transfer the deed for the farm to Pete and Angela Murphy. Could you help us with the right paperwork?"

"Jimmy, what's going on?" Ward said, sounding more alarmed. "Are you guys all right? Are you in any danger?"

"We're fine, Uncle Ward. We're honestly fine. I can't get into the specifics, but this is something we feel led to do—we know it's what the Lord wants. We have a real peace about it."

After discussing what was needed for another ten minutes, Ward finally agreed.

"Thanks for your help with all this; we're really grateful."

"I'd do anything for you, Jim, you know that. How soon do you need this?"

"Right away. That's kind of important; it has to be in place before the 15th."

"That's in three days..." Ward said in surprise. "OK, I'll get right on it," he promised.

There was an awkward silence on the phone before Jimmy cleared his throat... "I wish we could get out there to see you guys. Can we do a video call, maybe tomorrow night?"

"Sure, Jimmy, whatever you want." Ward couldn't help but feel concerned about the direction of their conversation. He knew, though, that if anyone could be trusted to do the right thing, it was Jimmy and Anna.

"Great," Jimmy acknowledged. "I'll send a meeting link for tomorrow night."

ANNA NUDGED him on the arm with her coat on; there was fresh snow on her shoulders and in her hair.

"Pete could use a hand in the barn setting up," she informed him. "So far, forty people are coming. Mom and Mike said they'll help with cooking."

"You're amazing," Jimmy said as he stood and kissed her. "You're the only one I know who could arrange a dinner party in just one day in the dead of winter."

"We'll see how well it goes tomorrow night," she said, sharing her considerable doubts. "Getting people to come is the easy part when you have a husband who's famous."

"Yeah, right," Jimmy dismissed. "A famous former International Terrorist and occasional podcast host," he joked.

"And don't forget time-traveling prophet," she added quietly with a sly smile.

Pete's wife Angela walked in behind her carrying their daughter.

"Wow, look how big she's getting," Jimmy noted with a smile.

"She's almost sixteen months," Angela said with a smile as she jostled the toddler in her arms.

Anna turned her attention to the baby while Jimmy grabbed his coat and headed out to help Pete.

⌘

34

COMMENDED

"Anna and I have received an important calling ..."

CENTER SPRINGS — MID-FEBRUARY...
Two days ago

Jimmy made his way through the secret passage on a mission to find *'the Stranger's'* journal. That was still the best description for the previous night's visitor. It was certainly a strange meeting; he still had difficulty accepting that he'd met an older version of himself. Over his shoulder, he carried a shovel and a large pry bar, expecting that he might need them.

Finally reaching the second staircase, he counted the steps as he climbed, coming to the twentieth step. To his surprise, it was the step just above the landing for the underground room where the provisions were secured. He never noticed before that this step was laid in place rather than carved into the natural rock like all the others.

It was a large slab of stone, eight inches tall and twelve deep, as wide as the staircase. Positioning two of the lanterns nearby, he examined the edges, noticing that small gaps had been filled with dirt, making them blend in with the surrounding rock. He was able to scrape most of it away, leaving a clear outline of the slab.

Jimmy had his doubts about moving it alone. He breathed a prayer for help, thinking he could sure use a hand from someone as strong as Chozeq right then. When no physical help arrived, he finally inserted the tip of his heavy pry bar into the gap at the back of the slab, placed the handle of his shovel behind it for leverage, then put his shoulder against it and pushed with all his might.

To his surprise, it moved more easily than expected, sliding back about eight inches before stopping. Examining the opening with a lantern, he could see that it concealed a deeper trough nearly as wide as the staircase; the lamplight reflected off something down inside it.

He carefully reached for it, finding a remarkable glass box. It was thick and heavy and appeared to be molded by hand. It was sealed at one end with a glass lid latched like a mason jar lid. Jimmy held it in his hands and swept the dirt from its surface. He could see the book inside, over two hundred years old but still reasonably well preserved — it was his own journal.

HE CAUTIOUSLY UNLATCHED THE LID, which burped as it opened, and carefully let the familiar book slide out into his hand. His heart raced as he held the aged journal, running his fingers over the embossed initials that his mother had added to the cover: 'JMM.' Its pages were yellowed but still sturdy; although the ink was faded, it was still readable. He ran his thumb along the open edge, letting the pages flutter past, realizing that it was full from front to back with words crammed tightly all the way to its last page. He debated whether to read its entries, finally unable to resist.

The opening entry was familiar to him, although now dry and faded. Its description of the night PJ is stabbed was stirring as he read it. *That will happen on the night of Chase's execution — Tomorrow night,* he reminded himself soberly.

Thumbing further ahead, he came to an entry he hadn't written —

at least not yet. It was with a different kind of pen — a quill, he guessed.

It's been two weeks since we arrived. The Tennents' hospitality has been amazing; they've put us up in a new caretaker's house beside the new church. It's a few meager rooms with little in the way of furniture, but more than sufficient for our needs. Members of the church have been very generous with clothing and blankets. Our son has more than enough hand-sewn clothes to keep him warm and clean.

We don't miss our modern conveniences as much as I thought we would. The air here is fresh, and the water is clean. The apples and fruit are incredible. We have the sound of conversation instead of television and the company of friends rather than phone calls. We do miss indoor plumbing, but I have some ideas for addressing that.

My work here has already become busy. Preparations for the new college are being made, and much work is still needed. Besides that, the church constantly needs repairs, which I'm happy to make. Rev. Whitefield has invited me along for several of his upcoming rallies, and I have plans to visit Rev. Edwards this summer.

I confess I'd taken for granted the convenience of traveling in the angels' way of doing it. Transportation here is by horse or carriage; getting anywhere takes forever. I suppose that building myself a car might draw a little too much attention.

Jimmy skipped ahead, deciding it'd be better to discover the coming days by living them rather than by reading about them. The next entry was more sobering...

The question of whether I'd ever travel again was answered tonight. Chozeg's welcome face greeted me as I stood alone in the church foyer, preparing to close it for the night. However, the expression on his face gave me pause.

"Radison needs thy help," his booming voice declared.

"Radison! Can I still help him from here?"

"God has called thee here to a task — it does not mean He has abandoned thy other work. There is still much that ye must do in His service, both here and at the end of the age."

The account described the first of dozens or hundreds of travels. Jimmy scanned them in amazement, realizing it would take days to read them all.

He stood and thought momentarily, deciding on the best place to protect the old journal while ensuring PJ would find it. His eyes fell on the huge chest in front of him.

He retrieved the keys to the vault-like chest from his backpack and opened it. With the chest's lid raised, he opened its long metal cash box and carefully laid the extraordinary old journal inside, setting it in the removable tray that covered the box's remaining coins.

It occurred to Jimmy that he'd been making weekly visits to this secret chest for the past seven years. Despite its familiarity, the remarkable storage vault still amazed him. He thought of Amos and all the effort that his nineteenth-century friend had put into its preparation. The fact that he could soon be the one making preparations for Amos himself carried tremendous irony.

While he knelt, looking at it, another thought struck him. He carefully unzipped the compartment in his backpack that contained Amos' journal and pulled it out, running his hand over it admiringly as he placed it in the tray beside his own.

LATER THAT EVENING

THE OLD BARN looked incredible with its decorations and well-set tables. Its large heat blowers had been running most of the day to combat the cold outside.

Dozens of cars filled the barnyard and lined the driveway as friends arrived for the hastily arranged dinner. Everyone was intrigued by the mysterious purpose of the occasion — a *special announcement* by Jimmy and Anna.

PJ and Baibina were notably absent since PJ had already promised to spend the evening with Chase.

Mike and Lena had prepared their specialty, Pasta Primavera, with choices of vegetable-only, seafood, and chicken sauces. The tables were filled with bowls of salads and warm bread, including hot garlic bread, of course, along with fresh olive oil and salad dressings.

While their guests enjoyed a dessert of tiramisu and hot coffee or tea, Anna and Jimmy stood to address the room. Anna suddenly felt moved to tears and turned to hide her face, quickly dabbing her eyes to dry them.

After collecting herself, she adjusted the laptop on the table in front of them to be sure the O'Malleys had a clear view. The room quieted to listen.

"THANK you all for joining us here tonight. All of you are really dear friends of ours," Jimmy began. "Over the past few years, we've been through a lot together. That's why we wanted to tell you about some pretty incredible news in our lives."

He turned to Anna and took her hand. She smiled at him through wet eyes. "Anna and I… are expecting our second child."

The room erupted in applause and cheers as everyone joyfully congratulated them. Anna's mom wiped tears from her eyes; even though she already knew about the baby, she couldn't help being moved by the emotional atmosphere in the room.

When everyone grew quiet again, Anna saw that Jimmy was struggling with the next thing he needed to say. She put her hand on his back and leaned against him supportively. His arm squeezed her shoulders as he drew strength from her support.

"THE NEXT PIECE of news is harder for us to share." He said as he scanned the room, looking into the faces of the people who meant so much to them. His uncle Mike and Anna's mom were listening attentively. Jimmy looked at their loyal friends Pete and Angela, then scanned the faces of Caden, Nyle, Pastor Wilkes, and his wife, and face after face of friends he'd grown up with or grew close to through the years. He remembered the laptop on the table and looked into the faces of Ward and Barbara O'Malley, who'd been like close family his whole life.

He drew a breath and prayed for courage and wisdom before continuing.

"Anna and I have received an important calling to minister in a place far from here. We won't be able to communicate with anyone." Jimmy and Anna shared a glance… "as far as we know, the move is going to be permanent; we won't be able to come back."

There were gasps of surprise mixed with cries of disbelief. Jimmy squeezed Anna tightly as they each worked hard to keep strong.

"You probably remember that God has had some unusual plans for us in the past."

There was a rustling of agreement and nervous laughter around the room as everyone remembered Jimmy's three-year battle with President Sheen and Athaliah, not to mention the incredible

Firestorm that shook the world and his very public battles with visible demons.

Jimmy held Anna tightly as he continued, "This is what we've trained for, and God has prepared us both for it. We've never felt more certain of anything in our lives. If we're going to follow His leading, then we have to do this. I honestly think that nothing we've ever been asked to do is more important than this.

"We're going to miss you all; there's no doubt about that." Anna brushed a tear from the corner of her eye as she looked at her mother and a few close friends. His uncle Mike looked like he was losing the last friend he had in the world. Jimmy cleared his throat and looked away to avoid choking up.

"I know, though, that we'll see each other again beyond this life. That day is closer than we think.

"That brings me to the most important thing I have to say. We've talked about the Lord's coming a lot in the past few years, but that doesn't make it less imminent. The signs are all around us like never before in the earth's history. Friends, He's at the door. Hold fast to Him, no matter what happens now. The times may get rough — we've seen rough times before, but He is faithful to carry us through the rough times. I know all of you will support and help each other through them as well. We've seen you do it.

"Please remember to pray for us — we need your prayers. We'll also pray hard for each of you for strength in the days ahead."

PASTOR WILKES CAME beside Jimmy and Anna, putting his arm around them as Jimmy finished his comments. "I can speak from experience that the Lord's calling on a person's life is a powerful and sacred thing. I know everyone here will agree with me that your faithfulness and courage in following that call have inspired us beyond words. We trust that whatever He has for you in the days ahead will be even more amazing.

· · ·

"IF ANYONE WOULD LIKE to join me in laying hands on Jimmy and Anna to commend them to this work, feel free to come forward."

There was a loud rustling of chairs as everyone in the room made their way to where they were standing. Surrounding them in a sea of support, everyone linked outstretched hands from shoulder to shoulder. Soon, the old barn rang with the cries and shouts of a gathering that rivaled any church meeting. Amos would have loved to see the barn he built being used this way.

Who knows... maybe he was seeing it.

⌘

35

PAINFUL FAREWELLS

"I am not ashamed, for I have known in whom I have believed, and have been persuaded that He is able to guard that which I have committed to Him until the last day."
~ 2 Timothy 1:12

FEBRUARY 15TH...
Yesterday Morning

Mike and Lena stayed at the farmhouse, talking with Anna and Jimmy far into the early morning hours. No matter how often they asked, Jimmy declined to reveal where they were going, saying only that God had arranged everything and that they'd be safe.

Jimmy was more concerned about Mike, Lena, and the others who remained behind. He knew the days were growing dark quickly; things in God's timeline would begin to happen rapidly now.

In fact, the feeling of imminence was clear to all of them, although none of them expressed it aloud. The couples were determined to spend as much of the remaining time together as they could. Anna offered Lena and Mike the guest room, finally admitting she couldn't stay awake another second.

A FEW SHORT HOURS LATER, little VJ's siren-like cries announced that he was awake and hungry. Jimmy retrieved him from the nursery while Anna warmed his breakfast in the kitchen. Soon, the smells of coffee and toast lured Mike and Lena as well, and it wasn't long before they were whipping up a fantastic breakfast together.

Jimmy went outside to get fresh eggs and met Pete, who was already busy with the farm chores. "Come on in and have some breakfast with us," he invited Pete as they worked together in the hen house.

"You've been an incredible help, Pete," Jimmy said as they walked to the large barn together. "I can't even begin to say how much it's meant. Without you, Anna and I could never have finished school and run the farm for the past six years.

"You and Angela know better than anyone what it takes to run this place and support the work of the food pantry. We've talked it over... we'd like you to have the farm after we're gone, if you're willing to have it."

"You're talking like you're leaving any minute," Pete worried. He stopped as they reached the porch and pushed the point. "I know you can't say where you're going, I get that— sorta, but you're acting like the two of you are leaving the planet — it's scarin' me, man."

"We'll be fine," Jimmy assured him. "I'm sure of that; we'll be safe in God's hands."

"I understand that you're being called to missions someplace that you can't talk about," Pete pressed, "but where are you going that you can't even be contacted? Don't you think there's a chance you could come back at some point?"

Jimmy struggled for a way to answer the question, realizing he couldn't explain it if he wanted to. "Plenty of missionaries have spent their whole lives in the mission field. Even today, there are places where missionaries have to operate under the radar. I can't say too much yet about where we're going; I wish I could. Maybe God will make it possible for us to see each other again at some point in the future; I just don't know."

"Wow, man. Your dedication is intense. I don't know how you do what you do." Pete looked down as he took it all in, then looked up at Jimmy with a new thought. "When are ya leaving?"

"We don't know the exact time, to be honest. It will be in God's time — at the time that He chooses."

JIMMY DEPOSITED the flat of eggs they'd just collected in the barn's walk-in refrigerator, choosing a dozen to take with them.

The gang at the kitchen table welcomed Pete as they entered. "You're just in time... the pancakes are almost ready," Anna informed them. Jimmy stole a quick kiss as he came alongside her and washed his hands in the kitchen sink. Lena was doting over little VJ in his highchair. Mike accepted the fresh eggs from Pete and cracked a few over the hot griddle, taking Anna's place as she carried a platter of pancakes to the table. Sizzling bacon filled the house with a delicious aroma that made their stomachs growl.

It wasn't long before the table was full of food, and everyone was seated. Everyone looked at Jimmy in an unspoken request for him to ask the blessing. He nodded and offered his hands to Anna and Pete, who grabbed hold of them and joined them with Lena and Mike, then bowed their heads.

"Lord, we're truly grateful for the blessing of family and friends. We marvel at the wisdom of your plan for us in creation, in placing us in families and friendships to share our lives' greatest joys as well as our deepest sorrows. Even if we are separated for a time, we know that the bonds created here will endure into eternity, and those we love who reside in You will one day be with us throughout ages without end."

Lena could be heard sniffling, and Anna squeezed her hand affectionately. Jimmy drew a breath to calm the sudden tightness in his chest, releasing it as he continued.

"Your great love for us makes that future possible. Thank you for your sacrifice to bear our sins and purchase our redemption. We know we're safe in your hands no matter what the future may bring. You are the rock that bursts forth with water springs in the desert and the strong tower that guards us. Keep each of us in your care, and equip us with all we need to fulfill your calling in the days ahead."

As they finished praying, Pete wrapped his huge arm around Jimmy's shoulders with a supportive squeeze. Then he slapped him on the back as he stabbed a stack of pancakes from the thick pile on the table and slid them onto his plate. "These 're wausum!" (*awesome*) he raved with a full mouth as he took a huge bite.

BROWNSVILLE, BROOKLYN...
Late Morning

BADRICK PULLED up to the tenement building that Rad and his friends called home and made his way to their rusted steel door. After knocking several times, it finally opened.

"Here are some clothes for ya," Badrick offered, holding out a box of folded items. "You can come an' use de showers at de Mission. We'll be havin' lunch b'fore leavin' to de prison."

Nacio accepted the box and began digging into it immediately.

"Chill it, Juice!" Rad warned him. Scamp and Jay-Jay both stepped back as Nacio nervously handed Rad the box. Rad slipped it under his arm; "We'll take it with us," he declared like a king issuing a decree.

Rad took the front seat while the others climbed in back.

"How ya holdin', mon?" Badrick asked Rad quietly.

Rad answered with a flurry of expletives… "The dude ain't hardly nothin'. I don't even know the man," he claimed defensively.

Badrick was quiet for a minute as he drove, finally breaking the awkward silence. "I never even met m' dad. Can't imagine what it'd be like havin' a dad who loved me like yours does. It's good that you're seein' im t'day, mon; I know it means de world to 'im. That's a big thing you're doin'."

Rad sat without answering while the scowl on his face fought to hide his undeniable deep sadness.

STOCKSLOCK PENITENTIARY…
3:00 PM

BADRICK STAYED OUTSIDE with PJ as Rad entered the small dining room, where Chase waited alone.

"Hi, son. Thanks a lot for comin'." Chase wanted nothing more than to embrace his son but kept his distance, reading Rad's tense body language. The boy's combative attitude when they last parted was still fresh on both of their minds.

Rad looked at the floor and shrugged uncomfortably. "Yeah… Sorry 'bout… tonight — 'bout what's happenin'."

"It's justice," Chase admitted. "It's what I deserve for what I done." He held out a hand, inviting Rad to sit across from him at the table. "You want anything? Water… coffee?" Rad just shook his head.

"Look, son, I know you hardly know me. I'm really sorry about that… more than anything. There's nothin' I wanted more the last few years than to be there for ya… to be with you. I know it's my own fault that I couldn't be, and that's the biggest regret of my whole life."

Rad stared at the table for a long minute, then released a deep breath. "Look… I ain't perfect either. There's stuff I've done. It sucks that they're gonna do what they're doing. Is it true you're takin' another guy's execution date? I hear he's a pretty bad dude — why would ya do that?"

"The execution doesn't worry me," Chase said, leaning forward sincerely. "I've made my peace with God; I want you to know that. The truth is, nobody gets outta this life alive — I'm just leavin' it on my own terms. I've got no regrets about that."

"Nobody can say you ain't brave, anyhow," Rad conceded, a little surprised by his father's sincerity. "I still say the other guy deserves it more."

"It's not bravery, son, it's trust. I know who I'm believing in, and I know God can be trusted to keep everything I've committed to Him — I know He's waitin' for me. I just wanna hear Him say well done when I get there."

"You sound like Reverend Jerome," Rad said. "That dude was always tryin' t'get me to go to church an' stuff. I don't believe in God. If ya ask me, my life is proof He don't exist."

Chase understood his son's pain; he knew it was useless to argue the point and didn't try. "Reverend Jerome looked out for ya while you were younger; I'm grateful to him for that," he noted instead.

"Yeah, guess so."

"So..." Chase began, changing the uncomfortable topic, "Last time you were here, you told me about your apartment. I'm proud of ya for havin' your own place already."

"Ah, it ain't much. I share it with a few other guys."

"Sounds like they're good friends of yours. Are these the same guys you used to skateboard and stuff with?"

"Jay-Jay, Scamp an' Juice... yeah. We been tight for, like, our whole lives."

The two of them talked for the next hour as Rad gradually opened up. Chase was careful not to offer advice that might come across as criticism, even when Rad described some pretty ill-advised choices. He realized he hadn't earned the title of *trusted father*, as much as it hurt him to admit it. Instead, He did his best to interject some of his own life's lessons, always pointing back to his decision to follow Christ.

It was tradition for condemned prisoners to be given their choice for their last meal. When it was time for Chase's last dinner, he requested a steak—he hadn't had one in years—and Rad opted for the same.

MEANWHILE, PJ and Badrick made their way to the prison chapel, letting Chase and Rad have the time alone. In light of the night's scheduled execution, the Warden approved a special chapel meeting with PJ for any inmates who wanted to attend. Soon, the chapel was packed. The impromptu prayer meeting lasted for the afternoon until it was interrupted by the prison's loud buzzer announcing the five o'clock dinner hour.

As the men filed out, Badrick and PJ made their way to a visitor's waiting room near the prison entrance.

"IT'S LOOKIN' like a storm front movin' in," Badrick said to PJ as they stood staring from the window. A bright flash of lightning lit the sky, followed immediately by a loud thunderclap, and the sky opened up with a sudden downpour of heavy rain.

"It's a storm, alright..." PJ replied.

IT WAS clear that he was referring to more than just the weather. He could feel it in his spirit — something else was also coming, something earth-changing.

⌘

THE EVENT

"Be vigilant on the night Chase is executed. That day is the keystone of your entire life."

In a Prep Room Behind the Prison Auditorium...
6:00 PM last night

C hase sat in front of the camera, checking his notes one last time. PJ and Mitch, the prison guard who had become Chase's long-time friend, were with him in the small room. Rad stood against the wall nearby, silently watching.

PJ LED the men in prayer.

"Lord, we're truly grateful for everything you've done in Chase's life and for how you've used him here to reach so many others. The light of your spirit that shines through him has led many souls to glory in this place.

"Today, we are here to support him in his most challenging calling of all. Please be close to him in this part of his journey. We know he desires for his final selfless act to be used in a powerful way to draw others to you, and we join him in that plea. Please give him the strength he needs to travel the most difficult steps in his journey and fill him with your supernatural peace."

Mitch looked shaken as he adjusted the camera to prepare for Chase's recorded statement.

Chase appeared exhausted but calm and serene as he looked into the camera and began...

"You are here tonight to watch me pay for crimes I freely confess and regret deeply. Saying that my punishment is deserved would be an understatement, but I don't fear death. I've made my peace with God. My reason for serving Him hasn't been for fear of Hell or because of any compulsion — my faith is not a fetter ...my belief is no bondage ...I wasn't dragged to holiness or driven to my duty to serve the Lord. No, ...piety — if that's what you wanna call it — has been my pleasure ...my hope in Christ is my greatest happiness ...my duty to him has been my delight."

A shudder went through Rad as he stood listening. He couldn't deny the absolute sincerity in his father's words, yet their meaning escaped him. How could they be true? He listened uncomfortably as Chase continued...

"The truth is that I already died years ago – the old me died on the day that Jesus Christ saved me from the darkness that was holding me – I was reborn that day as a new creature in Christ. On that day, I was called out of darkness into His marvelous light!

"I know that He's waitin' now to welcome me on the other side, and I'm ready to meet Him face to face – I want to thank Him with all my heart for all he's done for me.

"Some people have said I shouldn't have done what I did to take another man's place here tonight. They say that man deserved this more than me."

Chase looked at Rad with a sympathetic gaze before looking again into the camera as he continued to explain.

"Well, I didn't agree with that, but I didn't disagree either. Truth is, we both deserve it, me the same as him. The main difference, as I see, it ain't who deserves to die more, but who's more ready. I've prayed for that man… for his salvation, and I hope that whatever little bit o' time my choice gives him (only God knows how much that is) can be used to make him see his need for savin'.

"The other reason I done it was to let him know that Jesus has done the same for me, and this is what it feels like to have somebody do that. I want everybody to know that feelin' – the feelin' of bein' forgiven."

Rad shifted uncomfortably as his father looked over at him with a profoundly sincere and vulnerable look. There was no air of self-righteousness or hypocrisy. His heartfelt words penetrated Rad's calloused conscience like a razor-sharp sword.

"One thing I've come to know is that mercy and justice are opposite things; justice is gettin' what you deserve, and mercy is gettin' what you don't deserve. Only God can give a guilty man both things at the same time... he shows us mercy that we don't deserve and satisfies justice at the same time by takin' all the punishment we do deserve on himself. That right there is what love is all about... that's real love... there ain't no greater love than for a man to lay down his life for a friend. That's what Jesus done for me, and I'm humbled and honored to be able to show a little bit of his love to somebody else.

"My dyin' ain't nothing like what Jesus did, though... He took the blame for sins He didn't do – an' all I'm doin' is getting what I deserve for the crimes I've done. But I know that mercy is waitin' for me on the other side, all because of what He has done for me and not for anything I've ever done to deserve it."

Chase caught Mitch's eye as the huge guard wiped a stray tear from his cheek.

"I want to say goodbye to all my friends who cared to get to know me... I'm gonna miss you all for sure, but I'm prayin' that a good many of you will meet me someday in a better place. Jus' remember that every knee is gonna bow and confess that Jesus is Lord – You best do it before the day you're meetin' Him face to face, cause then it'll be too late."

He glanced again at his son with a deep love and a burning conviction reflecting in his eyes...

"There's one final thing I gotta say... and this is burnin' on my heart like an all-out forest fire – all of you need to take heed of it: Jesus is comin' back real soon. I can feel it stronger than I ever did before in my whole life – He's at the door! There's no more time for waitin' to make up your mind – it's time now to be gettin' ready.

"So, I don't think it'll be long before some of us meet again over there... until then, Goodbye for now, my friends."

JIMMY AND ANNA watched the TV coverage of events at the prison. It began with the Warden's comments, and then he passed the lectern to Mitch, who introduced Chase's recorded statement. The rugged guard's comments were sobering; his emotion could be felt, even over the TV broadcast.

Chase's recorded statement was played on air in its entirety. Jimmy felt a chill as he watched it. He'd seen these events before; the memory of that experience raced through his mind; it was now being brought vividly to life before their eyes. The words he heard from Chase were exactly the same as those recorded in his journal, where he'd written them years prior.

But it wasn't just those words that gave him chills. He also recalled the *old stranger's* words from Sunday night — reverberating like a jarring alarm bell: *Be vigilant on the night Chase is executed. **That night is the keystone of your entire life** — defining everything that happens before and after it.*

THE NEWS BROADCAST cut away to commentary from several experts discussing the merits of the country's new moratorium on executions. It was the fact that this was to be the country's very last execution that made it so newsworthy. For now, though, their live coverage at the prison was done.

Jimmy switched off the TV and leaned forward, resting his elbows on his knees as he bowed his head sadly. Anna hugged his shoulders and joined him as they quietly prayed together.

THE PRISON AUDITORIUM...
7:40 PM

THE DOCTOR STANDING beside Chase's gurney listened carefully with his stethoscope and felt for a pulse, then nodded somberly to the Warden, who sadly looked at his watch.

"Let the record show the time of death as seven-forty PM."

People in the crowded auditorium slowly stood. Everyone was silent as no one dared to disturb the solemn mood that permeated the room. Rad sat longer than anyone else — the last to stand. He had a dazed and despairing look on his face as he continued to watch the platform, where his father's body now lay shrouded under a white sheet.

There were no tears, but his eye twitched, and his hand trembled as he reached for the pack of cigarettes in his shirt pocket, extracting one and putting the unlit cigarette between his lips.

The Warden spoke quietly to Mitch, PJ, and the doctor, asking them to sign the death certificate as official witnesses. The three of them nodded sadly and followed the gurney from the room. As he turned, the Warden noticed Rad standing by himself with the unlit cigarette pinched between his lips.

"There's no smoking in here, son," he said sternly, not realizing the boy's relationship to Chase.

Rad's expression hardened in anger, and he glared at the Warden. Then he kicked over the chair in front of him, sending it tumbling into the row in front and knocking them over. Several guards quickly gathered around him. One recognized him from earlier in the day and let the others know he was Chase's son. They offered conciliatory glances, expressing their sympathy, then led him outside, where one of them offered to light Rad's cigarette.

IT WAS eight o'clock when PJ finally made it back to the auditorium. He asked around about Radison, eventually learning from one of the guards that Badrick had taken him home; they had already left. The guard shared that the boy seemed pretty shaken up.

PJ PULLED out the letter Chase wrote to his son and stared at it, immediately deciding to drive to Brooklyn himself to deliver it.

CENTER SPRINGS...
Midnight

JIMMY SAT RESTLESSLY on the couch. Anna leaned against him, sound asleep, while VJ rested in his playpen nearby. The old stranger's words continued to replay in his mind: *Be vigilant on the night Chase is executed...*

He still hadn't gotten used to the fact that the old man was a future version of himself. He honestly never expected that he'd live that long. Everything he'd seen in his travels suggested that the world didn't have long to go. He'd always figured they'd be *raptured* long before his sixtieth birthday.

He thought about the first time he traveled — when he first met Chozeq and Ardent. It was the night of Chase's execution. That was when he first saw PJ... Pastor Juan. It gave him a chill to realize that those events had now *arrived* — that was **tonight**. The shocking events of PJ's stabbing and near-death experience at the hospital rushed through his mind — they were still vivid despite seeing them almost ten years ago.

Jimmy looked at the clock on the mantle, realizing that those events must now be playing out — PJ was probably at the hospital by now.

HIS PHONE'S sudden ringing shattered the night's silence, waking Anna. She sat up with a start as Jimmy leaned forward and lifted his phone from the coffee table. They saw the caller ID... it was Baibina. He answered it on speaker...

They could hear a police siren and horns blaring as the patrol car she rode in raced through the streets. Baibina was crying, gasping as she spoke. "Juan has been hurt... he was stabbed.... I-I'm on my way to the hospital where they took him — in Brooklyn. They said it's pretty bad — h-he might not..." she broke down, unable to finish.

Anna looked at Jimmy, clearly distraught, a hand covering her mouth. Jimmy motioned to her supportively and grabbed Anna's hand as he spoke to Baibina.

"It sounds bad right now, I know... but he's in God's hands—God has him! He's going to be OK; he will come through this." He looked at Anna, who was shaking her head fearfully. We'll pray... we'll start a prayer chain..." he nodded to Anna, who grabbed her own phone and dialed her mom.

Anna urgently explained what had happened to her mom and Mike, and they quickly agreed to start calling others from the church. Anna called Pastor Wilkes next. They were still on the phone together when Nyle called the Pastor, asking permission to send a text blast to the congregation. Pastor Wilkes readily agreed.

They each received the text within minutes with a link to the conference line. "Join the conference call," Jimmy explained to Baibina as he heard it chime on her phone. "It's a prayer meeting — everyone is praying."

The conference line filled rapidly as word spread, soon growing to hundreds from the church and quickly expanding to the City Missions. As soon as Badrick heard, he headed for the hospital to meet Baibina, leading a prayer on the conference line.

> "God, you're a healin' God! Truly, we've seen you do
> healing' miracles through 'dis man o' God—'dis child
> o' yours. Now it be time for his own healin'—do a
> miracle, God! Do a miracle!"

An overwhelming sense of God's Spirit permeated the call—

everyone felt it. It was an anointing as powerful as anything they'd ever known. Even the patrolman who drove Baibina felt a tear escape the corner of his eye as he listened in.

IN HIS MIND'S EYE, Jimmy relived the incredible hospital emergency room scene. He could practically hear Ardent's words as they thundered:

> *"Ye have work yet to complete here below. There is much that ye still must do in the fields of His harvest. ...He has chosen to anoint thee with a portion of faith seldom known to the earth...."*

Others took turns leading in prayer as the throng of prayer warriors stormed Heaven. Eventually, there was a silent pause as people waited for the next person to lead in prayer. Jimmy began — his voice reflecting the confidence of having already seen PJ's miraculous recovery. It boosted everyone's faith as he declared…

> "A double portion, Lord! We ask You to anoint Juan with
> a double portion of Your Spirit! Make him like
> Elisha, who caught the mantle of Elijah as he was
> taken up to Heaven. Let it be a portion of faith
> seldom seen on earth. Make him a powerful
> messenger to the world in these closing days of
> time!"

Jimmy was still praying when Baibina broke in, interrupting the call…

"HE'S OUT OF SURGERY! H-he's alright… they say he's going to be alright. Thank you so much - thank you all so, so much!" They heard her disconnect as she distractedly dropped the call and ran to Juan as they wheeled him from the ER.

The conference line erupted in cheers and praises for several minutes. Pastor Wilkes finally closed the call with a prayer of thanks and then thanked everyone who joined.

ANNA TAPPED HER PHONE, disconnecting from the cacophony of beeps that announced each person leaving.

"Wow," she said as she studied Jimmy's face. "You knew... you knew that everything would happen just like that."

Jimmy was honestly surprised by her comment. "W-what makes you think that?"

"Everything. The way you spoke to Baibina... the way you acted... the way you prayed. You saw tonight — you saw it before."

Jimmy was quiet for a moment, then looked at her with a surrendered expression. "You're right... I did. It was one of the first times I traveled." He took her hands and studied her face as he continued. "In fact, believe it or not, it was on the night that we first met."

"At the Sub Shop — the night you fell and hit your head..." she said as it dawned on her.

"Yeah... I guess you could say I was still getting my footing back then. I'm surprised you remember that."

Anna smiled. "Who could forget that look in your eyes when you sold me that soda? I could see right inside you — I could tell you were feeling just like I was at that moment." She put her arms around his neck and smiled. "Like I still feel...."

The sound of VJ's crying interrupted their kiss. Jimmy managed to steal two or three more before she reluctantly pulled herself away and went to retrieve their son.

"I'll heat up his bottle," he offered.

"I think he's hungry; maybe make him some toast, too," she suggested.

. . .

JIMMY MADE his way into the kitchen and added some milk to a no-spill cup, placing it in the microwave, then dropped a couple of slices of bread into the toaster.

Turning to the kitchen table, he looked at his laptop and the arrangement of items beside it that he'd carefully prepared. His letter to PJ sat on top of an envelope containing the deed to the farm and the papers prepared by his Uncle Ward. Just beside those was an old wooden box containing the keys to the secret passage, the mausoleum, and the provision chest.

The microwave's beeping announced that VJ's cup was ready. He tested a sample against the back of his hand and headed back to the living room. Anna was pacing the floor with the baby as she accepted the cup and offered it to the restless child. She looked back at Jimmy searchingly. She'd been watching the way he had anxiously reviewed the kitchen table.

"STILL THINK IT'LL BE TONIGHT?" she asked, glancing at the mantle clock — it was past 1:00 AM. He could hear the trepidation in her voice. He just nodded and squeezed Anna's hand reassuringly, sensing her nervousness, then kissed VJ on the forehead.

The sound of the toaster popping summoned him back to the kitchen. Once again, he rechecked the items on the table, assuring himself that nothing was forgotten. He hugged the strap of a small backpack on his shoulder, which contained his unfinished journal, keeping it close.

Finally satisfied that he'd prepared for the unknown the best he could, he retrieved VJ's toast from the toaster and spread some jam on it, then switched off the light and returned to the living room.

He propped up one of VJ's stuffed animals on a small chair and pretended to feed it a piece of toast before handing it to VJ, who quickly munched on it. Anna sat their son on her lap while Jimmy opened his Bible to First Thessalonians chapter four and laid it on the coffee table. The verses resonated with meaning for him as he began reading out loud, beginning with verse 13:

Now, we do not want you to be uninformed, brothers and sisters, about those who are asleep so that you will not grieve like the rest who have no hope.

For if we believe that Jesus died and rose again, so also we believe that God will bring with him those who have fallen asleep as Christians.

For we tell you this by the word of the Lord, that we who are alive, who are left until the coming of the Lord, will surely not go ahead of those who have fallen asleep.

For the Lord himself will come down from heaven with a shout of command, with the voice of the archangel, and with the trumpet of God, and the dead in Christ will rise first.

Then we who are alive, who are left, will be suddenly caught up together with them in the clouds to meet the Lord in the air. And so we will always be with the Lord.

Therefore, encourage one another with these wor...[1].

Jimmy's voice was cut off abruptly as all three of them suddenly vanished from the room.

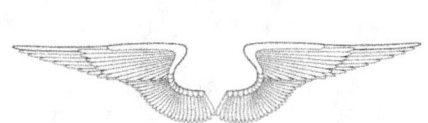

THE END

OF BOOK FIVE

―――――――

Sign up for Author Updates
at:
www.arkharbor.press

THANK YOU FOR READING!

PLEASE SCAN THE CODE BELOW TO LEAVE A REVIEW.

BOOKS BY

D. I. HENNESSEY

Books in the Within & Without Time Series:

Book 1: Within and Without Time

Book 2: The Traveler

Book 3: The Secret Door

Book 4: Evil Ascendant - Deliverance

Book 5: The Time of His Choosing

Book 6: A Mission Rarely Given

Book 7: An Unexpected Hour

Books in the Niergel Chronicles Series:

Book 1: Niergel Chronicles - Last Hope

Book 2: Niergel Chronicles - Quest

Book 3: Niergel Chronicles - The Tenth Mantle Bearer

Book 4: Niergel Chronicles - The Dragon's Tail

Available on Amazon

"www.amazon.com/gp/product/B09DFDM364"

NOTES

9. PRODIGAL

1. Police detective, Narcotics agent.

13. AWAKENING

1. Adapted from Edwards' writings, recounted in: Tracy, Joseph. The Great Awakening: A History of the Revival of Religion in the time of Edwards and Whitefield (p. 212). Counted Faithful.

15. UNLIKELY FRIENDS

1. Adapted from: Whitefield, George; Ryle, J. C.. The Collected Sermons of George Whitefield (p. 15). Jawbone Digital. Kindle Edition.
2. Whitefield, George; Ryle, J. C.. The Collected Sermons of George Whitefield (p. 26). Jawbone Digital. Kindle Edition.
3. Benjamin Frankin quote: Whitefield, George; Ryle, J. C.. The Collected Sermons of George Whitefield (p. 14). Jawbone Digital. Kindle Edition

16. MATTHEW TWENTY-FOUR

1. Matthew 24:4-14
2. AI: Artificial Intelligence

19. GROWING DARKNESS

1. Super PACs, officially known as "independent expenditure-only political action committees," are unlike traditional PACs in that they may engage in unlimited political spending (on, for example, ads) independently of the campaigns, and may raise funds from individuals, corporations, unions, and other groups without any legal limit on donation size.
    Wikipedia

21. ANGELS HEARD ON HIGH

1. Ezekiel 36:22-38

22. DOCTRINES OF DEMONS

1. Chozeq's words are adapted from: Joseph S. Exell, M.A., **The Biblical Illustrator,** Published in 1900; public domain.
2. Chozeq's words are adapted from: F. B. Meyer, B. A., **The Biblical Illustrator**

24. RESTLESS

1. 2 Thessalonians 2:8-11
2. Isaac Watts, When I Survey the Wondrous Cross, Hymns and Spiritual Songs, Published 1707
3. 2 Samuel 23:2-5
4. John Tennent's final words are excerpted from the account of these events recorded by: Alexander, Archibald. The Log College: Biographical Sketches of the Founder and Principal Alumni (Illustrated), 1845. Counted Faithful.

26. TROUBLE

1. Revelation 3:10

29. AN ANGRY GOD

1. Excerpted from: Edwards, Jonathan. Sinners in the Hands of an Angry God by Jonathan Edwards (p. 2). OSNOVA.
2. Excerpted from: Edwards, Jonathan. Sinners in the Hands of an Angry God by Jonathan Edwards (pp. 6-7). OSNOVA.
3. Edwards, Jonathan. Sinners in the Hands of an Angry God by Jonathan Edwards (p. 28). OSNOVA.

36. THE EVENT

1. New English Translation (NET) Bible, I Thessalonians 4:13-18

www.ingramcontent.com/pod-product-compliance
Lightning Source LLC
Chambersburg PA
CBHW062120170626
46813CB00002B/522